THE PARADISE OF DEATH

DOCTOR WHO
THE PARADISE OF DEATH

Based on the BBC radio series by Barry Letts
by arrangement with BBC Books, a division of
BBC Enterprises Ltd

BARRY LETTS

Number 156 in the
Target Doctor Who Library

First published in Great Britain in 1994 by
Doctor Who Books
an imprint of Virgin Publishing Ltd
332 Ladbroke Grove
London W10 5AH

Original script copyright © Barry Letts 1993
Novelisation copyright © Barry Letts 1994
'Doctor Who' series copyright © British Broadcasting
Corporation 1994

The BBC producer of *The Paradise of Death* was Phil Clarke
The part of the Doctor was played by Jon Pertwee

ISBN 0 426 20413 1

Typeset by Intype, London
Printed and bound in Great Britain by
Cox & Wyman Ltd, Reading, Berks

This book is sold subject to the condition that
it shall not, by way of trade or otherwise,
be lent, resold, hired out or otherwise circulated
without the publisher's prior written consent in
any form of binding or cover other than that in
which it is published and without a similar
condition including this condition being imposed
on the subsequent purchaser.

DOCTOR WHO
THE PARADISE OF DEATH

Chapter One

A well-rounded hand daintily selected a violet-flavoured chocolate cream as smooth and as plump as itself and conveyed it carefully to a pair of voluptuously cushioned lips. A sigh was mingled with a slight smacking sound as the confection met its end.

'How much longer, Tragan?'

'Nearly there, Chairman Freeth.'

The great figure pulled itself to its feet and stretched two arms like balloons about to burst.

'I find these flights increasingly tedious, the older I get,' he said petulantly.

Tragan's expressionless, pale eyes stared back at him. 'Don't forget the commercial,' he said.

Freeth glanced at the time. He spoke sharply. 'Turn it on then.'

Unhurried, Tragan moved to a small control panel and pressed a switch. Half-smiling tones flooded the small saloon: '... all that and more from yours truly and many other fabulous guests – after the break!' A synthesized burst of sci-fi music took over, only to retreat before a torrent of pseudo-urgent words: 'Feeling like nothing on earth? Come to SPACE WORLD and fly to the moon!'

'I nearly missed it! Why didn't you remind me?'

'May I point out, Chairman – '

'Sssh! I want to hear this.'

Freeth sank back onto his overstuffed overwide seat. The half-Cockney half-Yankee voice continued relentlessly, '... only ten minutes walk from Hampstead station, you can find the experience of a lifetime!'

A great deal was promised: Space Rides to take the breath away; light-sabre duels with the Robot of Death; challenges from the Mars Gladiator to beat; fabulous prizes to be won...

'...but best of all, the Monsters from Outer Space! Twenty-one alien creatures, so perfect in every detail, you'll have to believe that they're real! Come to SPACE WORLD – the great day out for all the family!'

As Tragan switched off the final dramatic sting of electronic sound, he glanced at Freeth. It was apparent that his ill-temper had vanished.

'Not bad. Not bad at all,' his orotund voice boomed out. 'Surprisingly good, in fact. Young Kitson is learning. I could have wished that they had mentioned the name of the corporation, though. That is, after all, the object of the exercise.'

'Perhaps we should have called it the Parakon Corporation Space Park.' It was difficult to tell whether Tragan's suggestion was intended seriously.

'Like a sponsored horse race, you mean? It lacks a certain *je ne sais quoi*, I would say. Wouldn't you agree?'

'If it did the job – '

'Ah well, you're a pragmatist, of course,' interrupted Freeth. 'The finer feelings are a closed book to you.' He chuckled comfortably. 'It must be the effect of consorting with those ghastly little pets of yours.'

Tragan looked at him with hooded eyes. 'You'd have been in a fine pickle without them last time.'

'Mm. A nasty moment. I'm duly grateful.' Freeth selected another chocolate with meticulous care. 'A pity about the screaming – and the blood,' he added.

'Most enjoyable, though.'

'True, true.' Freeth popped in a coconut delight and chumped it up with relish. 'It left us with something of a mess to clear up, that's all,' he said, a touch indistinctly.

Sarah Jane Smith was fed-up. Or was she? With a grumbling squeak, the sash window of her little studio flat allowed itself to be pushed up far enough for her to lean out and enjoy the fresh breeze coming from the Heath. She gazed across the greenery at the immense structure which dwarfed the trees on the night skyline, and felt again the spasm of frustrated irritation which had become so familiar. Outrageous even to think of building that thing. Who wants a space rocket in their back yard?

She returned to the matter in hand. Perhaps fed-up wasn't quite the word. Disgruntled? No, not that; but not particularly gruntled either. She giggled at the word and took a couple of deep breaths, savouring the spring smell of the trees beneath her.

What was she on about, for heaven's sake? Only a couple of years after taking the plunge into... into the murky waters of London journalism, she was... She pulled herself up, irritated by the cliché (murky waters, indeed!) and looked for a suitably wet thought to redeem the suspect metaphor. 'There is a tide in the affairs of men –' Oh yes, and what about women? ' – leads on to fortune?' Well, she wasn't doing too badly. A flat in Hampstead, no less. Well, an attic. And writers were supposed to starve in attics, weren't they?

Not that she was exactly starving, of course. A feature writer on a glossy woman's mag might not have found the pot at the end of the rainbow, in spite of the rumours, but she could always find a bob a two for a handful of rice. So what was it?

Was it that she had no project at the moment? Even the prospect of visiting some of the loveliest countryside in England had failed to get her excited about Clorinda's only suggestion. All power to the women who were muscling in on the age-old male world of sheepdog trials but... No. Her lack of interest was a symptom, not a cause.

Did she want a man? 'Well, since you ask, Sarah dear, no, not at the moment.' (First sign of madness, talking to yourself, that's what they used to say at school.) Huh! Overgrown schoolboys the lot of them. Especially... But Sarah wouldn't even let his name come into her head. Mr Zero; Mr Zilch; Mr Errgh: do forgive me if I throw up.

Talking of which... Sarah leaned perilously far out

over the window ledge at the sound of raucous singing coming down the alley. Yes, there they were as usual, coming out of the Dog and Duck. That song was yukky enough when Old Bleary Eyes wrapped his tonsils around it, but – 'Da da de da, I've had a few...' You can say that again, mate.

A memory floated from nowhere into Sarah's head: a slightly dandified figure dressed in a frilly shirt, a velvet jacket and cloak, standing outside an old-fashioned Police Telephone Box, holding the door open for her; and suddenly her grumpy mood was trickling away and she was flooded with a warmth which made her lift her eyebrows in surprise.

'Good heavens above,' she said aloud, 'I do believe I'm missing the Doctor!'

'I did it m-y-y-y-y way!'

With a deal of yawing, Bill and Nobby steered their uncertain course through the long grass in a vaguely north-easterly direction. They could hardly get lost using as their prime navigational aid the massive tower, shaped like the original Apollo moon rocket, which rose majestically above the high fence which protected the new theme park.

Bill stopped. 'Hang on,' he said. The singing continued. 'Belt up!'

'Wha'ssa matter?'

'Opens tomorrow, doesn't it?'

'Wha' you on about?'

'You know, all that fuss in the papers. Monsters and all.'

'Wha' about it?'

'Why don't we go and have a look? Come on!'

Bill set off purposefully towards the fence. Nobby took a couple of reluctant steps and stopped. 'Wha' if they *are* real? The monsters. Like it said in the paper?' Bill kept on going. Nobby slowly followed him.

'Yeah, but I mean, what if they are?'

'Don't be a berk. Come on, give us a leg up. Anyway, they'd be in cages, wouldn't they?'

Only half convinced, Nobby made his hands into a step the way he always had. But this fence was higher than the wall of old Wilson's garden where they used to go to steal the fruit dropping off the Victoria plum tree, or the corrugated iron barrier which had hindered their one and only attempt to do some real thieving some three years ago. In the end, on Bill's insistence that this was the opportunity of a lifetime, they dragged over a fallen beech log, victim of last year's gale, and climbed with precarious determination, up the stumps of its lost branches, towards the ending of their brief and unproductive lives.

Freeth wrinkled his nose fastidiously as Tragan returned to the saloon from the rear compartment. The sound of savage snarls was abruptly cut off by the closing of the door.

'Don't you ever give them a bath?'

'Would you like to try?'

'You could at least hose them down – or take them for a swim. I can't think why you want to get them out at all.'

'An elementary precaution. We'll be coming in to land in a few minutes.'

Freeth dabbed at his nose with a fine lawn handkerchief, scented with a perfume blended for his exclusive use.

'You're always such a moaner, Tragan. There'll be no trouble. Kitson would have warned us.'

Tragan's voice was as colourless as his eyes. 'That's just what you said last time,' he said.

It was hardly surprising that the building of the theme park had roused so much opposition. Rivalling Disneyworld in size and the scope of its attractions, not only did it swallow up acres of London's favourite open space, it also made it inevitable that the remainder would be trampled into an ugly death.

For the style of its odd-looking buildings, some as seemingly fragile as a spider's web, others weighing down the earth as massively as any of the edifices of ancient times, compelling awe in the beholder; the majesty of its wide avenues, lined with peculiar trees as elegant as they were strange (Not real? Run your hands over the bark, smell the flowers); the richness of the giant three-dimensional posters (Colour holography? But that's impossible!); everything was designed to lure the curiosity and wonder of the paying masses from all over the world.

Bill and Nobby, however, found Space World as disappointing as a visit to the seaside out of season. True, there were the vast pavilions of gleaming metal, cold and still in the light of the full moon; there were the alien carriages mutely waiting to carry the daredevil customer into improbable flights of fear; there were the gigantic structures, out of the pages of a science fiction comic, whose purpose could only be guessed.

But where was the fun in being offered a view of the Giant Ostroid – 'its kick could disembowel an elephant' – if the entrance to his lair was firmly locked? How could you 'fly through the Gargantuan Caverns of Southern Mars' or 'take a walk on the wild side of Mercury' if there was nobody there to let you into the Solar System? All in all, a total bust.

Until...

'Hey, look!' cried Nobby.

'What?'

'Only a bleedin' UFO, innit? It's landing an' all! That's a bit more like it!'

Nobby set off at a fair clip (in a reasonable approximation to a straight line) in the direction he'd been pointing.

Bill chased after him. 'Come back, they'll see us! Nobby!'

But Nobby kept going.

The two rows of space ships in Yuri Gagarin Avenue varied considerably in design. From a simple rocket shuttle to the most far-out alien space station which barely stopped short of boggling point, they offered a wide variety of simulated trips through the Universe. The western row had now been extended by one. The newcomer's domed shell had a unique particularity. It had, it seemed, no windows or doors – until, with the slightest of humming noises, a crack appeared which broadened to make an exit just wide enough to allow the massive form waiting within to alight and delicately step towards two figures waiting on the tarmac.

'Ah, Kitson.'

'Welcome back, Mr Freeth,' said the younger of the two. 'May I introduce Mr Grebber?'

'How do you do, Mr Grebber. We meet at last.'

The thickset Grebber grasped the pudgy little hand with one that could enclose a brick. 'An honour, Mr Freeth. I'm, er, yeah, that's right. Honoured and – and that.'

'The honour is all mine, my dear sir. Mr Kitson has told me of the excellent – nay, the magnificent – work your people have done in building our little playground. Allow me to express the gratitude of the Parakon Corporation.'

'Yeah, well, we aim to please. I've always . . .' But Freeth had turned away.

'No trouble, Kitson?'

'On the contrary. Everything's going very well.'

Freeth turned to the gaunt figure standing in the space ship entrance. 'There you are, Tragan. What did I tell you? An old misery guts, that's what you are.'

Tragan's head jerked sideways. 'Don't speak too soon,' he said. 'Look.'

Two figures were coming towards them down the long avenue at a shambling run. The first one stopped. He waved. 'Where's the li'l green men then?' he shouted.

His companion caught him up and grabbed him by the arm. 'Nobby! Let's get out of here!'

But Nobby was enjoying himself. He pulled away from Bill and performed an elaborate bow. He stood up and once more peered muzzily towards the frozen group of watchers. 'Take me to your leader!' he cried.

Tragan came to life. Stepping to one side, he turned and spoke into the ship. 'Go, go, go!' he snapped.

Neither Nobby nor Bill could have had time to realize that time had run out for them. With scarcely the chance to throw up an arm in a futile gesture of self-protection, they were as quickly dead as the victims of a sniper's bullets.

'That was hardly necessary,' said Freeth.

'You heard him,' replied Tragan, his eyes gleaming with satisfaction. 'He must have seen the ship landing.'

The savage snarling of the beasts had already dwindled to a mumbling slurping growl.

'Oh God! They're...' Grebber staggered into the shadows, retching. Freeth threw him an amused glance and turned to Tragan.

'Don't let them both be eaten,' he said. 'A mangled corpse could be good publicity.'

Chapter Two

The Doctor! Of course, that was it!

Sarah took a gulp of orange juice and spread a slice of wholemeal bread with soft, low fat, vegetable marge, feeling virtuous. Sort of. There was still a lot to be said for a thick piece of toasted white sliced, dripping with melted butter, or spread with half an inch of sugary fine-cut marmalade. Or both.

Well, perhaps not just the Doctor himself. It was all the rest of it. How could she settle down to the workaday world, albeit the supposedly glamorous world of the investigative journalist, after the sort of experience she had gone through with the Doctor? It was still difficult to believe that she'd actually travelled through time with him. A logical impossibility, time travel. She'd read it up. And yet...

They had first met when Sarah was working on a story. The rumour of an official cover-up of the mysterious disappearance of a number of research scientists had taken her, under a false name (she had pretended to be her own aunt, a scientist herself), behind the security barrier at the research establishment in question, only to have her cover penetrated in no time flat by this curious Doctor fellow.

Well now. What to do about it? (A sip of strong black coffee.) Kill two birds with one stone, that's what. (Cliché!) Here was a new project ready made. An in-depth interview with the Doctor, supported by boxes quoting the opinions of his colleagues and rivals. If she slanted it right, Clorinda might just go for it.

Now where did he hang out? He was scientific adviser to... What was it? Where was the telephone book?

Yes, here it was. The United Nations Intelligence Task Force.

She found herself grinning as she dialled the number. It would be just great to see him again.

'Now come on, Doctor. You're not seriously telling me that you travelled to *Atlantis* in that old Police Box?'

The Doctor had also seemed to think it would be great to meet again; and he'd agreed straightaway to the idea of an interview. He'd invited her along that very morning to 'have a bit of a chat' as she'd put it, on the understanding that she didn't stop him getting on with his work.

Perched on a high stool by the workbench, Sarah felt strangely at home. Though the Doctor's room at UNIT HQ was fundamentally the traditional lab with bunsen burners, various items of scientific glassware – test-tubes, of course; flasks and jars; even the obligatory retort, as if she were in a mediaeval alchemist's study – and odd bits of machinery and electronic equipment, the Doctor had made it peculiarly his own.

Quite apart from the TARDIS standing in the corner, there were innumerable objects lying about, some of which would have seemed more at home in a museum – and others in a junk shop.

There were odd pieces of clothing – a hat with an ostrich feather plume; a piece of rusting armour; a very long knitted scarf; a pair of pointed Renaissance slippers – piles of dried vegetable matter, including some horribly twisted fungi, a dusty stuffed albatross with wings outstretched (she'd had to duck underneath to get into the room), a large photograph of a man with a shock of white hair and a bushy moustache, (Could it be ...? It was, you know. Scribbled in the corner, it had, 'Many thanks for all your help, old friend.' and it was signed 'Albert Einstein') and so on and so on.

'Been having a bit of clear out in the TARDIS,' the

Doctor had said. 'Only trouble is, you never know when something might come in useful.'

Now he looked up from the complex piece of circuitry which was engaging more than half his attention. 'I'm so sorry,' he said. 'I think I've found the trouble. It's a matter of the temporal ... what did you say?'

'Atlantis,' Sarah repeated. 'You're having me on, surely.'

The Doctor returned to his work. 'My dear Sarah, as they used to say on Venus ...' His voice trailed away as he peered more closely into the intricate network in front of him.

'Can you come here a moment? There, you see that? Hold it still for me, will you, while I ...' His voice trailed away again.

'That little whojamaflip with the white bit sticking out?'

'That's the feller.' The Doctor picked up a strange-looking tool with tiny jaws shaped like a beetle's mandibles and poked it into the mess of wires.

'Used to say what?'

'Mm?'

'On Venus.'

'Oh yes. They had this proverb, you see,' the Doctor said absently, making some minute adjustments. 'That's when there were still people on Venus to have proverbs. Before the –' He stopped, grunting with concentration.

'So what was the proverb?'

'Mm? Oh yes. "You'd swallow a Klakluk and choke on a Menian dustfly."'

'A Klakluk?'

The Doctor stood up. 'A large lumpy beast. A bit like a moose with no horns. A nervous creature. It had two heads, so that a pack of pattifangs couldn't creep up on it. It never knew whether it was coming or going. A very confused animal, all in all. Thank you.'

'What for?'

'You can let go now.'

'Oh. Oh yes.' Sarah let go and wiggled the stiffness out of her fingers. 'So what's all that got to do with going back to Atlantis?'

'Well,' said the Doctor, 'you've travelled in the TARDIS yourself about eight hundred years back to Merrie England.'

'Merrie! That lot!'

Their hosts, if that's what they could be called, in the mediaeval castle to which the TARDIS had taken them seemed to spend most of their time killing each other – when not engaged in trying to kill the Doctor and Sarah.

The Doctor laughed and walked over to the TARDIS. 'Yes, a grim bunch, weren't they, old Irongron and his chums. But if you can swallow *that*, why choke on a mere three thousand years more?' He went inside.

Sarah called after him. 'Yes but Atlantis wasn't a real place. It's a fantasy, a legend!'

But the Doctor wasn't listening. He returned with a long wire which led out of the door and came back to the bench.

'Mark you,' he said, 'it was quite a hairy trip. The poor old TARDIS was nearly done for. Time Ram.'

Now what? What was the man talking about?

'Don't tell me,' she said. 'The TARDIS was attacked by a randy sheep with a clock for a face.'

The Doctor looked at her severely. 'Time *collision*! She collided with another TARDIS in the Time Vortex. They ended up inside each other.'

Eh?

'You mean the TARDIS was inside the other one?'

'That's right. And the other one was inside the TARDIS.'

At the same time?

'At the same time?'

'You've got it. Very disturbing. If you went out of one you found yourself in the other. And vice versa. No way of getting out. Like being inside a four-dimensional Moebius strip.'

Oh well. Perhaps it hadn't been such a good idea.

'I've got a feeling that you're not taking this interview very seriously, Doctor.'

'Interview?'

'My editor is going to say that it's all a load of old...' Watch it! '...bananas,' she finished feebly, avoiding 'codswallop' by a breath.

The Doctor stood up from the task of attaching the power lead to his circuit. He was not pleased. 'Do you mean to tell me that you've been *interviewing* me?'

'Well, yes. For my magazine. Metropolitan.'

The Doctor was haughty. 'Without even asking me?'

'But you know I'm a journalist. I thought you... I did say I wanted to have a bit of a chat, now didn't I?'

A flicker of emotion passed across the patrician face. What could it be? Disappointment?

Sarah floundered on. 'And I thought, since we got on so well, I mean, after all we'd been through together...'

The Doctor's lips were thin. 'My dear Miss Smith,' he said, 'you are hardly entitled to take such a liberty just because you saved my life a couple of times.' He looked up with irritation as the door swung open.

Sarah recognized the man in the army uniform who had come in. It was the officer – a Brigadier, wasn't he? – who had been in charge of security at the research establishment.

'Ah, there you are, Doctor,' he was saying.

The Doctor was even more irritated. 'Well, of course I am,' he said. 'Where else should I be but in my own laboratory?'

But the Brigadier had turned to Sarah.

'Good morning,' he said.

'Good morning,' she replied with relief. If only he knew what a welcome interruption he was!

But the Doctor wasn't going to let her off so lightly. 'This is Miss Sarah Jane Smith. A *journalist*,' he said icily. 'She's just leaving.' He switched on his circuit. It made a low humming sound.

Oh dear, oh dear. She really had blown it, hadn't she? 'Look, Doctor,' she said, 'I really am sorry if I've upset you but –'

'A journalist?' said the Brigadier. 'When we last met,

you were some sort of scientist, surely? Studied, er, bugs, wasn't it?'

Oh Lord! Things were getting more complicated by the minute. 'Bugs?' she said brightly. 'Oh, that sort of bug. Viruses and things. Yes. I mean, no. That was my Aunt Lavinia.'

The low humming of the circuit was getting louder and higher as the Doctor adjusted something in its innards.

'Really? I would have sworn – '

'Is it important, Brigadier? Because I'm trying to get some work done.'

'Good-bye, Miss Smith,' the Doctor added in a near shout, over the electronic screaming beneath his fingers.

'But, Doctor – '

'The Psycho-Telemetric circuit of the TARDIS has gone on the blink and – ' Pop! The unbearable noise stopped. A small wisp of smoke drifted up.

'Now look what you've both made me do. Brigadier! What do you want, for Pete's sake?'

The Brigadier seemed to be in no way put out. 'I want you to come with me to the opening of this new exhibition thing on Hampstead Heath.'

'Exhibition?'

'Theme park; funfair; whatever.'

'You mean Space World?' said Sarah, glad of a change of subject. 'I might come too. The press launch is at twelve.'

'Lethbridge-Stewart!' said the Doctor, 'Let me understand you aright. You have catastrophically interrupted a very tricky operation – on which, I may say, the entire navigation system of the TARDIS could depend – to invite me to a children's funfair?'

The Brigadier explained. The body of a young man had been found near the perimeter fence of Space World. He seemed to have been attacked by some sort of animal. Scotland Yard had turned the investigation over to UNIT and the Brigadier had thought it wise to take charge himself.

'I have to get stuck in straightaway. Before the Press arrive. Ask a few questions, that sort of thing.'

'Ask Miss Smith to hold your hand, then. She's very good as asking questions.'

Okay, okay, so she'd got it wrong. Did he have to go on about it?

'I need your help, Doctor. You see, the reason the police want us to be involved was – well, apparently the thigh bone had been bitten clean through. With one snap of the teeth.'

Hang on, there was a story here.

'There isn't a creature on Earth capable of doing that.'

'Precisely,' said the Brigadier. 'The pathologist said in his report that it looked as if the man had been savaged by . . .' He paused.

Well? *Well*? By what, for Heaven's sake!

The Brigadier continued somewhat hesitantly. 'It sounds absurd, I know, but – by a six-foot, sabre-toothed rottweiler.'

Oh Lordy! Was there ever a story here! Let them try to stop her coming too!

Chapter Three

As Billy Grebber swallowed a couple of aspirin for his breakfast in lieu of his customary fry-up, he noticed that his hand was trembling. Okay, he thought, so he was scared.

And it was all so unfair. He'd always tried to keep his nose clean. Well, more or less. What was the point of making a pile of dosh, if you were looking over your shoulder all the time for the fuzz – or worse? And as for duffing up the opposition, or having a ruck with every geezer who tried it on, well, leave it out. Look at Tel, who'd ended up splattered all over a car park in Bethnal Green for coming the old soldier with that tearaway from Brum. Or Tel's brother for that matter, going slowly crazy in Parkhurst.

And now, just when he was on the verge of making a couple of sovs for himself out of his share in Space World (he reckoned on half a million, give or take the odd grand), he'd got himself mixed up with a pair of maniacs who...

His stomach turned again as the image of the previous night rose up before his mind's eye. He groaned. What the hell was he going to do? The Old Bill weren't stupid. They'd soon make the connection. And then what? Billy Grebber, *finito*.

One thing was for sure: he was going to have it out with that brain-damaged cretin Freeth!

He swallowed the remainder of his tea to settle his still heaving stomach and set off for Space World.

The trouble was he'd left it a bit late. The deep sleep

he'd fallen into once his exhaustion caught up with him about five o'clock had lasted well into the morning. By the time he arrived, it was getting on for a quarter past eleven.

As he hurried through the spacious avenues to the comparative peace of the administrative block he could see that Space World was coming to life. No longer the deserted building site of yesterday, it swarmed with smartly uniformed 'Space Stewards', as the staff were designated. A bunch of metallic 'Robot Guides' (out of work actors glad to earn an anonymous pittance) were being rehearsed in their duties by an authoritative gentleman with a handlebar moustache and a Space Pilot's uniform. The sound of a technician's voice booming through the public address system and snatches of space age music competed with strange roars and shrieks apparently emanating from hidden monsters.

The interview with Freeth did not start well. Sweating with nerves as much as from his rush from the car park – why did these toffee-nosed gits always make him feel he was back at school? – he struggled in vain to dent the facade of well-upholstered confidence which the Chairman presented to the world.

'In any case,' said Freeth, imperturbably, 'you're too late. Two gentlemen from . . .' He glanced at a note on his vast mahogany desk. '. . . UNIT – some sort of Special Branch, I suppose – are e'en now plodding their way towards us.' He took a small handful of pink cachous and popped a few between his moist lips.

Billy Grebber could feel his guts tying themselves in knots.

'We've got to tell them the truth!' he said.

'The truth!'

'Well, not the truth as such, I suppose. We'll have to say it was an accident or something.'

He was certainly getting a reaction now!

'We shall do nothing of the kind!' Freeth's florid lips had tightened to a hard line.

Grebber was quick to seize his advantage. 'Now you listen to me, Mr Freeth – '

'You'd be better advised to listen to *me*!' Freeth spoke with a vicious sharpness.

In less than a moment, however, he had regained his customary urbanity. He gave Grebber a charming smile. 'I shall be ever in your debt for the excellent job your people have done on the site,' he said. 'That dinky little pavilion for the Love Worms! Sheer delight! And I promise that you'll see a more than worthwhile return on your investment. But you're playing with the big boys now.'

'That's all very fine, but – '

Freeth went relentlessly on. 'You saw last night how my esteemed colleague, Mr Tragan, ah, "gets his kicks".'

Grebber shuddered. Tragan's enjoyment was somehow the worst part of it.

'If I should drop the least little smidgeon of a hint – and I do assure you that it would hurt me more than it would hurt ... well, no. Perhaps not. But there, business is business. I have my shareholders to think of.' He chewed a few more of the scented sweets. The sickly smell caught the back of Grebber's throat. He swallowed.

'You wouldn't dare,' he said.

Freeth's face lit up. 'Oh, we're playing "dare" now, are we?' he said gleefully. 'What fun! Go on, then, try me.'

A buzzer sounded on his desk. He leaned forward. 'Yes, Tracey?'

'The gentlemen from UNIT are here, Mr Freeth.'

'Send them in, my dear.' He looked up at Grebber and twinkled at him mischievously. 'Now's your chance!' he said.

Determined not to lose contact with her source, Sarah had bummed a lift from the Doctor in his little old fashioned car, which he called 'Bessie'. He seemed more friendly now there was something real to think about. It was clear, however, that the Brigadier would not be pleased if she tried to muscle in on the investigation itself.

All the same, she could feel the rising excitement, the restless energy which told her that she was onto a good story. As she waited in the phone box opposite the door into which they had vanished, she found herself grinning cheerfully at a man standing waiting to make a call. Another journalist, presumably. He pointed at the phone and tapped his watch. She shrugged and turned her back on him as her editor came back.

'Yes, I'm still here. Who've I got?'

'Well, that's the thing. There isn't a photographer in the place. They're all on assignment.'

'What? Clorinda! Don't do this to me! I must have one!'

'How is it, Sarah Jane dear, that it's always "must" with you?'

The man outside rapped on the glass. 'You laying eggs in there?'

She desperately waved him away. Whatever he wanted, it could never be as important as her story. 'You've simply *got* to find somebody. I mean, if you can't supply the back-up, what's the point of employing the finest investigative journalist in the business?'

'Pause for hollow laughter,' replied Clorinda.

'Look, I'm in the driving seat on this one. I'll be able to find out if these monsters of theirs are real. I mean if they've been killing people – '

'Oh, be your age.'

'Well, the UNIT lot seem to think it's possible. Anyway, if they're not real, I can get an exclusive on how the wretched things are worked. You can run a "Metropolitan reveals all" on it. But let's face it, either way it'd be a bit naff without any pics. Come *on*!' The phone started to beep at her to put in some more coins. 'And I've run out of money!' she added in something of a squeak.

Clorinda sighed. 'Okay, you win. I'll do my best. But I can't – '

Her voice was cut off.

'About time too,' said the waiting reporter as she opened the door.

Sarah looked at him. 'Why didn't I go in for shovelling horse manure like my dear papa wanted?' she said.

*   *   *

Having been in Intelligence for many years, the Brigadier was quite accustomed to police-type questioning and the many different ways those questioned sought to deflect the questioner.

The man Grebber, for instance, he thought, with his one syllable answers. He didn't give the impression of a man who was easily scared and yet... And as for the fellow Freeth, well, he was too helpful by half. He should have been more exasperated that they'd turned up at such an awkward time, with the press view starting at any moment. Yet he'd welcomed them in, offered them a drink (which they'd refused), insisted on sending for this fellow Tragan – a nasty piece of work, if ever he'd seen one – and had fallen over himself to answer everything that either he or the Doctor could think to ask.

'You say that you and Mr Tragan arrived shortly after eleven o'clock. You're quite sure of that?'

Before Freeth could answer, Tragan interrupted in a hectoring voice obviously intended to intimidate. 'This is ridiculous!' he said. 'Badgering a man in Mr Freeth's position in this way! We can vouch for each other. And there's an end to it.'

The Doctor interposed a gentle enquiry. 'Were you once a policeman, Mr Tragan?'

'What of it?' he answered belligerently.

'I thought as much,' continued the Doctor. 'Similar characteristics the world over. One might almost say, universally?'

The Brigadier cocked an eye at the Doctor. Was there a particular emphasis on 'universe'? At any rate, it seemed to have silenced Tragan – for the moment, at least.

Freeth came in smoothly. 'Mr Tragan is now Vice-Chairman of the Corporation. He is the Head of the Entertainments Division.'

'Quite a career change,' said the Doctor. 'Fascinating.'

Tragan turned from him, his face as inscrutable as ever. His manner to the Brigadier hardly altered.

'Now, listen to me, Brigadier Whatever-your-name-is,

we've told you all we know, and that's nothing at all. Right?'

Cheeky blighter, thought the Brigadier. 'Just routine,' he said, in the time-honoured phrase. 'And my name, as I told you, is Lethbridge-Stewart.'

'Well, get to the point, man,' snapped Tragan.

'With pleasure. The point, Mr Freeth, is that according to the police,' the Brigadier said, glancing at his notes, 'your man was in the gatehouse having his supper, and therefore awake, from a quarter to eleven on. And Mr Kitson's car was the last one to come through the gate. How would you account for that?'

'Oh, God!'

All the heads swung round. 'What is it, Mr Grebber?' asked the Doctor.

'Nothing. Nothing,' blurted Grebber.

The Brigadier nodded to himself. The chap was scared. No doubt about it.

Freeth heaved a rich sigh. 'Brigadier, the company I have the privilege of serving is a very large one. In fact, I think I could say without fear of contradiction, that it is the largest multi-national in existence.'

'So what are you saying, sir?'

'It would be a pity, as I'm sure you would agree, if such a company were to begrudge its chairman the use of a teensy-weensy little corporate chopper.'

'A helicopter!' said the Doctor.

The Brigadier looked at him. Now what? He sounded as if this was practically an admission of guilt. But the Doctor hadn't finished. 'I see!' he added, as if this answered every question that could possibly be asked.

'And what exactly do you see, Doctor?' Tragan said grimly.

'Quite a lot, Mr Tragan. You'd be surprised.'

So should I, thought the Brigadier. 'Well, Mr Freeth,' he continued aloud, 'I think that covers everything for the moment. Thank you for your help.'

'Don't hesitate to contact me at any time,' said Freeth.

The Doctor eyed him beadily. 'We shan't. In fact, I

think I can promise you that we shall meet again quite soon. No, please,' he added to Tragan, who had not moved, 'we can see ourselves out.'

As soon as the door closed, Grebber burst into speech. 'They're on to us! That Doctor guy. He knows. He knows, I tell you!'

'Quiet!' hissed Tragan. 'They'll hear you!'

'Tragan!' Freeth's disarming air of helpless innocence had quite vanished.

'What is it?'

'I want to know who that Doctor is. Where he comes from; what his qualifications are; what was the maiden name of his maternal great grandmother. The lot! And I want to know a year last Tuesday. Right?'

Chapter Four

Oh Lor'! Here they come – and still no sign of any of Clorinda's photographers, thought Sarah, as she spotted the Doctor, deep in conversation with the Brigadier, coming out of the office block.

Pushing her way through the gathering crowd of journalists, she tried to get near enough to hear what they were saying. But what with the blaring sci-fi music coming through the loudspeakers and the usual ribald chat of her colleagues, it wasn't until she was almost on top of them that she could make out their words.

'You obviously noticed something about that shower that I missed,' the Brigadier was saying.

'Not a bit of it.'

'Thought you'd spotted that they'd all got Martian socks on. Or whatever.'

'That's just what I hoped *they* would think.'

Sarah lurked as near as she dared, elaborately pretending that she hadn't noticed them, still keeping an eye towards the entrance.

'You brought me here to find out whether there's an alien dimension to this death. If there is, and our friends are in fact involved, they'll be quite worried now. And a worried man is a careless man.'

'Ah,' said the Brigadier. 'Yes. Clever stuff.'

Oh dear, they'd stopped talking.

She sneaked a glance at them. They were both staring straight at her.

'Oh, hello!' she said brightly.

'We meet again, Miss Smith,' the Brigadier said drily.

'Yes, we do, don't we?' She gave a little laugh. It sounded unconvincing even to her.

There was an awkward pause.

'Are you going to join us on this guided tour affair? Due to start in a couple of jiffs.'

Was there a hint of reservation behind the polite words? The Doctor certainly had a sardonic lift to his eyebrow. But it was a chance too good to lose.

'Yes, I'd love to. I'm just waiting for the magazine's photographer.' Where was he for Pete's sake? She desperately scanned the chattering groups. And then she saw him: a slight figure bemusedly wandering through the throng, clutching a small camera case to his expensively clad bosom as though it might try to escape. Jeremy? What on earth did Clorinda think she was doing?

His face cleared as she called out to him. He hurried over. 'Sarah! Thank goodness I found you. All these people!'

'You're not a photographer,' she said in despair.

'Ah well, you see,' he answered in his impeccably upper class voice, 'I've got a message from Clorinda about that. She said to say that, er, "she told you she'd do her best and so she's sent me and you're not to laugh".' He frowned. 'I don't quite know what she meant.'

'I feel more like crying. You don't know anything about taking photographs.'

'No, no,' said Jeremy eagerly. 'You're going to do all that stuff. Clorinda's sent her own camera and if a monster eats it we're both sacked.'

Yes, very funny, she thought, noticing out of the corner of her eye the smile twitching at the corner of the Doctor's mouth.

'I'm so sorry,' she said, hearing herself echoing Jeremy's la-di-da tones. 'Doctor, Brigadier, may I introduce Jeremy Fitzoliver? Brigadier Lethbridge-Stewart and the Doctor,' she said to Jeremy.

'How do you do,' Jeremy said stiffly. Typical! Why couldn't he have said 'Hello'? Or even 'Hi, there'? 'How do you do' hardly went with his casual soft leather jacket (which must have cost a bomb and a half), or his designer jeans. Though on second thoughts, looking at that knife-edge crease...

The music stopped. The babble of the assembled men and women of the press died away, as the voice of a slim young man standing with Freeth on the steps of the first pavilion boomed across the open square: 'Ladies and Gentlemen! If you would like to gather over here?'

'Fitzoliver?' said the Brigadier, as they started to drift over with the rest, 'Any relation of Teddy Fitzoliver?'

'My Uncle Edmund, sir?'

Sarah knew Uncle Edmund – or rather knew of him. Only the majority shareholder in Metropolitan, wasn't he?

'Good Lord. I was at school with him.'

'I went to Holborough too,' said Jeremy. 'Only left last year as a matter of fact.'

The Brigadier chuckled. 'Haven't seen Pooh Fitzoliver for years.' His recollections were apparently tickling his sense of humour. 'Well, well, good old Pooh.'

' "Pooh"?' the Doctor said unbelievingly.

'Came of being called Teddy,' explained the Brigadier. 'Bear of very little brain, you know.'

That figures, thought Sarah, trailing along behind the newly established Old Boys' network.

Sarah couldn't pay proper attention to the Chairman's introduction – in which he contrived to mention the Parakon Corporation three times in as many minutes – because of her very real fears for his safety. Perched on the top of the flight of steps leading to the pavilion containing the Crab-Clawed Kamelius (the what?) he kept rising to the very tips of his elegant, over-polished shoes. Teetering on the edge, his massive form swayed with passionate intensity as he extolled the delights of Space World and the wonders they were all about to experience.

She was vastly relieved when, having invited them all to join him afterwards for a 'wee snifter and some munchies in the Space Restaurant at the top of the Apollo Tower', he handed over the running of things to his friend and colleague, Maroc Kitson, and tripped lightly down the steps and out of sight.

'Maroc? What sort of a name is that?' said the Brigadier.

'You may well ask,' replied the Doctor.

Kitson, having explained that the Crab-Clawed Kamelius was a native of the deserts of Aldebaran Two, a small planet about the size of Venus, invited them all to make its acquaintance. Before they could go inside, however, he stopped them.

'There's just one thing,' he said gravely. 'Although every precaution has been taken, I should point out that all the creatures I am going to show to you are killers. Keep on the right side of the barrier and, for your own safety, make no sudden moves or loud noises.'

This was greeted by laughter, combined with cries of 'Come off it!' and the like.

Sarah had her eye on the Doctor. He's not laughing, she thought. Nor's the Brig.

For that matter, it was plain that Jeremy had no idea why anybody should be laughing at all; and when Kitson continued, 'And, of course, no photography is allowed,' he glanced at Sarah as if he were afraid she would send him back to the office.

Kitson's dictum was greeted by cries of protest; it was only when it became clear that the Kamelius's guests would not be allowed past the lobby without surrendering their cameras to the large Space Cop at the inner door that it was ungraciously accepted.

'You'll get them back at the end of the tour,' said Kitson. 'Don't worry. You'll all be supplied with a handsome pack of shots in the hospitality room at lunchtime.'

Thank you, Clorinda dear, thought Sarah, slipping the mini-compact that Jeremy had brought into her jacket pocket.

Inside, the occupant of the pavilion was still not in view. A long handsome gallery in a vaguely classical-but-alien style was bounded on one side by a shimmering curtain of opalescent light, full with changing colour like the sway of shot silk. A murmur of appreciation rippled through the audience.

'I say,' Jeremy whispered to Sarah, 'this is something else!'

Something else? Honestly, he was always about ten years out of date! (Sarah was now feeling almost affectionate towards him.) Still, he wasn't wrong. She'd certainly never seen anything quite like it before.

Kitson made his way to the front of the gathering, as another security guard dressed as a Space Cop, carrying a heavy rifle which looked as if it would stop a rhinoceros charging, came in through a small door at the side. Sarah became aware of a low chattering gobble, apparently coming from behind the obscuring luminescence.

Kitson raised his hand for attention; the noise grew in a rapid crescendo to a great roar like the sound of an entire brass band playing together the ultimate discord; Kitson was forced to raise his voice to an undignified bellow.

'Ladies and Gentlemen!' he cried. 'May I present to you – the Crab-Clawed Kamelius!'

The curtain of light melted away. The Kamelius was revealed.

'Good grief!' said the Brigadier.

A remarkably realistic desert background seemed to stretch away into the distance, but the Kamelius was standing only a few yards away. In spite of its name, it had the merest suspicion of a hump. Its body was like that of an armadillo the weight of an African elephant, with legs of a similar size, though these too were clad in armour-like scales. Its cavernous red mouth, still gaping as it roared its displeasure, revealed two rows of teeth designed, it would seem, to crunch up a mouthful of rocks. Most fearsome of all, the claws – very like a crab's – at the ends of the two extra limbs attached to its shoulders, were clearly capable of snipping through the odd arm, or leg (or even neck) that ventured too near.

The ladies and gentlemen of the press drew back. Sarah felt Jeremy moving discreetly behind her.

'It's a real animal!' said the Brigadier, as the jabber of astonishment mounted in volume. 'It's the real thing!'

Sarah quite agreed with him. This was no animated puppet. She looked to see how the Doctor was reacting to the extraordinary beast.

'Have you ever seen a Crab-Clawed Kamelius before, Brigadier?' asked the Doctor.

'Of course not.'

'No. And you're not seeing one now.'

Was he saying it wasn't real? Was she supposed to disbelieve the evidence of her own eyes? 'Well, I certainly wouldn't like to meet it up a dark alley,' she said.

The Doctor raised his voice, over that of the Kamelius, which had subsided to the grumbling gobble they had first heard. 'Where did you say this beast comes from, Mr Kitson?'

'The deserts of Aldebaran Two,' he replied, 'which cover most of the planet.'

'I see,' the Doctor went on. 'Correct me if I'm wrong, but isn't Aldebaran about sixty-eight light years away from Earth? Something in the region of four hundred billion miles?'

'Quite right.'

'Then would you be so good as to explain how you managed to persuade the creature to come to Hampstead Heath?'

Kitson smiled. 'That, sir, would be telling.'

The assembled company, who had rather sheepishly regained their nerve now that the Kamelius seemed to have lost interest in them, laughed sycophantically.

What a lot of creeps, thought Sarah, pretending they hadn't been scared.

She looked over at the enormous creature, which was moving slowly away from them, its little red eyes scanning the ground as it swung the great head from side to side.

Kitson went on to explain that it was searching for its prey – a creeping land mollusc with a carapace as thick as a tortoise's, but Sarah was paying very little attention. She grasped the camera in her side pocket and tried to work out the safest way of snatching a quick shot – though the Kamelius's backside would hardly make the picture of the year.

'That's why it's got claws, I suppose,' said a rather dim columnist with scatty straw hair who normally wrote about the vicissitudes of living with her loveably madcap family. 'To get at the meat,' she explained helpfully.

'That's right,' said Kitson, eyeing her disingenuous bosom, which casually contrived to look as if it were about to spill out of her shirt. 'Though I don't suppose he'd object to a morsel of ready-shelled journalist.'

She nervously joined in the laughter.

Now! But Sarah started to pull the camera out of her pocket she felt Kitson's eye on her.

It's no good, she said to herself. If he didn't see me, that security guard certainly would. It wouldn't help much to get thrown out.

'I say,' Jeremy breathed in her ear.

'What?'

'Aren't you going to take a photo?'

'Oh, shut up!' she said.

Billy Grebber sat in his car and rubbed his damp palms with the clean linen handkerchief which, even in the midst of his morning turmoil, he'd remembered to select from the dozen or so in his drawer. He'd come a long way from his brickie days, he thought as, with trembling hands, he folded it carefully and stuck it back in his top pocket. Where did that Freeth get off, talking to him like he was his office boy? He was a flipping councillor, wasn't he? And if he played his cards right, he'd end up mayor.

A spasm of fear and anger clutched his belly. Why should he risk it all? It was murder, no two ways about it. And if it came out, he'd get done as an accessory, just because he was there, and because he'd lied to that Doctor geezer and said he didn't know nothing.

Suppose he went and got it off his chest? But if he did ... He heard again the screams and the sound of tearing flesh. Tragan's face flickered across his mind. He started to shake. He fumbled for his handkerchief and frantically tried once more to dry the cold sweat from his hands.

Chapter Five

Tragan covered the telephone mouthpiece with a bony hand. 'Do come in, Chairman,' he said, and watched with no discernible interest as Freeth turned diagonally to manoeuvre his immense width gracefully through the door.

Freeth said, 'Well?'

Tragan held up a hand. 'Thank you; you've been most helpful,' he said and put the phone down.

'I've found out what we need to know about the Doctor,' he said, anticipating Freeth's next question.

'And how did you manage to do that?'

'I rang UNIT and asked them.'

'A cunning ploy indeed,' said Freeth, sinking onto the sofa, which he neatly filled, designed as it was to accommodate two.

'The fools fell over themselves to give me the information. As much as they had, that is to say.'

Freeth frowned.

'Nobody seems to know where he springs from,' Tragan went on. 'He's the resident adviser, as the Brigadier said. He has a doctorate in practically all the scientific disciplines but he's a specialist in cosmology, space research and alien life forms.'

Freeth dug into his pocket and produced a small paper bag. 'Well, well, well. Maybe friend Grebber has good reason to be worried, after all. Where is he, by the way?'

'The Doctor?'

'Grebber.' Freeth started to unwrap a treacle toffee. 'In the circumstances I don't like the idea of his running

31

around loose. He could be a problem.' He placed the toffee in his mouth. His tongue flicked out and licked his finger and thumb.

Tragan rose from his desk and moved to the door. 'Maybe the problem needs a solution,' he said. 'A terminal one.'

Freeth chuckled. 'You'd enjoy that, wouldn't you, you wicked old Tragan, you?' he said, chewing stickily.

'How well you know me, Chairman,' replied Tragan without a smile and departed to look for the luckless Grebber.

Jeremy was thoroughly enjoying visiting the various monsters. Even the Giant Ostroid, he thought. A bit like an oven-ready turkey on stilts, she was. They didn't actually see her disembowelling an elephant or running at two hundred and twenty miles an hour, as Kitson told them she could. In fact, she didn't do anything much at all but look at them with her saucer eyes and occasionally give a loud belch which was jolly funny and made everybody laugh.

The Piranhatel Beetles were much more like it. They'd been thrown some sort of carcase just before the gang came in. They came swarming out of the undergrowth from every direction, hundreds upon hundreds of them: six inches long, with scarlet and black shells (did beetles have shells?) and these great tearing, biting thingies sticking out of their faces. They'd set upon the dead cow or whatever it was and in thirty-two point seven seconds – Kitson timed it with a stop watch – they'd stripped it down to its skeleton; just a lot of bare bones; just sticking up out of the grass. Made you think. Could have been you! Great!

But the best of all, so far, was the Stinksloth. He smelt worse than old Smellybelly Jenks in the third form – funny how his people took him away after only a term – and that was saying something. He lived in a pit of foul mud or worse – the Stinksloth, not Jenks, though that wouldn't have surprised anyone – and slurped around looking like a – well, a bit like one of those big sea lion thingies that lie around on the beach (the ones that have a thousand wives, and jolly tiring that must be, so no wonder they lie around!) only crossed with a jellyfish, sort of out-of-focus at the edges.

'The stench of putrefaction coming from his pit,' Kitson was saying, 'is due, I'm afraid, to his habit of storing the decomposing corpses of the giant slugs that he likes for breakfast in his sleeping corner. Ah, there! He's eating one now!'

Oh, yuck! Oh, double yuck! Jeremy thought.

And then, just when he was really enjoying himself, there was Sarah, pulling at his elbow and hissing in his ear. 'Come along, Jeremy,' she was saying as if she was his sister or something.

'Can't take it, eh?'

'Oh, don't be so silly. Come *on*!'

And she pulled him out of the pavilion and down the steps.

'Where are we going?' said Jeremy, desperately trying to keep up as she set off at a fast walk, almost a trot, while glancing from side to side as if she didn't want anybody to see where they were off to.

'I need you to keep watch,' she replied through her teeth. 'I'm going to get a candid camera shot of that Kamelius thing!'

Luckily, everybody they saw seemed to be far too busy getting ready for the afternoon opening to notice them, even when Sarah, with a quick secret-service-type look left and right, disappeared behind the Kamelius house. Jeremy blundered after her.

'Where are you going?'

'We can hardly march straight in through the front door,' she hissed.

'But what about that fellow with the gun?' he whispered, almost tripping over the mess of cables in the small back room which led to the side door.

'Sssh!' With infinite caution, Sarah eased open the

door and peeped through the crack. 'It's all right,' she whispered, 'there's nobody here.'

'Oh. I say,' said Jeremy as he followed her in, 'the beastly thing's gone.'

'No, there he is – coming out from behind that dune.'

Jeremy peered across the the heat shimmer rising from the sand. Oh, yes. But how could he be forty yards away, or more like fifty, when the pavilion itself was less than half that size? A phrase shimmered in his head like the hot air in front of him. Optical ... illusion? Yes, that was it. Sort of scientific conjuring. 'Oo look! He's eating a tortoise thingy!' He could hear the crunch as the Kamelius cracked open the shell with its immense claws.

Sarah already had the camera up to her eye and was muttering under her breath.

'Sorry?' said Jeremy.

'I said ...' Sarah took the camera away from her eye and turned to him. 'Oh, for Heaven's sake? Don't just stand there! Go and see if there's anybody in the lobby. Keep a look-out!' She spoke in a cross stage-whisper, sort of shouting at him under her breath.

Feeling got at – after all, she hadn't *said* – Jeremy went to peep through the main door into the reception lobby. No, there was no-one there either. If he stuck his head out a bit, he could see into the open square outside, but the odd member of staff passed by without a glance.

He could hear Sarah's voice, behind him, interspersed with the clicking of the camera: 'That's it, sweetheart, look this way. Lovely, lovely. Come towards me. Come on, I won't bite. That's my boy!'

The Kamelius had started its gobbling noise again – and it was getting louder. Jeremy looked round. Much to Sarah's delight, the creature was coming towards her at a fair old rate of knots. Perhaps he ought to warn her.

'Oi! You!'

He swung round in a panic. Outside, there was a tough-looking man about twenty feet away who was looking straight at him. 'Yes, you! I want a word with you!' He made for Jeremy with purpose in his gait.

'Sarah! Cave! There's someone coming!'

The Kamelius was almost on top of her and she was clicking away like mad. 'Sarah!' shouted Jeremy.

'I'm on my way!' she said. As she lowered the camera, the Kamelius swung at her head with a claw gaping wide. She fell backwards with a strangled squeal.

Scrambling to her feet, she scuttled to Jeremy's side. 'He nearly got me,' she gasped. But Jeremy was by now more concerned about the man coming up the steps.

'What are we going to say?'

Sarah took in the situation. 'Leave it to me,' she said. 'Pretend to be a bit dim-witted.'

'Eh?' said Jeremy.

She threw him a glance. 'On second thoughts, just stay as sweet as you are.'

Shoving the camera into her pocket, she walked straight through the lobby and out of the front door, meeting the man as he reached the top of the steps. 'Hi there,' she said. 'We were just having a bit of a look round.'

Grebber was looking for the Doctor. Once he'd made up his mind what to do he'd begun to feel a bit better. Of course, he'd never grassed on anybody before. After all, it wasn't as if he'd always been a plaster angel himself. But it wouldn't be like turning in a mate who'd bought a load of dodgy marble, or saved a bit here and there on the architect's specification. These people had got to be stopped.

As for Tragan, well, he'd just have to keep out of his way. 'As long as he doesn't know it was me what landed them in it, I'm safe,' he said to himself, as he hurried through the endless avenues and squares of Space World, searching for the guided tour. If he didn't find them soon, though ... He could feel his resolution ebbing away. He stopped and wiped his forehead. He was back outside the Kamelius House, where the tour had started.

Now, there was a face he recognized. It was that kid who'd been with the Doctor. He'd seen them out of the window of Freeth's office. He'd know. He called to him and hurried over; and as he reached the top of the steps the other one, the girl with the bobbed hair, came out with the kid behind her.

'Hi, there,' she said. 'We were just having a bit of a look round.'

She looked at him curiously as he panted his enquiry about the Doctor. 'Well,' she said, pulling the press release out of her pocket and consulting it (Now why hadn't he thought of getting hold of one of those?), 'I should think they must have got to the Moon Walk by now. If he's still with them.'

'You're a doll,' he said. 'Look. If you catch up with him before I do, will you give him a message for me? Only for God's sake don't tell anyone else, see. Only him or that Army guy. Okay?'

'What is it?'

'Tell him I lied to them this morning. Tell him – '

'Ah, Mr Grebber. There you are.'

Oh God, it was Tragan! Had he heard?

Apparently not. 'I've been looking all over for you,' he continued in a cold but courteous voice. 'Mr Freeth would like a word.'

Billy Grebber's first impulse was to run; he didn't give in to it, but he couldn't tell whether the reason why he allowed himself to be led meekly away, albeit with a covert look of entreaty at the girl, was courage – or simple terror.

When, on the night the Americans landed on the moon, Brigadier Lethbridge-Stewart had watched Neil Armstrong on TV jumping onto the surface – and fluffing his entrance line – and had immediately gone out onto his balcony to look at the full moon a quarter of a million miles away, his prime emotion had been envy. And yet, standing, or so it seemed, on that very surface, under the immense black dome dotted with untwinkling stars, the clouded blue disc of the Earth hanging above his head, he was content to watch with the Doctor while the more mobile members of the group performed the low-gravity acrobatics which were the main attraction of the Space World Moon Walk.

'He doesn't believe a word of it,' he said to himself, with an eye on the Doctor, as Kitson came out with a load of scientific gobbledegook – as far as the Brigadier was concerned – which purported to explain how the thing worked.

'What do you think, Doctor?' he asked as they followed the others into the next side-show, a wonder by the name of 'ER', which promised, yet again, to blow their minds.

'They should make a lot of money.'

'Yes, but what do you *think*?'

'Well, in the first place, neither centrifugal force nor centripetal force exists, as such; the use of the terms – indeed of the concepts – betrays either a naive misunderstanding or a cynical intention to mislead. In the second place, in the context of anti-gravity – '

He stopped abruptly and shushed the Brigadier, giving him a severe look as if he had been the one talking. Kitson was holding up his hand for silence.

'Ladies and Gentlemen,' he said, 'Space World can, I think you'll agree, be justly proud of the wonders you have seen so far. However, the next call on our itinerary will more than astound you, it will introduce you to something which is destined to become an integral part of your future lives. If you will follow me, I shall show you a way to the fulfilment of all your secret hopes – and an escape from all your secret fears – Experienced Reality!'

Oh yes? thought the Brigadier.

Chapter Six

'ER – Experienced Reality! The Wonder of the Millenium!'

The Brigadier surveyed Kitson with a somewhat cynical eye. He'd come across too many of these smooth-talking johnnies. Trying to sell something, this fellow was. Like Chuffy Knowles. Perfectly decent cove when he was at Sandhurst, and then, only eighteen months after he left the Service, turned into a smoothy just like Kitson and tried to sell him a life insurance policy. Over lunch at the club, at that.

'Now, this may look like a rest room to you,' Kitson was saying, 'but these luxuriant ergonomically perfect couches can offer you the chance to know for yourself all the thrills this great old world of ours can offer. Like to go skiing? Can't ski? Oh, yes you can. You can ski as well as next year's Olympic champion. Skin-diving, windsurfing, hang-gliding, you name it – and not just on a colour telly screen. I'm talking about a real experience. A leisure experience beyond your wildest dreams!'

He was interrupted by the blurred voice of a member of his audience who had obviously been anticipating the promised 'wee snifter'.

'That's not the sort of thing I dream about, when I'm on my luxuriant couch,' it said coarsely.

The Brigadier looked round. He recognized the leering face at once, which was not surprising, since it not only graced the top of his daily column, but appeared with nauseating regularity on every sort of chat show, as he could always be relied upon to supply a generous measure of thinly veiled innuendo and implied smut. Septimus Hardiman, that was the name. Were there really six more at home like him? God help us all.

'Well sir,' replied Kitson, obviously treading very carefully, 'although it wouldn't be appropriate to offer such delights to the general public, the technology is available to cater for every imaginable taste to the utmost, er, *satisfaction*.' He invested the word with a multiplicity of meaning.

There was a feverish scribbling of notes, and a clamour of voices, led by Hardiman's demand that he expand on the notion. But Kitson was into his prepared spiel once more.

'An opera lover, perhaps? You can not only be present at the first night of the new Traviata at La Scala, Milan, but if you wish you can experience the joy of singing the lead role yourself, of *being* the star. A boxing fan? You can choose to watch from the best possible ringside seat or, if you so desire, you can be up there in the ring yourself, fighting for the championship of the world!'

All very fine and dandy, thought the Brigadier, but why didn't the man stop nattering and let them all have a go? As the thought passed through his mind, it was voiced, a deal more crudely, by the obnoxious Septimus.

Kitson was only too pleased to oblige, and the Brigadier was soon reclining at his ease, wearing a lightweight headset, trying to decide which of the many buttons on the control panel to push. There had been a mild altercation between himself and the Doctor as to who should be first, as there weren't enough places to go round. Since, however, it soon appeared that the Doctor wasn't really concerned, apparently on the grounds that ER would be a more sophisticated version of something he called VR – Virtual Reality – the Brigadier allowed himself to be persuaded.

'Well now,' he said, finger poised, 'how about "A Day at the Races"? I've always enjoyed an outing with the gee-gees.' He stabbed the appropriate button.

'Good grief!' he exclaimed. 'I'm there! I'm really there!'

As if in the far distance, he heard the Doctor's voice: 'Not a computer model, then?' but it was almost drowned by the noise of the crowd, the shouting of the bookies, and the general din he knew so well. For, yes, by jiminy, he *was* really there. At Epsom, of all places. He was walking down towards the paddock. He could feel the grass under his feet and the breeze in his face, and the smell of the horses mingling with the tempting aroma of cooking meat, drifting down from behind the crowd. He might pop over presently and get a bite. It seemed a long time since he'd had his breakfast.

With a jolt, he remembered what was really happening and became aware of the Doctor's voice: 'For Pete's sake, Lethbridge-Stewart, speak to me. What's going on?'

By concentrating hard, he managed to regain a rudimentary consciousness of his real situation, like a far-off unwanted memory. He could feel his body lying on the couch like the ghost of a thought at the back of his mind; and he was able to reply to the Doctor. But even as he described his experience, he found himself leaning on the rail, surveying the runners. There was Murphy Muffin, the Irish winner of the Oaks. Should stand a very good chance. He glanced up. Yes, of course. He would be favourite. Odds on.

The Doctor was almost shouting at him. 'Brigadier! I said, "Try turning round and walking back the way you came".'

Wretched fellow! 'Frankly,' he said, 'I don't want to. I'm quite happy as I am.'

'A scientific experiment, man! Remember why we're here.'

Oh yes. Yes. The Brigadier managed to remember, but it seemed to be quite impossible to get his recalcitrant body to obey him. But it didn't matter. As he told the Doctor, he was doing exactly what he wanted to do. Beautiful creatures, racehorses.

'You're doing what the program wants you to do,' the Doctor was saying in the distance.

Fred the Frog looked to be in good nick. He might be worth a few bob each way.

'May I change the channel for you?'

'What? Oh, if you must. But I must say that I – oof!'

It was like hitting an air pocket. Epsom Downs vanished in an instant; the Brigadier felt himself falling through a cloud of – black cotton wool? No sound, no sight, no touch; until, abruptly, but with no sense of a sudden stop, he landed on a beach somewhere.

The shock of the change had forcibly reminded him of the object of the exercise. He made a firm effort to make some sort of report to the Doctor. 'At the seaside. Lord knows where. Pretty darn hot. Strong smell of flowers. Can't quite place the perfume. I seem to be in my bathers. Been for a swim, I suppose. I can hear the surf behind me and I'm walking up the beach towards a bunch of ... dollybirds ...'

His intention faded away as he looked at the group of girls, half a dozen or so, sitting on the sand in the shade of some palm trees and smiling a welcome. Absolute stunners, all of them, thought the Brigadier; there was something about a tanned female figure in a bikini – or half a bikini, some of them! As he sat down with them on the hot sand, he tried to work out what to say, casting his mind back to the wilder days of his youth when he had acquired a number of very fruitful chat-up techniques. But before he could open his mouth, he suddenly became aware of his legs, as he stretched them out in front of him.

'Good Heavens above!'

'What is it?' he heard the Doctor say.

'Those aren't my legs! Those are *not* my legs!'

'Are you sure?'

'Of course I'm sure. Since when have I painted my toenails pink? Those are female legs for Pete's sake; and yet they're *my* legs – but they're not, if you see what I mean.'

Utterly disorientated, the Brigadier made a great effort

and raised the phantom hand at the back of his mind and pulled off the headset.

In an instant, the beach was nothing but a memory and he was back with the Doctor, blinking at the change of light; hearing the cries of wonder coming from the other couches.

'Extraordinary experience,' he said. 'Bit beyond my ken, if you follow me, but quite fascinating. Here, you'd better have a go.'

But before the Doctor could take the headset from him, Sarah's head appeared round the door.

'Psst?' she said.

'And that's all he said?' asked the Doctor when Sarah had got them outside and told them what had happened.

'It was all he had time for,' she said.

'What was he like, this fellow?' said the Brigadier.

'Bit of an oik, actually,' said Jeremy.

Well, really! Sarah thought. How snobbish could you get? Giving Jeremy a reproving look, which obviously went right past him, she explained that the man was nothing of the kind – just that he had a London accent; sort of Cockney.

'Grebber, by Jove,' said the Brigadier.

The Doctor said nothing. He walked a short distance away from them, where he seemed to be in close contemplation of a nearby bush covered with silver roses. After a minute or so, he turned round. His face was grave.

'This merely confirms what I feel about this place,' he said. 'It could pose a serious threat. There's danger here.'

'What, you mean the monsters?' said the Brigadier.

'No, no, no,' the Doctor said impatiently. 'I'm talking about real danger. It's this place. This ER. This "Experienced Reality".'

If it was true that the Doctor was over seven hundred years old (and that's what he'd told Sarah) it was perhaps fair enough that he treated the Brigadier like an adolescent schoolboy – and really the Brigadier took it very well when the Doctor told him that he was talking rubbish saying that ER was only another form of telly.

'Even if you consider it in that light, how many people are there who have to have a nightly fix of their favourite soap operas?' he said. 'As harmless as being addicted to the caffeine in a cup of coffee, you might think. Well, television is to ER as caffeine is to heroin! Think, man! Think how it must work!'

'Haven't the foggiest. How does it work?'

The Doctor explained that at first he'd assumed it must be a subtle form of suggestion; a type of electronic hypnotism which merely provided the seed of an experience, which the subject's own brain expanded.

'Two things gave me the clue, however. Firstly, the way the program went its own way, no matter how much you tried to change it; and secondly, Lethbridge-Stewart, your painted toenails.'

'Painted toenails! The Brigadier?' In spite of herself, Sarah couldn't help giggling.

'Yes, well,' the Brigadier said gruffly, 'we won't go into that.'

'Oh yes, we will,' said the Doctor. 'Don't you see? Somebody *had* those experiences. Somebody went to Epsom races with a sensory transmitter implanted in his brain. The same with the woman on the beach. Every sense impression she had was transmitted to a polygraph recorder. And those sense impressions were reproduced in the Brigadier's brain, even down to the scent of the flowers.'

'Bougainvillaea! I knew I'd smelt it before,' said the Brigadier. 'Must have been the Caribbean.'

Sounded great, thought Sarah. How could he say it was dangerous?

Jeremy echoed her thought, saying it sounded 'wizzo-wicked' to him.

The Doctor explained. 'The program took charge of the Brigadier's will,' he said. 'He *wanted* to go where he was being taken. He lost any intention of his own.'

'Not entirely,' said the Brigadier, remembering his plans to chat up the girls on the beach.

'For all practical purposes,' replied the Doctor. 'But it's even worse than that. If these people, wherever they come from, have the technology to transmit brain signals – *and to control the receiver's will* – they have the means to control a country, a world.'

A shiver ran down Sarah's spine. If what the Doctor said was true, and she'd never known him wrong before, this was the story of a lifetime, and it was all hers!

Chapter Seven

Tragan carefully placed the implantation gun back into its case, put the case into the drawer of his desk and locked it.

Freeth looked at the recumbent figure on the sofa. 'He doesn't look at all well,' he said. 'Decidedly peaky. He's not dead already? A high profile death – what you might call a public corpse – is useful publicity. A private corpse might be something of an embarrassment.'

'I know what I'm doing,' replied Tragan, walking over to make a close examination of two small red punctures, one on each temple. 'The transmitter needles are a little larger than usual, that's all. His system will soon recover.'

He lightly slapped the flaccid face. 'Wake up, Grebber.'

There was no reaction. Without any change of expression, Tragan lifted his hand and delivered a vicious backhander to Grebber's cheek. His head jerked to one side and he started to moan.

'Mr Grebber!' called Freeth, in dulcet tones, 'Open your eyes, there's a good boy.'

Grebber complied. 'Where ... where am I?' His eyes tried to focus. 'What happened?'

'You passed out, that's all,' answered Tragan.

'Me?' said Grebber, sitting up and looking vaguely round the room. 'I never fainted in my life.' He stood up, and promptly sat down again.

'You'd better be getting home, dear boy,' said Freeth, his evident concern creasing the folds of flesh around his little eyes. 'If you don't feel well in the morning, you'd do well to go and see your doctor. It could be anything.'

'Good advice, Mr Grebber,' said Tragan, opening the door.

For the first time Grebber seemed to register who Tragan was. He dropped his eyes. 'Yeah, yeah,' he muttered and made his way uncertainly out. Tragan closed the door behind him.

'I hope you do know what you're doing,' said Freeth, wriggling his bulk into the vacated sofa and searching for his toffees. 'That headset is larger than the normal ER type,' he added suspiciously.

'Well, of course it is. I'm transmitting and receiving live, not just plugging in to a recording. Now, if you would be so good, Chairman? I have to concentrate.'

Grebber stood outside, trying to make up his mind. He was still feeling groggy, in spite of getting away from Tragan. Indeed, it was the sight of him that had revived his indecision. He recognized dully that the intensity of his fear had been transformed into a fatalistic acceptance of his doom.

'It don't make any difference what I do. I've had it either way,' he said to himself, rubbing his forehead as if to charm away his throbbing headache.

Freeth was right. He'd be better off at home. What could happen today? Sweet FA, that's what. So he might just as well sleep on it. He set off towards the car park.

He couldn't have gone more than a dozen paces when he was pulled up short. An idea had come into his head, almost as if it had been injected from outside; an idea of such blinding clarity that there could be no question of rejecting it.

He stood for a moment, contemplating its elegant simplicity. If he were dead, he'd have no more worries. Of course. It was the only way out.

He turned and strode purposefully towards the Apollo rocket which towered over the rest of Space World.

'Got him,' said Tragan.

'Bye-bye, Grebber,' Freeth said lightly, through a mouthful of treacle toffee.

The seaside donkey with good feed in his nosebag happily follows wherever he is led. In spite of much evidence to the contrary, there is a widely held view amongst those in the PR business that the ladies and gentlemen of the press can be bribed into a good opinion by offering them the equivalent of prime quality oats. In Sarah Jane Smith's case, they happened to be right (other things being equal).

'Smoked salmon!' she said, taking another large mouthful. (Must be a thousand calories a bite. So what? She could always go without supper.) 'They're doing us proud.'

'I'm bored with smoked salmon,' said Jeremy, piling his plate with little Nuremburger bratwurst sausages. 'Every party you go to, they – '

'Listen to the deb's delight. Think yourself lucky it's not a pickled onion on a toothpick.'

Happily munching, she peered through the bodies of her ever hungry (and thirsty) colleagues milling about the Space Restaurant. She mustn't let the nosh get in the way of the job. She frowned. 'Where's the Doctor got to?'

'The Observation Gallery. I saw him going up with the Brigadier.'

'Oh, Jeremy, why didn't you tell me?'

Pausing only to add a dollop of fresh asparagus mousse to her heaped plate, she pushed her way through to the glass lift in the middle of the circular room, closely followed by Jeremy – and up they sailed like a couple of weightless astronauts to the gallery above.

As she stepped out, her attention was caught by the view through the big picture windows, which was even more spectacular than the one from the restaurant below. Of course, on the south side you had to look through the scaffolding framework holding the exterior lift which had brought them all up, just like the original Apollo rocket which went to the moon, but that merely served to emphasize the incredible distance you could see. The whole of Greater London, with the winding ribbon of the

Thames, was laid out like a giant's toy; and beyond, the greens and browns of the Surrey countryside, shading off into a far blue haze; and beyond that even – yes, it was! Glinting in the noonday sun: the sea!

'Not a bad Chablis, all things considered.'

The Brigadier's voice broke into her thoughts. He and the Doctor were alone, the other members of the party having found more important things to do down below. Poking a gourmet forkful into her mouth, Sarah wandered casually round the gallery to the other side, hoping to be as unnoticed as a familiar piece of furniture.

'All the circumstantial evidence,' the Doctor was saying, 'points to their having come from the other side of the Galaxy.'

Now, this was something interesting. She stopped chewing in case she missed something.

'What evidence?' asked the Brigadier.

'Those creatures; the extremely advanced brain technology used in ER; the – '

'But you said the monsters were fakes,' interrupted the Brigadier.

'I said nothing of the kind. It's the names that are fakes. "Kamelius!" "Ostroid!" I'm surprised they didn't show us a two-trunked Elephantiasus from the Planet Junglon.'

A chortle from Jeremy drew a filthy look from Sarah. He became aware that they were all looking at him.

'Sorry,' he said. 'It just tickled me, that's all. There isn't really a planet called Junglon, is there?'

'Of course there isn't. I just made it up.'

The Brigadier brought them back to the matter in hand. 'So if they are in fact real,' he said, 'we're on the right track, after all. One of them could have killed that poor chap on the Heath.'

'If I'm correct in my suspicions, Lethbridge-Stewart, you'd be as safe with those creatures as you would be in a field of new-born lambs!'

Sarah's indignation overcame her discretion. 'But that Kamelius thing nearly got me!'

'Yes,' said Jeremy, 'it could have had her head off. If I hadn't been there – '

'Well, of course, they've programmed the things to appear savage. But I assure you that you were never in any danger at all.'

'Programmed?' said the Brigadier.

'Nevertheless,' the Doctor went on, ignoring him, 'I think it must be true that this gang know more about the killing than they pretend. I'm looking forward to having another word with our friend Grebber.'

'Ya,' said Jeremy. 'I shouldn't trust him all the way though.'

This time Sarah's look of disapproval registered. 'Well, I thought he was an oik,' he said, sulkily. But Sarah wasn't listening, for through the window on the other side of the gallery, she could see the man himself, standing on the far side of the scaffolding, desperately keeping his balance by clutching one of the supports.

'Doctor! Look!' she cried.

'He's going to jump!' exclaimed the Brigadier.

The Doctor was already on his way. 'Brigadier!' he said as he ran to the lift. 'Get the Fire Brigade with a long ladder. Sarah! Persuade him to turn round. Try to keep his attention!'

'Where are you going?' she cried, but the lift was already speeding him downwards.

Billy Grebber had no fear of heights. One of the star workers on some of the tallest developments in the City of London (fastest brickie in the East, they used to call him) he'd always enjoyed the sense of freedom he got when he was way up high, the sense of being above the petty concerns of the ordinary mortals on the ground.

But he was afraid of dying.

It had seemed so easy as he'd climbed the last thirty feet from the lift platform. Even now, as he gazed at the Lilliputian inhabitants of Space World, hundreds of feet below, he still knew with unshakeable certainty that the only way out of his present troubles was straight down.

And then? A wave of vertigo swept over him. He swallowed and hung on even more firmly. Perhaps he was being too hasty. Even to be banged up for life might be better than – what? Other certainties, inherited from a long line of chapel-goers, and largely ignored in latter years, now presented themselves with the inevitability of the predestination he'd learnt about at Sunday School.

What if he weren't one of the elect? If ever there were creatures from hell, Tragan's were. Maybe he'd had a glimpse of the torments waiting for him in the Eternal Pit. He started to shake uncontrollably.

Dimly he became aware of a banging noise which had been going on for some time. There was a voice. 'Mr Grebber! Over here! Please turn round! Please!' He turned his head. The voice was coming from behind, but climbing up towards him was the Doctor himself, the very man he had thought to help him.

'Don't look down, Mr Grebber,' the Doctor called in a calm, firm voice.

Grebber opened his mouth to try to explain, but nothing would come out but a feeble croak. The Doctor was now on a level with him, about ten feet away.

'Look at me,' he was saying. 'Look at me. That's it. We'll soon have you safe.'

'I – I wanted to finish it all, but... Help me, Doctor! Help me!'

'Hold on tight,' replied the Doctor. 'Help's on its way. Just hang on!'

Grebber could feel a dreadful compulsion to let go. His fingers were starting to loosen, as if against his will. 'I can't hold on much longer,' he gasped. 'I shall fall! Help me! Please!'

'Very well,' said the Doctor. 'I'll come to you.'

Grebber watched as the Doctor, with one hand on the wire rope above his head, edged along the scaffolding pole, holding out the other hand. Suddenly, Grebber knew exactly what was going to happen. Although he was still shaking in the extremity of his fear, he reached out and gripped the proffered hand with his own bricklayer's paw. He let go with his other hand.

For the first time, there was alarm in the Doctor's voice. 'What are you doing, man! Hold on! You'll have us both over!'

'I'm sorry, Doctor!' he managed to gasp and then, with a great cry of desolation and despair, Billy Grebber surrendered himself to whatever fate his God had decided for him at the beginning of time.

Freeth stopped chewing in alarm as Tragan's shout of terror echoed round the mahogany panels of the office. He leaned forward as his Vice-Chairman pulled off the headset. 'Are you all right?' he said.

Tragan was sitting with his eyes closed, panting slightly. 'Oh yes,' he answered, opening his eyes after a pause, 'I'm fine. I stayed with him too long, that's all.'

He looked up at the mass of flesh sitting opposite. His face was as impassive as ever, but his normally flat voice was rich with overtones of gratified desire.

'I played him like a fish, Freeth, letting him go and reeling him in, with his fright all the time growing in intensity; growing, growing; and at the end, his mortal dread of dying. I couldn't resist going with it. It was ecstasy, I tell you, utter ecstasy!'

Freeth shuddered. 'Delicious,' he said.

Tragan stood up and stretched. 'We've been given a bonus,' he said. 'We can relax. We shan't have any more trouble from that meddlesome Doctor. He came over with me. The Doctor's dead.'

Chapter Eight

Sarah turned away sadly as the flashing of the ambulance disappeared. Jeremy was quietly waiting and watching. 'Did you know him well?' he asked.

How could she begin to explain to anybody else how she was feeling? She couldn't even explain it to herself.

'Not really,' she said. 'But he was a good man. And a brave one. It's silly, I know, but I feel as if – as if I'd lost my best friend.'

How inadequate words were, after all!

'I don't think it's silly at all.'

She looked at his concerned face, and then felt guilty that she should be surprised. 'You're rather sweet, Jeremy,' she said.

The excited crowd which had gathered was melting away. A uniformed constable was removing the temporary barriers which had been erected around the area. Sarah looked for the Brigadier – to keep in touch with him would almost be like being with the Doctor still – but there was no sign of him. He was probably with the police somewhere. He'd have plenty of official stuff to keep him busy. She was being childish.

'This is no good,' she said. 'Life must go on.'

'Well, that's what he would want, isn't it?'

He'd surprised her again. 'You're right, of course. Come on. We'd better get back to the office and get these pictures developed.'

As they walked the length of Galaxy Avenue, with its alien water-sculptures (to call them fountains would be an insult; how could a simple fountain twist into such shapes?) Sarah could hear a sound like the roar of an impatient football crowd. As they approached the main entrance, the gates swung open and Space World's first real customers started to pour through in their hundreds.

Life would go on, with or without the permission of Sarah Jane Smith.

By the time the CID man from Golders Green had satisfied himself that the double death was probably not connected with the body on the heath, the Brigadier was getting impatient. They'd been closeted together in the little room Kitson had found for them for what seemed like hours. At last, he closed his notebook with a snap.

'Seems clear enough,' he said. 'We'll need to find out a bit more about Mr Grebber's background, but that apart ... and there's the autopsy, of course. But that's more or less a formality in the circs.' But the Brigadier was hardly listening. The Doctor's death didn't mean that his own investigation had come to a full stop. So what now?

'My dear Brigadier, I cannot begin to tell you how devastated we are,' said Freeth, rising nimbly from his gargantuan swivel chair to greet his visitor.

'Kind of you,' grunted the Brigadier.

'We have our own occasion of grief, of course,' Freeth continued. 'The man Grebber, poor foolish troubled soul. But nothing compared to the loss of a colleague – and a friend?'

His unctuous voice vied with the fleshy solicitude of his face. He seated himself on the sofa, which was covered with a richly coloured Gobelin tapestry, by a coffee table surfaced in mosaic – an apparently genuine ancient mosaic, as if from a Roman villa, but portraying a fearsome alien beast under a hyacinth sky. He motioned to the easy chair opposite. *This is a social occasion*, the gesture said. *Let us be intimate together, let us mourn together.*

The Brigadier remained standing.

'Be that as it may,' he said. 'I am here on official business. I have to ask you to cancel the opening of Space World.'

Freeth's manner changed instantly. His eyes narrowed and the soft curves of his face noticeably hardened.

'Do you indeed?' he said. 'And I have to tell you that I have no intention of complying.'

The Brigadier's face was equally hard. 'Then I shall be forced to close it down.'

'I understood from that boy who described himself as a detective sergeant that his enquiries here were closed. On whose authority do you propose to take this officious action?'

'My own, sir.'

'I see. On what grounds?'

For a moment, the Brigadier hesitated. It would not be acting outside his powers to shut Space World with no explanation at all. Freeth's cool arrogance deserved no less.

However, it might not be good policy. He needed Freeth's co-operation.

'Before he – he died,' he said, reluctantly, 'the Doctor told me of certain suspicions he had. Until I am satisfied that these suspicions are groundless, I cannot allow you to proceed with your plans.'

As Freeth listened, he seemed to relax. He spoke more gently. 'My dear Brigadier, you should have come to me sooner. You're too late. If you listen you'll no doubt be able to hear the baying of the Great British Public bent on pleasuring itself. Or is that the phrase I'm after?'

He smiled winningly, his head tilted to one side like a manipulative toddler. His manner had quite reverted to its habitual bantering lightness.

'We shall have to clear them all out then,' said the Brigadier, harder than ever. 'As Officer Commanding the United Nations Intelligence Task Force in the UK, I am empowered, under the treaty, to take any action I consider necessary to safeguard international security.'

'Ah, but there are so many forms of power, aren't

there?' Freeth rose from the sofa. In spite of the situation, the Brigadier couldn't help thinking of a hot-air balloon casting off its moorings. As Freeth walked back to his desk, he smiled again.

'Before you get stuck in the political mire of exactly who has the power to do what – and to whom – I would strongly advise you to read this.'

He opened a drawer and produced a letter.

The Brigadier's lips tightened as he saw the impressive letterhead. He glanced down at the signature. Not only was the letter from Number Ten, it was signed by the Prime Minister himself.

Freeth was clearly enjoying himself. 'It hurts the pride, doesn't it, falling flat on one's face? Never mind,' he added comfortably, 'I'm sure Mummy will kiss it better.'

'But, General, it was a personal letter guaranteeing him and his precious corporation freedom from interference of any kind whatsoever!'

The Brigadier was sitting in the Doctor's car, speaking to the world headquarters of UNIT in Geneva. In such a delicate matter, it would be most unwise to use a public phone, or worse still, one in the Parakon office block.

The General was sympathetic but ultimately unhelpful. His authority, wide though it undoubtedly was, could not override that of the government of a host country in such a situation.

The Brigadier was determined that Freeth should not get away with it. 'Would you have any objection, sir, if I went over your head to New York then?'

'To the Secretary General? None at all. I don't hold out much hope though. Use my name if you like.'

Armed with this authority, it took the Brigadier a surprisingly short time to get through. The Secretary General of the United Nations, however, intercepted on her way to a meeting of the Security Council, was clearly not pleased. Her trans-oceanic accent, a fitting symbol of her position, sometimes obscured the meaning of an individual word, but her total message could not have been clearer.

'No, Brigadier Liffbrish-Stute,' she replied to his urgent plea. 'I shall not speak to Mr Freeth. To the contrary. You would be well advised to butter up his feathers, as the saying goes. It is of the utmost imperative that he is not to be made upset.'

The Brigadier tried again; in vain.

'Understand me clear,' she went on. 'You will be held personally responsible if, through any action of yours, there is any hitches in these delicate negotiations.'

The Brigadier sat up. 'What negotiations?'

But the Secretary General, saying that she had said quite too much already, put the phone down on him.

'Blast,' said the Brigadier.

Sitting in the little yellow car, he reviewed the situation. To his chagrin, he soon came to the conclusion that his pursuing of Freeth over the closing of the theme park was a displacement activity designed to stop himself facing a most disturbing fact: he had no idea what to do next.

If he hadn't had the assistance of the Doctor at all, it would have been quite clear. Even if Freeth had claimed the protection of the Great Panjandrum of Outer Mongolia, he would have applied for a warrant to search the whole of Space World – a large task, but not impossible with the help of the Met.

'But what would I be searching for, for Pete's sake?' he said to himself. 'The creature that killed the fellow, presumably. Traces of blood. All that stuff.'

But the Doctor had said the monsters were all harmless.

He allowed himself the luxury of thinking about the Doctor, and found to his surprise that his prime emotion was anger. Not that he'd been left in the lurch; more that a long established friendship, a friendship of unacknowledged depth, had been so unmercifully cut short.

The wretched fellow had no need to risk himself. Help had been on its way. It was a foolish, sentimental, unnecessary way to die.

After all they'd been through together; the very real

dangers they had faced. His mind went back to the early days: that brush with the Yetis in the London Underground; those uncanny Cybermen – living creatures or robots? Or both? And then ... But as usual, his mind shied away from the thought of his next encounter with the Doctor; a Doctor utterly changed, with a different face, a different personality – but undeniably the same individual he'd known before. What had he called it? Regeneration, or some such poppycock! How could anybody believe such arrant nonsense? And yet ...

In spite of himself, the Brigadier felt a faint stirring of hope. But it soon faded. There had been no sign of anything of the sort in the limp figure carried away by the ambulance men. The Doctor had been dead, dead, dead.

Hang on, though. What about that time at Devil's End? At first he'd been given up for dead, only to revive something like ten hours after having been frozen solid.

The Brigadier's melancholy abruptly disappeared. If there were the slightest chance ...!

But he'd been taken away a corpse. He'd be in the mortuary by now, and as the sergeant had said, there'd have to be an autopsy and in the very nature of things they didn't hang around.

Regenerating might prove a little difficult with ones tripes taken out.

'So what delights have they found for us today, Brian?' said Mortimer Willow to his assistant, as he donned the green surgical robe the mortuary attendant had put out for him. His voice bounced satisfactorily off the white tiled walls. The Professor was famous for singing at his work. Better than the bathroom, he always said.

'It's the two chaps who fell, Professor.' Brian Prebble switched on the big central light, dispelling the early evening gloom.

'Of course. Took a swallow dive from the top board. Pity the pool was empty.'

Dr Prebble peered at him through his thick spectacles. 'No, no,' he said earnestly. 'They fell from –'

'Manner of speaking. Manner of speaking.' Glory be to Gladys! thought the Professor, none of these youngsters seemed to have a sense of humour any more.

'There's something very odd about one of them,' said Prebble.

'First things first.' The Professor eased on a pair of surgeon's gloves. 'Where've you got to?'

His assistant picked up a piece of paper. 'Apparently there's no question of how they died, so there's no need for a full forensic investigation. But the investigating officer would like to know if either of them . . .' he squinted at the paper ' " . . . had been ingesting or otherwise introducing into their systems any substance which might have impaired their bodily co-ordination or powers of judgement".'

'In other words, were they pissed or stoned? Why couldn't he say just that? In any case, he's wrong. Even if these fellows had been found dead after falling from the top of the north face of the Eiger, we should still have to check for possible causes of the fall: some sort of vascular incident, perhaps; a myocardial infarction or a cerebral haemorrhage, for example. Things are not necessarily as simple as they seem. Still, I feel sure we should be able to satisfy your verbose friend one way or another. Have you taken the fluid samples?'

'I have. And the subjects are all ready for you. But the odd thing is – '

'Let's have a shufty, eh?'

'A what?'

'A look-see, a viewing, an ocular demonstration.' Ignorant as well! 'Where's Tom? As if I didn't know.'

He strode to the door and pushed it open. A large and puzzled-looking man in the corridor looked up from the telephone. 'I'm sorry, I got to go,' he said into the mouthpiece. 'I know, but – I tell you, I got to go! I'm sorry!' He put the phone down and came into the room. 'Sorry, Prof,' he said.

The Professor followed him in. 'How is your love life then?'

'Sorry?'

'Getting our oats, are we?'

The attendant looked even more puzzled. 'That's just it. Never stops whingeing, does she?'

'I should be infinitely obliged to you if you could tear yourself away. Dr Prebble and I would like to get home some time tonight. We have our own oats to consider.'

'Sorry, Prof,' said Tom and pulled out one of the drawers.

Willow looked down at the naked figure with the front of its skull smashed in, several ribs protruding from the chest, and a compound fracture of the right arm. There was a label tied around the left foot. On it was written 'William Jephthah Grebber'.

'Nothing odd that I can see.'

'It's the other one. Thank you, Tom.'

The attendant pulled out the next drawer. 'This one hasn't got a name, Prof,' he said. The label simple said 'Doctor?'

Willow looked up. 'Wrong body, Tom,' he said. 'Where'd you get this chap?'

'No, no, this is the one. I was here when they were both brought in,' said Dr Prebble, hopping from one foot to the other like a schoolboy bursting to pee.

The Professor looked again. Surely this man had never fallen over two hundred feet? Perfect in form, the alabaster figure was without blemish or mutilation of any sort.

'How very – odd,' he said.

'I told you! There's not a single bone broken!'

' " 'Curiouser and curiouser,' said Alice." ' The Professor's eyes gleamed in the harsh light. 'In the circumstances, I think we should give this gentleman a certain priority.'

As his assistants lifted the body onto the stone slab in the middle of the room, he walked over to the table where his instruments were. He surveyed the range of scissors, saws, chisels and the rest, spread out for his choice. He picked up a fine-pointed dissecting knife with a four-inch blade as sharp as an old fashioned cut-throat razor.

'Now, what'll it be?' he said. 'A selection from White Horse Inn?'

Chapter Nine

The Brigadier had tried no less than twelve times to get through to the mortuary and had eventually been told by the operator (having said that he'd been trying for nearly forty minutes, which was stretching the truth by a factor of four) that the line was 'engaged, speaking'. Driven as much by his frustration as his concern for the Doctor, he had decided to go straight there in the Doctor's car. After all, it was only a matter of ten minutes away.

Now, as he was hurrying down the bare corridor of gloss-painted brick, he was guided by the sound of a powerful baritone voice singing, only slightly out of tune, 'I wish you all a last good-bye,' which did nothing to allay his anxiety.

Pushing open the door after a perfunctory knock, he was greeted by the sight of the singer in question, with a knife in his hand which was about to be plunged into the neck of a clearly unregenerated Doctor. 'Stop!' he cried.

The concert came to an end. The soloist lowered the knife, looking up in mild irritation. 'Who are you, sir? What do you think you're doing?'

The Brigadier took a deep breath. It had been a damned close run thing. 'The name's Lethbridge-Stewart', he said.

'Ah yes. You're in charge of the investigation into the Heath case. You'll forgive me if I don't shake hands.'

'You're Doctor Willow?'

'It's Professor Willow,' one of his companions said in a worried manner.

'Oh, I'm sorry.'

'For my sins,' said the Professor. 'The chair of Forensic

61

Pathology. But you can call me Doctor if you like. I'd answer to Rover if you offered me a bone.'

Looking down at the Doctor, he added, 'Speaking of bones, we have a most interesting case here. Every bone intact, yet he is reputed to have fallen from the top of a high tower.'

'Indeed he did. I saw him fall.'

'Really? He's still as dead as last Sunday's joint, though. We're just about to take a look at his innards.'

He raised the knife again.

'No!' said the Brigadier.

'Not squeamish, are you?'

'No, no, of course not. It's just that I happen to know the Doctor and, well, it's just possible that . . .' Good grief, how could he possibly explain?

'You see, there was at least one other occasion when he'd been given up for dead.'

The Professor looked at him sceptically. 'If you're suggesting that there's the remotest chance of reviving this man, I can assure you that you're mistaken. Spontaneous remission of death is somewhat rare in my experience.'

Saying which, he placed the point of his knife on the skin of the Doctor's throat and –

'Ouch!' said the Doctor.

'Oh my God!' said Brian Prebble.

'You see!' said the Brigadier.

Tom said nothing. His mouth hung open slackly and his eyes were very wide.

Professor Willow had not moved. Staring unbelievingly at the unruly corpse, he tentatively made another small jab with his knife.

The Doctor squinted down at it. 'Would you be so kind as to take that a little further away?' he said. 'You'll do me a mischief. Thank you.'

'But you were dead,' said Willow. 'No question of it. You were as dead as – '

'As last Sunday's joint? Yes, I heard you say that. Well, clearly I'm not now.' The Doctor sat up. 'Ah, Lethbridge-

Stewart. Do you think you could find my clothes? It's a trifle parky in here.'

Like many before her, Sarah had found some relief from having to face the unfaceable by plunging into her work. But Clorinda was proving hard to convince that the experiences of the morning could provide the material for a piece in Metropolitan.

'No, Sarah dear, it's all rubbish,' she said, pushing aside a stray tendril of her fashionably untidy Titian hair (nee mouse).

'I mean to say, Atlantis!' she went on. 'Alien monsters roaming around Hampstead Heath! I'm not the editor of a Sunday tabloid, you know.'

'Of course you're not,' replied Sarah, wheedling. 'You're the dearest sweetest cleverest *loveliest* editor of the best glossy on the market.'

'You noticed,' said Clorinda, unmoved.

'It would be a sort of – oh, I don't know. A sort of *tribute* to the unknown genius in our midst. "Who was this man?" All that stuff.'

'If he's unknown, why should anybody be interested in him?' said Clorinda, unanswerably.

But Sarah tried to find an answer. It wasn't the first time she'd had to persuade her hard-headed boss to change her mind.

'Well,' she said, getting out of her stark (more modern even than post-modern) chair which was really rather tough on the bottom bones, and walking over to the window to seek inspiration, 'you could – '

Jeremy came in. 'I say!'

She flapped a *shut-up* at him and continued desperately, 'You could . . .' She looked across at the hideous construction going up on the other side of the road, the latest glitzy tourist trap to disfigure the West End. 'You could link it with environmental pollution, the destruction of our heritage and all, the disgrace of building a theme park on London's historic Hampstead Heath – '

'I say – ' said Jeremy.

'In a *minute*,' said Sarah, taking in Clorinda's impassive face.

'And you could use the shots of the Crab-Clawed Kamelius to sauce it up a bit,' she concluded lamely.

'But that's just it,' said Jeremy. 'There aren't any.'

'What?'

'There aren't any shots of the Crab-Faced Whatsit. I just got the contacts back from Anthony. Waste of a film, he says.'

Clorinda picked up her camera which was lying on her desk. 'Oh Sarah! Did you forget to take the lens cap off?'

But Sarah was gazing incredulously at the sheet of prints. They couldn't be hers, she thought. He must have got them mixed up. And yet the ones of the outside of the pavilion were okay and they were on the same film.

But the ones she'd taken inside didn't even show the desert, let alone the Kamelius. There was nothing to be seen but bare walls. This was more than strange, it was impossible.

The Brigadier needed to know about this. He should be back at UNIT HQ by now. Unless he'd gone home.

'May I use your phone, Clorinda?' she said.

The Doctor put on his jacket. 'You're right, Brigadier,' he said. 'Much higher and last Sunday's mutton could easily have become next Sunday's lamb. You could be talking to a new version at this very minute.' He looked in the mirror on the wall and ran his fingers through his hair. 'Though not necessarily an improved version,' he added, pushing at his face as if to make sure it was still the same one he had woken up with in the morning.

No, he hadn't changed, thought the Brigadier, with an inward smile. 'Lord knows why you weren't killed, though,' he said.

The door of the little office lent to the Doctor as a dressing room swung open. 'Tom's made us all a cup of tea,' said the Professor. 'I'm afraid we don't run to anything stronger.'

'Okay if I make a quick phone call, Prof?' asked Tom as he left the room.

'Nectar,' said the Doctor sipping his tea. 'I sometimes think I only stay on this planet for the tea. Nothing like a good cuppa. A chap in India got me hooked. Name of Clive.'

'General Clive?' said the Brigadier, doubtfully.

'That's the fellow. A thoroughgoing bad lot, but he knew his tea.' He took another sip and continued, 'The reason I wasn't killed, Brigadier, was that I used a technique I learnt a few years ago from a wise old Neanderthal.' A gulp of tea. 'Well, not as wise as all that, perhaps. They were a relatively dim lot, but they certainly knew how to fall down cliffs. A simple matter of bone relaxation, do you see.'

'*Bone* relaxation?' said Professor Willow, who had been listening with a settled look of disbelief on his face.

'That's right. As you know, muscle relaxation can save you some nasty bruises if you, say, slip on a banana skin. Well, if you find yourself falling from a great height, bone relaxation can be just the ticket.'

'But that's physiological nonsense!'

'A colloquial shorthand. More strictly speaking, it is analogous to the breakdown and regeneration of larval tissue in the formation of a pupa.'

The Professor could take it no longer. He put his mug down with a bang. 'I have never listened to such unmitigated poppycock in all my born days! I don't know who you are, sir, but I can tell you what you are. You are a charlatan, sir! A pseud!'

The Doctor eyed him coldly. 'And if I knew who you were, sir, I might be able to decide what you are!'

The Brigadier leapt in. 'I'm so sorry. This is Professor Willow. This is the Doctor, Professor, my scientific adviser.'

The Doctor's face cleared. 'Professor *Mortimer* Willow? Who wrote that paper on the post-mortem agglutination of red blood cells in victims of carbon monoxide asphyxiation?'

'The same,' the Professor said suspiciously.

'I'm very pleased to meet you, sir. An excellent piece of work.'

'Thank you,' answered the Professor a little stiffly. 'I quite agree.'

The Brigadier looked from one to the other and decided to give a little help to the budding rapprochement. 'What's more to the point, Doctor, is that it was Professor Willow who wrote the post-mortem report on the victim of the attack on Hampstead Heath.'

This did the trick. The two scientists were soon in deep consultation and mutual agreement on the unaccountable nature of the injuries inflicted on the body in question.

'And you have it here?' asked the Doctor, eagerly.

'You were in the fridge with him.'

'Any chance of a quick glance?'

As they walked back down the corridor Tom, looking up from the phone more puzzled than ever, said, 'Sorry, Prof.'

He followed them into the room, but not before the Brigadier had heard the end of a conversation of an apparently terminal nature, culminating in an angry 'Well, I'm sorry!' and a noisy clatter as the receiver was banged home.

'Sorry,' Tom said again, at the Professor's over polite request for his assistance. 'If you ask me,' he said, pulling out the appropriate drawer, 'I was better off with Imogen.'

'You can see for yourself,' said Willow, as they gazed down at the pitiful horror which had been Nobby (it said on his label: Bartholemew Clark). 'The marks of the teeth and the tearing of the flesh are extremely atypical.'

The Brigadier, for all his experience in battle (and indeed, in the bloodier aspects of his UNIT job), found the sight extremely disturbing, reminiscent of a butcher's stall in an Eastern street market.

'What's more,' continued the Professor, 'since the preliminary report, I have found even more reason for puzzlement. I have analysed the traces of saliva on the deceased's clothes, what was left of them; and of all things, it turned out to be acidic.'

So? thought the Brigadier. What had that got to do with anything? The Doctor, however, was of a different opinion.

'Acidic?' he said with great satisfaction. 'Then that settles it. The creature who perpetrated this horror is not of this planet. We have our proof.'

Typical! 'There's still nothing to connect Freeth and his friends with the attack, Doctor, and that's what we need.'

The Doctor was scornful. 'You have the mind of a six-and-eightpenny lawyer, Lethbridge-Stewart. It's good enough for me.'

So they were no better off! But the Doctor hadn't finished. 'Stop!' he said, as Doctor Prebble started to close the drawer, Tom having disappeared again.

'What is it?' asked the Professor.

'There's a hair.'

'Where?'

'There, man, there! As plain as the nose on your face. Under the nail of the second digit of the left hand.'

Brian Prebble flushed. 'There can't be,' he said. 'I collected scrapings from every fingernail. It's standard procedure. There were no hairs; in fact, there were no fibres of any kind.'

The three doctors were bent over the body, peering at its hand. The Brigadier tried to get a glimpse between their heads. He was blowed if he could see any hair.

'See for yourself. It's nearly half a millimeter long. Well, don't just stand there, Willow. Get me a microscope slide and some tweezers! Jump to it!'

Appalled at such lese-majesty, Prebble jumped to it instead.

'Sticking out a mile,' said the Doctor, carefully retrieving it. 'I can't think how you came to miss it, the two of you. If you want to get on in this profession . . .' His voice trailed off in concentration.

'Don't mind the Doctor, Professor Willow,' said the Brigadier. 'He's apt to get a little excited.'

The Professor smiled. 'Please don't apologize. It's getting on for thirty-five years since anybody treated me like a backward student. I find it strangely exhilarating.'

The Doctor was soon peering down the powerful microscope and grunting as he adjusted the focus. 'Aha!' he cried.

'What is it?'

'Take a look.'

'Mmm,' murmured the Professor. 'How very strange. The cuticle is . . . But on the other hand . . .' He stood up. 'It is clearly a hair of animal origin, but no ordinary hair. I have certainly never seen anything of the sort before. What is without doubt is that this did not come from a mammal. And if he wasn't attacked by a mammal, what in heaven's name did attack him?'

Chapter Ten

Sometimes the Brigadier found that the Doctor seemed to be taken over by a manic energy which brushed aside all forms of normal behaviour. Their exit from the mortuary was a case in point. Talking, talking, talking what seemed to be a farrago of nonsense – although the Professor and Doctor Prebble, forced by politeness to follow him to the front door, seemed to understand him – he suddenly darted back 'to fetch his handkerchief', waving away all offers to get it for him.

The Brigadier was left with the two pathologists listening to the distant voice of Tom ('Yes well, I'm sorry but . . . The thing is, Imogen, I wondered if you were free tonight . . . Yeah, I know, I'm sorry, about that . . .'), until the Doctor returned, waving the missing handkerchief above his head, and swept the Brigadier out to Bessie amid a torrent of thanks and cordial farewells.

'Get a move on,' he hissed.

'What's the rush?' said the Brigadier, falling back into his seat as the little car shot away like a Formula One at Brands Hatch.

'I want to get away before they find out, of course.'

'Find out what?'

'That I've nicked that hair.'

'Whatever did you do that for?'

'I have a hunch we're going to need it,' the Doctor said and refused to say another word.

'Space World will be closing in fifteen minutes' time.

Please proceed to the main gate or to the car park. Space World will be closing in fifteen minutes' time...'

The distant voice on the public address system could barely be heard in the hushed luxury of the Chairman's room.

'A very satisfactory day all round,' said Freeth, as he inspected the returns from the box-office. Tragan watched him inscrutably as he ambled over to the Sheraton sideboard and poured a quarter pint of crème de menthe into a crystal tumbler, topping it up with a dollop of Campari.

'Nevertheless,' he went on, sucking his teeth after a first luxuriant gulp, 'it would be as well if you were to return to Parakon forthwith and take, er, "Fido" and "Fifi" with you.'

'And if there's more trouble here?'

'The only possible trouble would be if that soldier person,' he continued disdainfully, 'should manage to connect us with the death of the intruder. If you've removed the creatures, the problem can't arise.'

'I wish I could agree, Chairman Freeth.'

Freeth took another large sip of his greyish concoction. 'The point is academic,' he replied. 'As you say, I am still the chairman and I shall decide. The only other person who might have posed a threat has been dealt with. The Doctor is dead.'

A single knock and the door swung open to reveal the putative corpse, followed by the 'soldier person'. For a moment, Freeth's jaw hung open, a little dribble of his cocktail trickling from the corner of his mouth.

'Forgive us for barging in unannounced,' said the Doctor. 'Your secretary seems to have gone home for the evening.'

Freeth quickly recovered. 'I'm delighted to see you so hale and, one might almost say, hearty. We were given to understand that you'd left us.'

He wiped the trickle with the back of his forefinger and licked it off, with every appearance of enjoyment.

'Space World will be closing in five minutes time. Thank

you for visiting us. Please tell your friends how much you have enjoyed yourselves. Space World will be closing in five minutes time...'

'I say, Sarah Jane –'

'Sssh! Keep still!'

Honestly, she'd have been better off by herself. But he'd pleaded, saying how good he was at keeping watch and saving her life and stuff, so she'd relented; and now she was stuck with him in the little service room behind the Kamelius House, listening to the booming voice outside and waiting for everything to shut down. They'd incautiously peeped through the door and seen the Kamelius lying down, chewing like a cow, and were just in time to catch the last visitors being ushered out. So it wouldn't be long now.

'But I've got pins and needles.'

'If you don't be quiet...!'

UNIT had refused to give her the Brigadier's home number, but they'd checked for her. He wasn't in Bessie either, because they had given her that one, and she'd tried three times. So she'd decided that, Clorinda or no Clorinda, it was too good a story to pass up and if necessary she'd sell it to one of the Nationals and –

A voice in the Kamelius's chamber! Jeremy was by now delivering himself of a sort of sotto voce groan. She pinched his arm hard, and with a little 'Eek!' he subsided.

'Maybe tomorrow night. Mavis'll have got the chips on. See you.' Oh, Lor'. The voice was getting closer!

She pulled Jeremy down behind a big grey metal box near the wall. The door opened, momentarily flooding the room with light. She could hear footsteps coming towards them; the sound of a key and the opening of a metal cover; switches; the lid slammed shut. She involuntarily shrank back as she saw through the gloom the legs of a man passing less than two feet away. The outer door opened. There was a click of the snib on the lock and the door slammed. Sarah gave a deep sigh of relief.

'He's locked us in!' Jeremy squeaked.

'Oh, don't be so silly, it's a Yale lock. Come on, let's have a look.'

Still being careful to keep fairly quiet, she picked her way to the little door and opened it a crack. At first she couldn't see anything. The glare of the Aldebaran sun had gone, leaving the sort of nondescript twilight found in a cinema after the audience has left and the attendants are clearing up the mess.

She pushed the door wider. 'Well, well, well,' she said, stepping through.

'It's all gone,' said Jeremy. 'Desert and everything.'

And so it had. There was nothing to be seen but a large hall with bare walls and a bare floor littered with sweet wrappings and soft-drink cans.

'Switched off,' she said. 'They've just switched him off. No wonder he didn't come out on the film.'

The Brigadier had been content to listen as the Doctor told of the anomalous discoveries made by the forensic pathologist. He did not intervene even when Freeth apologetically interrupted to tell Tragan to put in hand the arrangements they had been discussing before the arrival of their guests.

He watched him go, wishing that he had enough hard evidence to tell him not to leave town, like a marshall in a Western.

Freeth, however, now turned to him. 'I gather you've been having a little chat with an old friend of mine, Brigadier.'

'Sir?'

'In New York.'

'Ah. Yes. That's right.'

'You'll no doubt be gratified to hear that your attempt to go to the top of the tree had borne fruit. I am, so to speak, a peach ripe for plucking.' He smiled archly at the Brigadier.

A bit overripe?'

'Sir?' he said again.

'We have agreed that I should keep no more secrets

from you. In her own words, that I should "come clean as the driven snow". I'm sure you recognize the style.'

He turned back to the Doctor. 'If I understand you aright, you are suggesting that one of our little "monsters from outer space" escaped from the park last night and did the naughties? Well, since we're playing the truth game, let me tell you something – '

The Doctor held up a hand. 'I'll save you the trouble,' he said. The Brigadier listened hard as the Doctor launched into a highly technical explanation of how the creatures came to be there, ending with the words: '... by means of a radiated matrix of modulated psycho-magnetic beams.'

Was he saying they were mere hallucinations?

'Indeed,' he was going on to say, 'the whole thing is really a more complex version of your Experienced Reality technology.'

He was!

'My, my!' said Freeth. 'Aren't we the clever-clogs? I hate to admit it, but you have it exactly right. It's all an illusion.'

'Good heavens above!' exclaimed the Brigadier. 'I could have sworn they were as real as my old basset hound.'

'If you tried to pat one of our little family,' said Freeth, 'your hand would go right through it. So how could one of them have harmed that poor fellow?'

But if those animals were a form of ER, thought the Brigadier, then the experience of them must have been recorded. Although they were only images, they must be the images of real creatures.

This apparently was the point the Doctor was making. 'I recognized your so-called Crab-Clawed Kamelius as soon as I saw it,' he was saying.

'You *recognized* it?' said Freeth. 'Who are you, Doctor?'

'Somebody who spent a long weekend on Aldebaran Two a few years ago. Too long a weekend – the food was disgusting.'

A fat chuckle of agreement. 'Indeed. How many recipes are there for cactus pulp?'

So it was true. They weren't from Earth at all.

'You come from the other side of the Galaxy, don't you?' the Doctor said quietly.

'It's a fair cop,' said Freeth. 'I'll go quietly.'

What? He was admitting the whole thing, just like that? 'You mean that you accept responsibility for the death?'

'No, no, no! I have no idea how that poor young man died.' Freeth glanced longingly at his drink, which stood half-finished on his desk. 'I was merely agreeing that I and my friends are, so to speak, an ethnic minority on your planet.'

Bit hard to swallow, that there was no connection at all, the Brigadier thought. 'Something of a coincidence, isn't it?' he said. 'I mean to say, fellow killed by some sort of alien beast – and you admitting that you're aliens too.'

'Brigadier,' said Freeth, 'if you found a body that had been savaged by a tiger, would you arrest Mr Patel from the corner shop?'

He'd got a point certainly.

'No,' said the Doctor drily. 'But we'd certainly have a few questions for the proprietor of the travelling circus which had just arrived in town.'

Freeth giggled. 'Touché!' he said. 'Let me bare my breast and tell all, as I promised. Then you'll be in a better position to make a judgement.'

The Brigadier glanced at the Doctor. His face was as cool and distant as it had been from the start of the interview. He gave no answer.

'We're not in the business of making judgements, Mr Freeth,' said the Brigadier. 'It's our job to get at the facts.'

'And facts are what you shall have. But first, allow me to offer you a sherry – or perhaps you would prefer a "wee dram"?'

For an alien from the other side of the Galaxy, he managed a very plausible Scots accent.

Jeremy was most impressed by Sarah's skill as a burglar.

Luckily, all the back doors had Yale locks, so the well-known credit card technique (which she'd first tried when she had locked herself out of her flat, with packing to do, a train to catch, and a story fast escaping) had already given them entry via the tradesman's entrance to the residences of the Thousand-Legged Zebroid (who in fact had a mere one hundred and twenty-eight if you bothered to count them on the poster, which Jeremy did while Sarah did the necessary) and the Philosophical Phwat. Neither was at home.

On the other hand, it was all a bit scary. Apart from the fact that they were nearly caught by a roving watchman (when Jeremy had just reached the one hundred and twenty-sixth leg), you never knew what might be lurking in the dark corners where the security floodlights didn't reach. He was beginning to regret volunteering.

'Why are we having to check them all?' he whispered. 'If one monster's a fake, they all will be.'

'Second rule of investigative journalism,' she answered in low tones, as they peered round the corner to make sure that the coast was clear, 'never take anything for granted. That body on the heath wasn't torn up by the vicar's pussy cat. There's something nasty in the woodshed. There must be.'

This wasn't at all reassuring. 'And what if we open the woodshed door and it jumps out at us?'

'Scared?'

'Yes. No. Yes. Of course I am!'

Sarah grinned and took off across the brightly lit avenue. He scuttled after her.

'What's the first?' he said as he caught her up at the back door of the Flesh-Eating Gryphon's house.

'Eh?'

'The first rule of investigative journalism?'

'Oh that,' she said, starting on the lock. 'Get your expenses sorted out.'

The Gryphon was as inhospitable as his co-stars; the Blue-Finned Belly-Flopper and the Vampire Teddy-Bear having proved no better. Jeremy found his fear rapidly turning into boredom. When Sarah, deciding that to check all twenty-one monsters was perhaps being over scrupulous, changed the immediate aim of her quest and started looking inside the rides in Yuri Gagarin Avenue, his insides were churning so much that he couldn't stop himself complaining again.

'I don't understand *why* we're looking inside all these spaceship thingies. I mean, they never pretended that they were anything but simulations all the time.'

'That's right,' answered Sarah, as she came out of the 'Flight to the Edge of Chaos', closing the door with a gentle click. 'But we didn't see inside all of them, did we? Perhaps they're using one of them as a kennel.'

'Ssh!' she added, drawing back into the shadows. Jeremy peered over her head down the avenue. Two men were coming towards them from the direction of the central square. As they approached, he could hear what the very thin one was saying.

'. . . and be prepared to return at once to pick up Chairman Freeth. He may need to leave in a hurry.'

'Yes, Vice-Chairman Tragan.'

'It's that one who took Mr Grebber away. I'm going to follow him,' Sarah breathed into Jeremy's ear as the men went by. She started to move forward.

'No, wait!' hissed Jeremy, grabbing her arm. 'They're stopping.'

They had stopped by the last spaceship on the opposite side of the avenue. Jeremy could still just hear them. Tragan was speaking again. 'Shouldn't we feed the guards before we go, Crestin? You know what they can be like when they're hungry.'

As his companion replied, he held out an arm towards the spaceship. The doors slid back and the two figures were silhouetted against the brightness from inside.

'They've had two cats apiece, a labrador and a cocker spaniel,' said Crestin. 'They're quite satisfied.'

'They don't sound very satisfied to me,' responded

Tragan as he led the way inside; and, indeed, faintly across the deserted way, they could hear an unearthly howling.

'The rotten lot,' said Jeremy.

'What did I tell you?' said Sarah, ferreting in her pocket. 'Here, take this.'

'What is it?'

'I wrote down the Brig's phone numbers. You go and ring him. Get him here. ASAP.'

'Whatter how much?'

'For Pete's sake! Get a move on!'

Before Jeremy could stop her, she was gone, sprinting across the broad avenue, up the ramp and into the ship; and as Jeremy watched in paralysed horror, the doors slid smoothly closed behind her, leaving no crack of light to show that there was anybody inside.

Chapter Eleven

Freeth fussed over his guests like a middle class hostess with social pretensions who had been surprised by a visit from royalty. The earnest discussion as to the precise degree of dryness the Doctor preferred in his sherry and the connoisseurship displayed over the Brigadier's choice of whisky formed a lengthy prologue to the disclosure of the long awaited facts which Freeth had promised.

These turned out to be something of a disappointment. It seemed that Freeth, holding the position of Interplanetary Ambassador of the planet Parakon, as well as that of chairman of its sole commercial corporation, had for some time been secretly negotiating a trade agreement with the leaders of the world community.

'Secret negotiations? About a funfair?' said the Brigadier, not convinced.

Before Freeth could reply, the Doctor spoke. 'Is that good Scotch, Lethbridge-Stewart?'

What was he on about now, thought the Brigadier, impatiently. 'Best drop of malt I've tasted since my grandfather died,' he said. 'Why do you ask?'

'And this sherry can only be described as noble,' replied the Doctor. 'Mr Freeth wants to get us on his side.'

Freeth laughed appreciatively, little drops of minty Campari spluttering from between his thick lips. 'I said you were a clever-clogs, Doctor,' he said. 'I'll go further. You're a smartypants. Do go on.'

'He knows how wary the human tribe is of foreigners,' the Doctor continued to the Brigadier, 'What sort of welcome do you think a gang of alien carpetbaggers from outer space would get?'

Freeth took this insult as an example of the purest wit. Wiping his eyes as he strove to control his mirth, he managed to speak at last.

'Not quite the expression I might have used myself, Doctor, but fundamentally you've hit it. On the button. Or even the nose.'

He went on to describe the benefits a treaty could bring to Earth: a valuable new export market for a new product, large enough to satisfy every country participating; cheap imports of every kind; the banishment of hunger. Indeed, the advanced technologies on offer would guarantee a life of ease and luxury to the vast majority of the world's population.

'We want to share the paradise we have on Parakon,' he concluded. 'However, you can lead a horse to the water...'

'But in case he won't drink,' said the Doctor, 'you offer him a twenty-five-year-old GlenMactavish instead.'

'You've lost me,' said the Brigadier.

'Public relations are of the essence,' explained Freeth. 'The Doctor's quite right. We have to tread carefully. I have come to know the people of your world very well over the last thirty years or so.'

He'd been here for thirty years? There'd been alien undercover agents here for *thirty years*?

'I fell in love with your pretty little planet, and indeed with your exquisitely quaint country, when I came on an early scouting mission as a young man.

'Hardly out of short trousers; a mere child,' he added hurriedly. And it wasn't a joke, thought the Brigadier.

'And you've been visiting ever since?' asked the Doctor.

'Waiting until the time was ripe,' agreed Freeth.

The flying saucers, by Jove!

'So,' said the Brigadier, working it out, 'you plan to get the public on your side before it's revealed that you come from outside the solar system. Give them a spoonful of honey to help the pill go down. Right?'

'Exactly right. Except that in this case, it'll turn out to be honey, honey, honey all the way.' He fluttered his eyelashes at the Brigadier and with a little tilt of his head, smiled at him lovingly.

Jeremy found a phone box very quickly; there was a row of them at the end of the avenue just opposite the space ship thing. However, when he got through to the duty office at UNIT, it took an age for them to answer, even longer to put them through to the duty officer, a Captain Yates – which they insisted on doing when he asked for the Brigadier – and even longer still for Captain Yates to discover that the Brigadier wasn't at home.

So by the time he rang the other number, he was pretty frantic. Anything could be happening to Sarah, anything at all. He kept his eyes fastened on the dark, silent dome of the saucer-shaped ship and waited. What else could he do but wait?

'Sounded fair enough to me,' said the Brigadier.

Freeth had shown every intention of escorting them all the way to the car, but the Doctor had refused to allow it, politely but firmly.

'Maybe we've been misjudging him,' added the Brigadier as they walked down the stairs.

'On the principle that anybody who knows his malts as well as he does can't be all bad?' the Doctor said.

Not such a bad principle at that, thought the Brigadier, but before he could answer, the Doctor went on, 'Lucrezia Borgia put her poisons into only the finest vintages, or so she once told me.' They stopped for the night porter to open the massive teak door for them.

Declining to enter such deep waters, the Brigadier said, 'Actually, I meant this PR idea. Softening up the public and all that.'

The Doctor said, 'Oh, it'll work. It's the same as throwing maggots into the river to attract the poor fish you hope to have for dinner.'

Bessie was waiting patiently at the bottom of the steps.

'Your choice of metaphor is hardly flattering,' said the Brigadier as they got in.

'It wasn't intended to be,' said the Doctor, starting the engine.

The phone rang.

'Greyhound One. Come in please, over,' said the Brigadier into the receiver.

'Oh Lord,' said an agitated voice. 'I think I must have got the wrong number. I wanted to speak to the Brigadier.'

'That's the phone, not the RT,' the Doctor said in slight irritation, switching Bessie's engine off again.

'Oh yes, of course. Lethbridge-Stewart here. Who's that?'

'Jeremy Fitzoliver. Sarah Jane Smith asked me to ring. It's sort of urgent, really.'

'What's up?'

'We've found those dog thingies that killed that man. At least we think we have...' The further into his tale, the higher Jeremy's voice rose. By the time the Brigadier had got through to him the urgent necessity of saying exactly where he was speaking from, it was a frantic squeak.

'That's just it, you see, Sarah's gone into one of those space ship thingies after the dogs and they've closed the doors!' By this time, the Doctor had restarted the engine, swung the car round and was driving flat out towards the centre of Space World.

'Wait there, Jeremy. We're on our way. Can you see anything?'

'Not really. It's in the shadows, you see, and the thing's almost black and since they closed the doors, I can't – oh no!'

'What is it, man?'

'It's going up in the air! It's taking off! I mean it's not a fake at all, it's a real – Oh Lor', they've gone! They've gone off with Sarah Jane!'

As Bessie swung round into the centre square, the Brigadier saw, far off at the other end of Yuri Gagarin

Avenue, a thickening in the sky, a darker darkness, a flash of black against the stars. They were too late.

When the doors closed behind Sarah, she was more excited than afraid. It was only a small complication, after all. As long as she kept out of sight, she was quite safe. She could always escape by going through the little service room – there was bound to be one, like all the others – and out of the back door.

She found herself in an entrance lobby, with walls of the same dark material as the outside of the ship. There was a ladder (not very imaginative, she thought; it was like the sort you'd have on a boat) and three doors. The growling, which was a little more subdued now, came from dead ahead, through the only door that was open.

She crept forward, her steps deadened by the thick pile of the black carpet, and peeped inside, breathing deeply to try to quieten the excitement of her heart. It was okay, the room was empty. But it clearly wasn't intended for parties of Space World punters.

To start with it was too small, but even more conclusively, it was fitted out in the most luxurious manner possible, with plump cushioned seats apparently covered with black velvet, walls patterned in grotesque but fascinating shapes which seemed to move as you looked at them, and the hi-tech equipment, some familiar, some utterly strange, that you might expect in the first class saloon of a private spacecraft of the future.

A voice! It was the voice of Tragan, pitched over the top of the continuing growls, coming through a door on the other side of the saloon: 'Crestin!'

Quick, where to hide? Only one place: behind the large seat like a small sofa which was up against the right hand wall. If she got right down on the floor and wriggled ... Yes there was just enough room, and she could still see the bottom of the farther door.

'Warn me when you're about to make the jump into hyper,' Tragan was saying.

'Will do,' came a quacking intercom voice in answer.

'You've quite a while yet. I'm sorry, Vice-Chairman, but in normal circumstances I'd have completed all the pre-flight routine in advance. And even after we've taken off, we have to clear the solar system first.'

Sarah had no time to digest the implications of the interchange, for not only had the weird growling turned into a savage snarl which almost drowned out Crestin's voice, but her restricted view of the open door showed not only a pair of shod feet – obviously Tragan's – but also the feet of some sort of beast; feet such as she had never seen before; feet which she wished she were not seeing now. About the same length as Tragan's highly-polished footwear, but as broad as a teaplate, webbed toes spread wide, with knife-edged claws longer than a man's hand, they were treading the floor like a caged leopard impatient for its dinner.

'Very good,' said Tragan, in acknowledgement of the pilot's report, and moved forward to the open door, closely followed by his companion. He stopped.

'I think you'd better come out now,' he said. Sarah put her face down to the carpet, her eyes squeezed tightly shut, as if she could block out the reality of what she'd seen as well as the sight.

'You, I'm talking to,' Tragan went on, 'behind the seat. Or would you like me to ask my friend to come and fetch you?'

As Sarah crawled out backwards she found that she was shaking so hard that it was doubtful if she would be able to stand up. By dint of clinging on to the back of the sofa, she managed to haul herself to her feet, but her knees nearly gave way again when she saw the creature standing behind Tragan.

Even more fearsome than the sabre-toothed rottweiler guessed at in the pathologist's report, it stood nearer to seven foot than six. Its overall shape was dog-like, with the muscles of a pit-fighter rippling under a leather skin denuded of all but a few hairs. But its face, a mongrel mix of demon and dinosaur, could have been used as a model by Hieronymus Bosch in his most graphic depictions of the denizens of hell gnawing at the entrails of those eternally abandoned by God. Its eyes, blood red, seemed to glow with the fire of an internal furnace; its teeth, unlike any earthly creature's, were jagged and long, each with a number of stiletto points to pierce and tear. It smelt of decay.

'Well, well. It's the journalist girl.'

'I warn you,' said Sarah, the fluttering of her diaphragm belying the courage of her words, 'the Brigadier knows that I'm here.'

'Is that so?' said Tragan. 'And where's the Brigadier?'

Sarah could find no answer. Even if Jeremy had managed to get through to him, it was going to be some time before he could do anything to help her.

'Exactly,' said Tragan, his pale face inexpressive.

The snarls behind him had doubled since Sarah's appearance from behind the sofa. It was apparent that it was only the presence of its master that inhibited the brute. Its own preference would have been to make a meal of her.

'Could you ... Would you ... please put that ... creature away?' she said.

'By all means,' he said and turned to the beast. Then he turned back. 'You won't run away, will you? Sit down; make yourself at home,' he said.

Oh, ha ha, thought Sarah as Tragan, with a combination of gestures and quiet commands, drove the animal back down the short passageway. Quite the comic, wasn't he? As if he'd ever let her go now that she'd seen that thing. But she did sit down, sinking into the depths of the velvet sofa, because she was afraid that if she didn't, her knees really would give out.

As he returned, the intercom crackled again. 'Vice-Chairman,' said Crestin, 'the weight ratio has changed. We're carrying more than we should. I think we should check.'

'We have a stowaway,' Tragan answered.

'Everything all right, sir?'

'Thank you, yes. Everything's under control. The lady has decided to come with us. Haven't you, my dear?'

Sarah said nothing. She hadn't much choice, had she?

'Stand by for take-off then, Vice-Chairman,' said Crestin.

Only the slightest of vibrations, very nearly masked by the trembling of her body, told Sarah that they had left the ground. 'Where... where are we going?' she managed to say.

'To my home planet, Parakon. Though, to be honest, to arrive with you as a passenger might prove something of an embarrassment.'

'What are you going to do with me?'

'A good question, to which I'm sure I shall find an answer. But in the meantime, we must try to make you comfortable.'

Eh?

'Or would it be more fun to make you uncomfortable?'

That's right, stay in character, mate.

'You see,' continued Tragan, sitting down opposite her and arching his fingers like a pedantic bank manager discussing an overdraft, 'although by definition the journey through hyper-space takes no time at all, subjectively, it's tediously long.'

'So?' said Sarah, not wanting to hear the answer.

'I shall be glad to have something to distract me. We must think up some little games.'

He looked at her with heavy eyes.

'I'm very good at thinking up little games,' he said.

Chapter Twelve

The Brigadier would remember the ride back to UNIT in Bessie as one of the most hair-raising experiences of his life. Having established who it was that Sarah had followed, the Doctor swung the little car around, barely giving Jeremy time to jump in, and took off even faster than when he left the mortuary.

It wasn't too bad while they were still shooting through the broad empty avenues and squares of the theme park, but once they were out into the narrow crowded streets of upper Hampstead their lives were in the hands of the Doctor. It could not be said that his skill was unquestionable, as it was questioned innumerable times in forceful terms by many of those on the other end of his near misses and vigorous admonitions.

'If you don't know the width of your car, you shouldn't be driving it!' he shouted at the elderly driver of an old sit-up-and-beg limousine, as he swung out of Platt's Lane into the main road.

'For Pete's sake, slow down! You nearly clipped that one,' said the Brigadier.

'You heard what Jeremy said. Sarah is in the hands of a ruthless sadist. We have to get after her.'

'What? How?'

'In the TARDIS, of course,' the Doctor said, speeding up even more in an attempt to beat the lights. In this he was unsuccessful. Through the resulting disharmony of protesting car horns, the Brigadier heard a siren obligato: the inevitable police car was after them.

'Now you've done it,' he said.

'Leave the talking to me,' the Doctor said as he pulled into the side, after a brief attempt to escape was frustrated by the usual Swiss Cottage traffic jam.

'Good evening, sir,' said the large policeman. 'Would you be so good as to explain why you are driving down the Finchley Road at one hundred and forty miles an hour?'

The Doctor was calm and reasonable. 'I can understand your concern, Officer,' he said, 'indeed I would commend it. It's perfectly safe, however. Bessie is fitted with – '

'Bessie?'

'The car. She's contained in an inertial stasis field.'

'A what?'

'It's a primitive form of anti-gravity, operating in the horizontal plane,' the Doctor explained helpfully. 'As you know, gravity and acceleration are fundamentally indistinguishable. Einstein showed conclusively that – '

The policeman seemed willing to lose the opportunity to increase his knowledge of Einstein's General Theory. 'Out!' he said, in a most impolite manner.

'I beg your pardon?'

'Out! Get out of the car!'

The Brigadier felt that it was past time for him to intervene. He leant forward. 'Excuse me, Officer. May I have a quiet word?' he said.

The Doctor was still grumbling when he pulled up in the UNIT car park, having completed the journey at a demure thirty miles an hour. Policemen were all the same: illogical; rigid; domineering. Didn't he realize, thought the Brigadier, that he could have spent the night in the local nick instead of merely receiving a reluctant caution? As the Officer had said, he was lucky in his choice of friends.

Ignoring Captain Yates's attempts to report a couple of irate phone calls from Professor Willow, he marched into the laboratory, saying that they had more important things to think about than self-important jacks-in-office; they had to repair the psycho-telemetric circuit of the TARDIS, for a start.

'Otherwise,' he said, 'we'll never get to Parakon.'

'What do you mean?'

'Well,' he said, peering into the slightly sooty tangle of wires on the bench, 'we know whereabouts the planet is in the Galaxy, within a few light years, don't we?'

'Do we?' said the Brigadier.

'I do,' replied the Doctor, 'Plug in the soldering iron will you, Jeremy old chap?'

Jeremy, who had been staring round the room with his mouth agape, came to with a start and hurried to obey.

'We could spend an eternity searching, though,' went on the Doctor, carefully taking a tiny component out of the circuit. 'The TARDIS will take us to the right neck of the woods and then home in on Parakon using this in her psycho-telemeter.'

He produced a roughly folded envelope from his breast pocket. 'What is it?' asked the Brigadier.

'The hair of the dog, to coin a phrase,' said the Doctor, carefully unwrapping a microscope slide, and examining it closely. 'Or rather the non-dog. I told you it would come in useful.'

The Brigadier was beginning to experience his usual feelings when dealing with the Doctor; that the ground he stood on was not as firm as usual; that the whole world might decide to operate upside down for a while. He clung on to the facts of the case. The immediate thing, the urgent thing, was to try to stop any harm coming to Sarah Jane Smith.

'Freeth must be in touch with his man,' he said. 'If I put the fear of God into him ... How long are you going to be, Doctor?'

'Long enough for you to make a phone call,' answered the Doctor, tweaking something deep inside the telemeter.

Interrupting his dinner, a fact which he was careful to make clear, Freeth was, of course, most concerned that Miss Smith – through her own foolish curiosity, as he felt bound to point out – was on her way to Parakon. He felt sure that Mr Tragan would extend to her the hospitality of the Corporation and do his best to entertain her during the trip. No, it wasn't possible to get in touch – for technical reasons – as he was sure Brigadier Lethbridge-Stewart would understand. And now, if the Brigadier would excuse him?

As an exercise in putting the wind up the Chairman, it could hardly be counted a success.

'And of course,' the Doctor commented, 'if Tragan's into hyper-space by now, or out the other side, it's perfectly true that there's no way of contacting him.'

'I don't know what you're talking about half the time. Well, actually, nearly all the time,' said Jeremy, who was holding a selection of screwdrivers, pliers and more exotic looking tools. 'Does that mean you can't catch them after all? I mean, what about Sarah?'

'Don't worry,' said the Doctor, switching on the circuit, which responded with a solid-sounding hum. 'The TARDIS has a trick worth two of that up her sleeve. By doubling back in the Time Vortex, she can effectively start before Tragan. We can be on Parakon waiting for him to arrive!'

But surely that was impossible, thought the Brigadier. Hadn't the Doctor said that even the TARDIS couldn't take you back to put something right if you got it wrong the first time round? 'But what about the, er, the limitation thingummy you told me about?' he said.

'The Blinovitch Limitation Effect?' said the Doctor, unplugging the psycho-telemeter, picking it up with eggshell care and carrying it with the power lead back to the TARDIS. 'That only prevents her taking us back into our own past. Really Lethbridge-Stewart, I sometimes think you have a very shaky grasp on the Special Theory of Relativity!'

Sarah hadn't expected to be tied up. After all, she certainly couldn't escape, or even avoid compliance with Tragan's demands – as she had quickly learnt a few minutes earlier when he had first produced the rope – and what seemed to be a length of clothes-line somehow didn't fit the futuristic ambience of the saloon. In fact, when he was tying the knots which secured her to the upright chair by the control desk, he even apologized.

'If I'd known I was going to have such a stroke of luck, I'd have come prepared,' he said. 'Do believe me when I say I have far more efficient means of restraint at my disposal at home. I should hate you to think that we don't know how to enjoy ourselves properly on Parakon. Keep *still!*' he said, giving the rope a vicious tug as she shifted to ease the pain in her arm from the blow which had sent her flying across the room.

'But why do you want to tie me up at all? I can't do you any harm.'

'Ah well, you see,' he answered, 'it's all part of the game we're going to play.'

'What game?' Sarah asked faintly.

'It's called: "How far do I have to go before she . . ."' He paused. 'There,' he said, with a final tug, 'that's it. Not too tight? It won't be long now before we make the hyperjump.'

Sarah just managed to speak. 'Before she what?'

'Well, that's just it,' he answered. 'There are so many variations. "How far do I have to go before she begs me for a kiss? Starts screaming? Dies?"'

His voice seemed to have become very distant, yet there was no possibility of mistaking his meaning.

Jeremy, if he had had any expectations at all, had been thinking that when the Doctor had finished his repairs he would take the circuit thingy outside somewhere and get in to some sort of space rocket with the Brigadier and he would be left standing on the ground; and then what? So when the Doctor called to him to bring the tools into the old police phone box standing in the corner he had no idea what was going on. And then the box turned out to be bigger on the inside than it was on the outside – a whole room! With doors and stuff, and this big control thingy in the middle where the Doctor was fitting the psycho-whatsit. It just didn't make sense; and yet the Brigadier seemed to be taking it all quite for granted.

Now the Doctor was adjusting some dials, and the outside doors were shutting. He looked up and saw Jeremy.

'What are you doing here, boy?' he said.

'You asked me to bring the tools,' Jeremy said plaintively.

'Yes, well, it's too late now. I've activated the coordinates. You'll have to come too.'

A thingy in the middle of the thingy-in-the-middle started to go up and down, and a noise came from nowhere, from everywhere, that sounded like the trumpeting of a demented elephant.

'What's happening?' gasped Jeremy.

'Next stop: Parakon!' said the Brigadier.

Sarah closed her eyes and took a series of deep breaths. When the swimming in her head cleared a little, she tried to force herself to be objective about her situation. What was it they always said you should do if you were taken hostage? Try to see things from your captors' point of view; treat them as rational human beings in the hope that they would begin to see you as human too? That was it, wasn't it?

'I don't think you've thought this through, Mr Tragan,' she forced herself to say.

He seated himself on the sofa and stared at her with his empty eyes. 'Really? Do tell me.'

'You said that I would be an embarrassment to you on Parakon. Wouldn't a, a corpse, or a . . . a . . .' She couldn't find the words.

'A mouthing white-faced creature scared literally out of her wits?' supplied Tragan.

Sarah gulped. 'Yes,' she said. 'Wouldn't – one of those – be even more embarrassing for you?'

He didn't answer for a long moment. Could she really be getting through to him? At last he spoke. 'Have you ever travelled through space before, Miss Smith?'

Sarah hesitated. Would telling a lie help? What was the truth anyway? Did travelling through time count as space travel?

'No,' she said, hoping it was the right answer.

'It's very big, you know. And our garbage disposal system is very efficient. But I do appreciate your concern, believe me.'

All hope fled. 'How can you be so inhuman?' she cried.

'Oh but that's exactly what I am,' he answered, as if he were surprised that she hadn't realized the fact. 'Indeed, unlike Chairman Freeth and his compatriots, I am only humanoid in the literal sense, in the shape of my body. That is why, when I go on trips such as the present one, I have to wear this.'

Tragan put up his hand and peeled off his face.

Sarah had thought that nothing could ever make her feel worse than she did when she saw the monstrous dog creature. But now, as well as being frightened, she felt as if she were going to be sick. Yes, the face underneath the face had eyes and mouth in the same relative positions as a human, but there the resemblance ended.

A sickly pale purple, the skin was covered with warts and what appeared to be suppurating pustules. As if melted by some unburning flame, the substance of his face sagged in liquid folds, which changed shape as Tragan moved. Unlike the passivity of his pseudo-face, which now hung limply from his hand, his expression constantly changed – as if the subcutaneous flesh had a life of its own – but if there were any emotional content, it was so alien as to be unreadable.

Sarah, hanging on to consciousness with an almighty effort, turned away her head and screwed her eyes shut; and behind the high white noise ringing in her brain she heard him laugh. For the first time, she heard him laugh – and she prayed that it might be the last.

Chapter Thirteen

Travelling through space wasn't at all how Jeremy had imagined it would be.

To start with, they didn't all get into special lying-down seats and have their faces pulled out of shape. In fact, the TARDIS didn't seem to be moving at all; and though the Doctor and the Brigadier kept up a desultory conversation about worm holes through space-time and stuff (worm holes!), it was difficult to tell exactly how long the trip took. It was sort of the same as getting really interested in something, like that time he got caught up watching a slug crossing the path in the kitchen garden, and was late for tea and Nanny got so cross. Yet in the TARDIS there was nothing going on to be interested in.

But in no time at all – or was it an hour or more? – the noise came to an abrupt and noisy end. The Doctor was bending over the dials, checking them, and seemed to be in no hurry to leave.

Jeremy wondered what happened next. 'Are we there?' he asked.

'Oxygen eighteen per cent. Mm? It would appear so,' the Doctor answered, looking up. 'On the other side of that door, according to Mr Freeth, we shall find a paradise, a paradise called Parakon. Of course, it rather depends on your definition of paradise. Ready, Brigadier?'

'Ready, Doctor.'

'Then here goes.'

Jeremy could feel his heart thumping as he followed the others outside. But what awaited them was a sad disappointment.

As they walked away from the TARDIS, it was difficult to see very much at all for the thick oily mist that swirled about. There was half a collapsed wall nearby and a glutinous mud beneath their feet. A dull rumbling was interrupted by the sound of a distant explosion. Almost immediately the unmistakable swoosh of an approaching missile or shell filled their ears.

'Get down!' cried the Brigadier.

Jeremy flung himself to the ground. A noise so loud that it became the whole of the world flung bricks and mud over his head. Dimly he heard the Doctor's voice. 'Everybody all right?'

Tentatively pushing himself into a sitting position – ugh, he'd got a mouthful of the disgusting mud – Jeremy checked. Nothing seemed to hurt.

As his hearing recovered, Jeremy could pick out other warlike noises from the general rumble of faraway guns. There was a machine-gun somewhere in the neighbourhood, and more explosions, though none so near as the first.

'Over here!' called the Brigadier; and in a crouching scramble through the rubble and the mud, Jeremy joined him in the inadequate shelter of the ruined wall, now half its former size.

As he reached the wall, his foot turned on a lump of brick and he stumbled forward on to his hands, on to a softness and a wetness that – oh God! He'd landed on a body! Lying face down in the mud, the dead man had been torn apart by an earlier explosion. Jeremy recoiled in shock and fell at the feet of the Brigadier.

'Hold on, lad,' the Brigadier said, picking him up. 'Better get back to the TARDIS, Doctor!' he shouted. But the Doctor, walking forward apparently oblivious of any danger, peering through the murk in the direction of the sounds of fighting, seemed not hear him.

'Keep your heads down! You want to get killed?' A rasping voice preceded the appearance of a mud-covered figure, heaving himself along on his elbows the better to keep a gun which looked like a short thick rifle off the ground.

'Who are you? What are you doing here?' His leathery face was the colour of the mud beneath him, and his totally bald pate was streaked with blood. As he raised his gun and aimed it at the Doctor, another scattered broadside of shells landed close ahead.

'Is this Parakon?' said the Doctor. He had to shout to be heard over the renewed attack.

'What?'

The Doctor moved over and squatted by the man. 'This planet? What is its name?'

He lowered his gun. 'Just landed, have you?' he said. 'No this isn't Parakon, may it be cast into the Everlasting Pit of Serpents! This is Blestinu.'

Blestinu? So the TARDIS had brought them to the wrong place?

A line of explosions detonated behind them, the last one splattering them with mud. 'They've got us bracketed, Doctor,' shouted the Brigadier. 'We'd better get out of here!'

'If you've got somewhere to go, then go!' the soldier said in his croaking voice, and heaving himself to his feet, he ran slantways into the fog, gun at the ready, with the lumbering gait of exhaustion.

The Brigadier didn't wait any longer. Disdaining to crouch, he ran to the TARDIS (which Jeremy could only just see – just to think if they'd lost it in the fog!) with Jeremy coming after him just as quickly as he could squelch through the mud. The Doctor arrived at the door at about the same time as the Brigadier. 'Come on, boy,' he called, as Jeremy sank his left foot deep into a mud puddle of a more than usually viscous nature.

'I'm stuck!' he squeaked, as he tried in vain to pull it out. What the Brigadier said remained private, as an even nearer explosion quite drowned it. Nevertheless, he ran back to Jeremy, and with a strong pull, yanked him free.

'My shoe! I've lost my shoe!'

'Come *on*!' cried the Brigadier, and hauled him, hobble-dy-skip, across the mud to the TARDIS.

The post-mortem started as soon as they were safely inside and the door closed.

'How could the TARDIS make a mistake like that? Is that circuit still broken?' the Brigadier asked rather testily.

'The TARDIS didn't make a mistake,' said the Doctor. 'I did. I foolishly made the assumption that the hair in the psycho-telemeter came from a creature that is a native of Parakon.'

'Ah, I see,' said the Brigadier.

'Well, I'm hanged if I do,' said Jeremy, sulkily. 'I don't know what's going on at all. And I've only got one shoe now.'

'The psycho-telemeter guided the TARDIS to the place of origin of the hair,' explained the Doctor. 'Just as it was intended to do, in fact. But the creature came from Blestinu, not Parakon.'

'So what are we waiting for?' said the Brigadier.

'What do you mean?' said the Doctor.

'Now we know, we'd better get a move on.'

'And how do you propose to do that?' said the Doctor. 'We are in the right sector of the Galaxy, certainly, but there must be several thousand possible planets to choose from. You like a flutter on the horses it seems. If there were two or three thousand runners, you wouldn't risk a ha'penny on the favourite, let alone an outsider. And we'd be gambling with Sarah Jane's life.'

Tragan seemed to lose interest in Sarah once he had shown her his real appearance. He leaned back in his chair and closed his eyes, becoming quite still. It was almost as if he were meditating.

The pause gave Sarah the time to gather her shattered defences. After all, she thought, it didn't really matter what he looked like, though she couldn't stop herself from shuddering when she tried to look at him with an objective eye. It was sheer prejudice to judge people by their appearance.

'Never mind his looks,' shrieked another voice in her head. 'It's what he's doing to you – what he's going to do!'

She closed her eyes and took a few deep breaths. He hadn't really done anything yet, apart from tying her up. Maybe it had all been just talk. Maybe he was just trying to frighten her.

She opened her eyes and realized with a shock like touching a live terminal that his eyes were open and he was staring at her with his colourless heavy-lidded eyes. That was another thing, she realized. He never blinked.

Okay, mate, she thought. You're trying to frighten me; and you're succeeding. But I'm not going to give you the satisfaction of knowing it. Okay?

Realizing that an attempt to stare him out could only end with her as the loser, she closed her eyes again and did her best to forget her surroundings. At once her mind filled with the events that had brought her to this pass; and her heart sank anew. The Doctor was dead.

The sound of the pilot's voice on the intercom interrupted her thoughts: 'Vice-Chairman?'

'Ready when you are, Crestin,' Tragan replied, a slight ripple passing over his face. 'More than ready – eager!'

'No, it's . . . I've got Chairman Freeth for you.'

'Oh. You'd better put him through, then.'

She felt an irrational hope – surely his boss, even if he were a crook, surely he wouldn't let Tragan . . . wouldn't allow him to . . . Sarah's mind refused to go on.

But Tragan had continued, 'Oh and Crestin, don't tell him about our guest.'

'I already have. Sorry, sir.'

Tragan's fluid face trembled like a badly made blancmange, but whether in fury or disappointment it was impossible to guess.

'Never mind. Put him on. No wait! Ask him to hold on.'

'He's very impatient to speak to you, sir. It seems he's been trying to get through ever since we passed the Asteroid Belt.'

'I shan't keep him a moment,' replied Tragan.

'I must apologize for cutting you short so impolitely,' he said as he muffled Sarah's protests. The taste of the cloth in her mouth was alien and nauseating. 'I'm sure you understand the necessity,' he went on. 'Right, Crestin. Let us discover what our esteemed chairman wants.'

Freeth's concern became apparent very quickly. He knew already that Sarah was with Tragan.

'Let me speak to her,' he said.

Tragan paused briefly and then said, 'I'm afraid she's a little tied up at the moment.'

Sarah tried to shout through the thick folds of the gagging cloth, but if Freeth heard the muffled sounds, he preferred to ignore them.

'Up to your old tricks, are you?' he said. 'Well, I'm sorry to spoil your fun, but I've had a call from the Brigadier. He claims to know that you have Miss Smith on board.'

Oh, dear old Jeremy! Well done!

'I denied all knowledge of you and your disgusting doings, of course, but since we are "the goodies" at the moment, it might be as well if she were to remain, er, *intacta*. So to speak.'

'She's seen one of the guards,' said Tragan, in his flattest voice.

'I see. Pity. Very well, keep her incommunicado, but safe. She's more useful to us alive – and well. You understand me? But of course you do.'

Tragan started to protest. At once Freeth's voice hardened. 'No argument. No discussion. You will do as I say. The situation has changed now that we know the Doctor is still alive.'

What! Not dead? But that was impossible!

'You said yourself that we should be safe provided I removed the guards,' said Tragan.

'I've had a long talk with the Doctor. He is even more dangerous than I thought. We must tread very carefully.'

Oh, blessed be! The world was in step again! Even her sinister prison with its dark walls and black furniture had changed its dull threat to a brightness of aspect that almost sparkled.

Now Tragan was wheedling, trying to make Freeth change his mind about Sarah.

'After all, Chairman,' he was saying. 'They've no way of following us to Parakon. They'll have to believe whatever tale we choose to tell.'

'You're greedy, Tragan. You know that?'

'I do. I am.'

'Don't worry,' said Freeth, in a kindly voice. 'Once the hue and cry has died down, you can have her back. You can play even better games with her at home, now can't you? I might even join you. We could have one of our special parties, with Miss Smith as our star guest. Now, wouldn't that be fun?'

The intercom switched off. Removing the gag, Tragan sat down opposite her once more and stared at her as he had earlier. The movement of his face under the skin was like the slow rolling swell of the ocean after a storm.

This time, Sarah stared back at him. Forcing himself to speak coolly, she asked if there were now any reason to keep her tied up. A safety precaution, he answered.

His answer was a lie, she was convinced of that. Her discomfort and the demonstration of his power over her were a small compensation for losing his 'little games'. He'd have to untie her when they arrived on Parakon, after all.

'I presume that we shan't be landing at your equivalent of Heathrow,' she said.

'I have my own facilities in my own – backyard, I think you could call it.'

'Fortress Tragan. With a nice selection of hungry beasties roaming the grounds?'

'One might almost think you'd been there,' he said, and licked his thin lips.

All at once, Sarah was filled with anger. That this – this creature should dare to treat her so! 'I'll tell you this,' she said, filled with the righteous courage that rage bestows, 'I nearly lost my bottle back there, I freely admit – '

'Your bottle?'

'It doesn't matter. What does matter is that the Doctor is still alive. I don't know what your game is, but you're evil through and through, and I give you my word that I'll go on fighting you to the end, whatever that might be.'

Tragan sighed a deep sigh of satisfaction. His face had come alive: bumps of fluid-filled skin appeared and disappeared, bubbling like a saucepan of boiling porridge.

'Aaah!' he said. 'The brave ones are always so much more rewarding. When at last they break, the extremity of their fear resonates like the shriek of a thousand out-of-tune violins. Oh, how can I bear to wait?'

Chapter Fourteen

On board the TARDIS, it seemed at first that nobody could think of any way of following Sarah. Certainly Jeremy had no opinion to offer. He just had to trust that the Doctor would eventually come up with some notion of how to get out of the hole he'd dug for himself and the others.

'The only course that seems to offer any hope is to go back to Earth,' the Doctor said at last.

'I can't see any alternative,' said the Brigadier. 'But how does that offer any hope? It's more like giving up.'

'We could start again, with the psycho-telemeter focused on some artifact from Parakon that Freeth has taken to Earth – if we can identify one. He and his friends seem to have gone native. We don't want the TARDIS to end up in Fortnum and Mason's.'

'And if we do go home,' said Jeremy, 'I could grab another pair of shoes.'

'What did you say?' said the Brigadier, his concentration broken.

'Well, I can't go wandering round the jolly old Universe like diddle diddle dumpling, now can I?'

'What are you talking about?' said the Brigadier, quite exasperated.

'My son John,' said Jeremy, equally exasperated. 'You know, the nursery rhyme.'

The Doctor's face was alight. 'Eureka!' it announced to the world. 'Of course!' he said, diving for the controls. 'Stuck in the mud outside the door! Thank you, Jeremy. That's the answer!'

'My shoe?'

As the Doctor ran through the opening door, an almighty bang blew smoke and smatters of mud into the TARDIS. 'Good grief!' said the Brigadier. 'Come back! You can't go out there!'

But before he could follow, they heard the Doctor cry out, 'Got it!' and moments later he dived back through the door clutching Jeremy's shoe.

'Oh super!' said Jeremy, as the Doctor tossed it to him and closed the door.

'And what's more to the point...' said the Doctor, rubbing the mud off an object in his hand.

'What is it?' said the Brigadier. 'What have you got there?'

The Doctor took the object over to his bench and began to wash it clean. 'From the way that soldier was cursing it, I'd say that Parakon is involved up to its eyes in this war. And knowing how our friend Freeth operates –'

'They supplied the arms!' cried the Brigadier.

'More than likely. So, a lump of shrapnel in the focus of the psycho-telemeter...' The Doctor held up a piece of jagged metal, carried it over to the control column and carefully placed it on the little platform in the centre of the telemeter circuit. He activated the TARDIS. 'And with a bit of luck...'

Clever stuff, thought Jeremy, lacing up his shoe as the trumpeting started again.

The President's Palace of the Parakon Head of State – who was, after all, the titular leader of an entire planet – was considerably less palatial than might have been expected. A large house, certainly, but nevertheless a straightforward dwelling of simple balanced lines, sitting in an open green park surrounded by high walls, it seemed to offer a smiling welcome to the Doctor and his companions.

Their arrival on the planet had created something of a problem. The appearance of a strangely shaped blue box in the centre of a manufacturing complex which would have made the Ruhr valley of Nazi Germany look like Toytown stimulated a full-scale security alert. However, the emergence of the 'Mission from the United Nations of the Planet Earth' from inside their curious spaceship reduced the problem to one of protocol.

In the absence of the Chairman and the Vice-Chairman of the Corporation, it was apparently decided to follow the usual procedure for dealing with representatives of other worlds.

Of course, it was clear that they were heavily if discreetly under the guard of their courteous escort in the distinctive purple uniforms of the Corporation Security Service. Even after they had left the purple flycar which had landed in the palace grounds and, at the entrance to the palace itself, were handed over to the Presidential Guard (who were wearing a dark green far more restful to the eye), they were never left alone. Even when they reached the President himself, which entailed working their way through a hierarchy of increasingly grand functionaries, the Captain of the Guard remained within earshot.

The President, as yellow and dry as the page of an ancient paperback, was clearly very old indeed. Sitting in a high-tech wheelchair which seemed as much a life support system as a means of conveyance, he nevertheless was clearly in full control of all his faculties.

Indeed, when the Doctor – with many an apology – explained how a member of the mission, through an unfortunate misunderstanding, was travelling with Vice-President Tragan, the uncertainty of age quite vanished and he became a model of command. Dispatching the Captain to meet her, he assured them that she would be perfectly safe in the hands of the Vice-Chairman. Perfectly safe, he repeated, emphatically.

'Now, why should he find it necessary to say that?' thought the Brigadier, and noticed with alarm that the Doctor seemed as worried as he felt.

What Sarah had expected to find when she stepped out

of the spaceship she was not quite sure, but she hadn't anticipated finding herself standing under a cloudless blue sky in a beautiful flower-filled garden. Leaving Crestin to deal with the two animals, Tragan gestured to Sarah to precede him down the steps of the landing pad onto a wide path paved with marble.

As she walked down the long winding path, Sarah began to feel that the vista wasn't so beautiful after all. On each side were banks of strange fleshy blooms, some of which, with a simulacrum of teeth in the centre, seemed almost to be grinning at her. It was a kaleidoscope of rich discordant colours, backed by swirling shrubs and the tangled foliage of thick squat trees. Although there was only a gentle breeze, everything in sight was in constant edgy motion, almost as if the vegetation was on a wary lookout.

'The largest collection of alien life forms in the whole of Parakon,' murmured Tragan, behind her.

'I'd advise you to keep to the centre of the path,' he added.

'Why? What do you mean?' she asked – and immediately had her answer. A small creature the size of a squirrel or small cat darted from the undergrowth and tried to cross the path. But two plants with blooms like giant orchids swooped down and both grabbed it in their – yes, their mouths!

The flowers' contest for their screaming capture was soon settled by a natural judgement of Solomon. The disputed prey split down the middle, a final squeal abruptly cut off, and the plants resumed their former positions; the excited flurry of movement around them settled down; and all that could be heard was the sound of chewing.

Sarah had stopped short. As Tragan impelled her onwards with a hand on her shoulder, she was gasping for air, to keep herself from throwing up.

The path going round a bend, a high stone wall was revealed, with an ornate archway containing a heavy gate. As they approached the gate, which Sarah had expected to swing open, it slid sideways into the wall.

Another push between her shoulders and she walked through the arch – and nearly fell over. She appeared to be on a narrow walkway or bridge, with no sides, thousands of feet in the air. As she heard the door close behind them, she saw that in fact she and Tragan were in a transparent tube, leading from the top of an enormous building to the uppermost floor of another even larger; and each building was perched precariously (or so it felt; oh, how precarious it felt!) on the top of a long stalk or tower. She realized with a jolt that the garden, extensive as it was, was on the roof of a structure which would dwarf the most colossal skyscraper ever built on Earth.

Even though she now knew it was safe, it was all that Sarah could do to cross the twenty yards or so to the other side without dropping to her hands and knees. Beneath her feet, far below, she could see busy roads criss-crossed by elevated fly-overs no less busy, with small flycars buzzing in and out and under like a swarm of gnats. So high was she that she felt as if she were flying herself. Even the rest of the vast city spread out on either side was beneath her, for none of the buildings, large as they were, could compare in height with the gargantuan twin towers of – Fortress Tragan?

'Welcome to – what did you call it? "Fortress Tragan",' said her host, gesturing to her to go through the door at the other end of the bridge. 'Very appropriate,' he added.

She went through the door, across a small anonymous lobby, and into a vaulted hall as luxurious, and impersonal, as the palazzo of a renaissance prince. Heavy tapestries showed scenes of alien battle, with the appearance of some of the combatants as far from the comparative normality of Tragan's as his was from Sarah's. Large humanoid statues echoed the theme of combat and bloodshed, some even representing episodes of torture, from which Sarah quickly averted her eyes. Thick, strangely patterned carpets intermittently softened the ringing of their footsteps as they advanced across the marble floor.

'This is your home?' she said, unbelievingly.

'It is.'

Good heavens above!

'This building is the headquarters of the Entertainments Division of the Parakon Corporation, of which I am Vice-Chairman. I live over the shop, so to speak.'

They had arrived at a smaller chamber set back from the main room, furnished as sumptuously but on a more domestic scale. Tragan walked to the wall and pressed a concealed button. 'We must find you somewhere to sleep,' he said. 'And I'll order some food.'

It looked as if he was going to obey Freeth, then. For the moment at any rate, she was to be treated as a guest, rather than as a captive or as a... Again Sarah's mind refused to go on.

A voice responded to his summons, a voice which filled the echoing spaces of the hall. 'Is that you, Vice-Chairman?'

'Who else could it be, Odun?' snapped Tragan, the warts on his face riding the ripples.

'I told Captain Rudley you were still away.'

'Rudley? What did he want?'

'He's here now. He – '

The worried voice was interrupted by the strong confident tones of a younger man. 'Tragan? I'm coming in.'

'You can't go in there! Come back!'

But Captain Rudley ignored the feeble protest. A door in the wall which Sarah had not even noticed, disguised as it was by the ornate carvings, slid open and a tall young man dressed in a dark green uniform strode into the room, followed by a small agitated man uttering feeble protests.

'This is insufferable!' said Tragan, his face flushing a deeper shade of purple. 'You've really gone too far this time, Rudley.'

'Is this Sarah Jane Smith?'

'How did you know that?'

Rudley turned to Sarah. 'Are you all right?'

'Just about,' answered Sarah. It looked as if the cavalry had arrived, even if he hadn't got a horse!

'Good,' said Rudley. 'If you would like to come with me – '

'The Presidential Guard has no jurisdiction in this sector,' Tragan said. 'I'd be within my rights to have you kicked out. Literally.'

'I shouldn't advise you to try,' said Rudley. 'I'm here on the direct orders of the President himself. Ready, Miss Smith?'

'I certainly am!'

Tragan interposed himself between them. 'Miss Smith stays here.'

The Captain didn't even raise his voice. 'Get out of the way,' he said.

Tragan's face was shaking and shivering as if agitated by a sudden squall of wind. He spoke as quietly as Rudley, but the intensity of his anger was shaking his voice as well as his face. 'You are of very little account in this society, Captain Rudley. If you take my advice you'll – oof!'

Sarah's cry of surprise was followed by a giggle of delight as Tragan fell to the floor, doubled up by a powerful short-arm jab from the Captain.

'Come on,' he said, leading the way to the door, where Odun was standing, pressed back against the wall. 'Don't worry, I didn't hit him very hard. He's only winded.'

'That's a pity,' said Sarah.

Tragan struggled to get his voice. 'You, you young puppy! I'll make you sorry for that! I'll ... I'll ...'

But they had gone; and what could have been a useful warning to Captain Rudley of a very real threat was heard only by the cowering servant.

Chapter Fifteen

Having sent Captain Waldo Rudley on his way, the President resumed the universally observed ritual of a host and offered his guests refreshment – a deliciously refreshing drink with a taste not unlike the best mango juice – and politely asked them if they had had a good journey, for all the world as if they had arrived on the Intercity Pullman from King's Cross.

The Brigadier was a little taken aback when the Doctor talked of their unfortunate landing in the middle of a battle. Apart from the possibility of the story being construed as a criticism of one of the planets in the Parakon Federation, his own instinct, sharpened by years of intelligence operations, was to reveal as little information as possible.

'A war? On Blestinu? Surely not,' the President said in a worried, thin voice.

'It looked uncommonly like a war to me,' replied the Doctor.

'That beautiful green world. The very first I visited on behalf of the Corporation, oh, a lifetime ago. They have been one of the most successful members of our Federation ever since. You were unlucky. A little local quarrel, no more.' He was squeezing the palm of his right hand with his left, as if to soothe a pain. His hands were shaking.

'You must be right, Your Excellency,' said the Brigadier with a reproving look at the Doctor.

'Please,' replied the President. 'We don't go to such extremes of ceremony. "President" will do very well. We are a democracy, after all.'

His agitation subsided as he went on to tell them at some length of his early days on Blestinu; of the excitement of exploring such a primitive tribal society and of being the instrument of their progress into the peace and prosperity shared by all the planets in the Federation.

'During your stay on Parakon,' he said, 'you will see members of many different alien races, living together in harmony; although I must admit it has taken a while to achieve.' The President stifled a yawn and added drowsily, 'I can't tell you the pleasure it gives me to welcome the representatives of the United Nations of Earth. Too many of the planets we visit are very far from united.'

'I think the word expresses a pious hope, rather than a reality, President,' said the Doctor.

This was greeted by a rueful smile and a nod of understanding. There was a longish pause. The President's head drooped. 'Now what?' thought the Brigadier. They obviously couldn't leave until it was indicated that the audience was at an end.

A tall woman who had been standing unnoticed in the shadows at the side of the room, moved easily to the President's side. With a smile of apology to the company, she bent her neat dark head and checked one of the dials on the chair. She put out a hand to adjust a control. The President lifted his head and blinked, as if he had been touched by sleep. He gave the woman the slightest of frowns. 'Please stop fussing with my pulse rate, Onya,' he said petulantly. 'I assure you that I find my guests more stimulating than tiring.'

'Of course, President,' she said gently, and returned to her place by the wall.

'You will of course ...' the President said then stopped as if he had lost the thread of what he was going to say. 'You will of course ... be accorded the status of Ambassadors during your stay,' he finished triumphantly.

'Super,' said Jeremy.

The President lifted an eyebrow. The Brigadier, with his antennae alert to the slightest nuance, gave the boy a little shake of his head.

'And your staff will be given the accommodation proper to their rank,' continued the President, stifling a yawn.

Jeremy apparently got the message. 'Oh,' he said. 'Yes, of course.'

'Just as long as I don't have to muck out the Stinksloth!' he added, with an attempted chortle, which died as it became apparent that nobody was joining in.

It was clear to the Brigadier that the audience was coming to an end. The wretched boy should have noticed how tired the President was becoming, he thought. The old man was nodding in his chair, for Pete's sake. How to retire gracefully, that was the problem.

It was a problem postponed, however, for through the door came Captain Rudley, his mission successfully completed.

'Doctor!' cried Sarah, running forward.

Thank the Lord, thought the Brigadier.

'I can't tell you how relieved I am, Sarah,' beamed the Doctor.

'Same here,' she said, a great grin spreading across her face. 'Why aren't you dead? Oh Doctor, am I glad you're not!'

'I'd have to admit, if pressed, that I'm quite chuffed myself,' he replied. 'And you? You're sure you're quite all right?'

'Sort of. I am now. I must admit I nearly freaked out a couple of times. That Tragan – '

A warning cough came from the Brigadier; Sarah stopped abruptly. 'Well, let's just say that he has some weird ideas,' she finished, with a glance at the President, who had been benignly watching the happy reunion.

'Don't let him worry you,' he said. 'Vice-Chairman Tragan has a somewhat bizarre sense of humour.'

'Oh sure,' said Sarah. 'I never stopped laughing.'

The arrival of Sarah seemed to have provided the President with enough momentum for him to be able to give his guests leave to depart, by inviting the Doctor and the Brigadier to dinner that evening. Sarah and Jeremy were confided to the particular care of 'my brave Captain Rudley', who had then escorted them all to the magnificence of the Ambassadorial Suite, which was in one of the other buildings clustered round the palace like a brood of ducklings round their mother. Sarah and Jeremy, as obvious underlings, were to be relegated to the smaller suite adjoining.

The guest-house seemed to be outside the jurisdiction of the Presidential Guard; the purple tunics of the Security Force could be seen lurking in the entrance hall. Captain Rudley agreed to arrange the moving of the TARDIS to the courtyard behind the guest-house and disappeared.

Almost as soon as the captain had left them, to their surprise the woman addressed by the President as Onya turned up to ask, with the gracious hospitality of a hostess, whether they would like some food.

'Who's she?' asked Sarah, impressed, sinking into the depths of a luxurious armchair. 'The President's daughter or something?'

'Lord knows,' said the Brigadier. 'And frankly, my dear, I don't give a damn. If she can provide us with a boiled egg or a ham sandwich or whatever, she could be the Princess Baldroubadour for all I care. I've had nothing since breakfast.'

'I gave you a perfectly good meal in the TARDIS,' said the Doctor, mortally offended.

'Two red pills – and a green jelly baby for pudding?'

'Quite adequate, nutritionally speaking.'

'Try telling my stomach. Roll on the steak and chips.'

'Hear, hear,' said Jeremy in a small voice.

Sarah could only agree with them. In Earth terms, it was now long past Sarah's bedtime, and yet here on Parakon, it was the middle of the day. She must be suffering from hyper-lag or something, she thought to herself. All she wanted to do was grab a bite to eat and zonk out for a few hours.

But, of course, first she had to tell the others all about Tragan with his purple face and general yukkiness ('A

Naglon,' said the Doctor. 'I've had trouble with them a number of times.') and about the dog thing and all.

'Fascinating!' said the Doctor. 'Parallel evolution. A reptilian canine! Did you notice the skin of the Blestinu soldier, Lethbridge-Stewart?'

'Can't say I did. I had other things on my mind at the time.'

'Ya,' said Jeremy. 'Like being blown up.'

'His face was leathery, like the dog's skin. Reptilian. The very word that leapt to my mind.'

'Anyway,' said the Brigadier, 'this is the proof we needed. Tragan and Freeth were responsible for the killing on Hampstead Heath. We've got them.'

'Have we indeed?' The Doctor was not going to forgive the Brigadier in a hurry, thought Sarah. 'So we can go home now, can we?'

'Well, that was the object of the exercise, after all.'

'True. May I come and watch when you arrest Tragan? You mustn't forget to warn him: "Anything you say will be taken down in writing and may be given in evidence at your trial". And did you remember to bring the handcuffs?'

'Mm,' the Brigadier said stiffly. 'See what you mean.'

Sarah's quiet amusement at the prickly exchange was interrupted by the return of Onya and a pair of obsequious servants with a Lucullan breakfast, or dinner, or tea; what did the name matter? It was food! Not steak and chips, nor a ham sandwich or a boiled egg, but plate after plate piled high with every conceivable type of dish: meats, vegetables, fruits, cooked and uncooked, sauced and unsauced. Some of it seemed familiar, like the dozen or so different types of bread, some very strange, like the large whelk-like snail thing with staring dead eyes which nobody touched.

Even the Doctor, in spite of his feast on the TARDIS (the thought of the Brigadier eating a jelly-baby still made Sarah want to giggle), succumbed to the gourmet side of his nature and sampled a goodly number of the treats on offer.

Whether it was due to the simple relief of tension or the effect of the drinks, which tasted like – what? Like Australian wines, rich and chewy (Wasn't that the word? Sarah would rather have had a cuppa. Still . . .) – they all became very merry, chatting and laughing with their mouths full, waving their arms about (especially Jeremy, who knocked over a pile of spherical objects like marbles which turned out to be hard-boiled God-knows-what eggs) and their talk became more like gossip than the grave deliberations of an interplanetary mission.

Inevitably, though, their thoughts returned to their situation. What to do? Wait for the TARDIS and slip away, back to Earth? Or stay and try to find out more about the paradise they were supposed to share?

'I'm all for that,' said Sarah. What a story! she thought. But what about Tragan? And Freeth if he arrived on the scene?

'I get the feeling that we're safe as long as we're under the official protection of the President,' said the Brigadier.

'I quite agree,' said the Doctor.

'That's why I stopped you telling us about Tragan in front of him,' the Brigadier added to Sarah.

'I thought he was rather a dear old duck,' she answered through a mouthful of fried feathers (crunchy and nutty in flavour but apt to get between the teeth).

'Ya,' agreed Jeremy. 'Not much sense of humour, though.'

'A charming man,' said the Doctor. 'And he seemed honest enough. But Freeth and Tragan are his envoys, after all. And they seem to be selling a few serpents along with their paradise.'

Yeah, thought Sarah. But did Parakon spawn nothing but baddies? Apart from the President there was the Onya woman, for instance. Somehow, she gave the impression of being more 'together' – okay, modern cant word, almost a cliché, but what else would do? – than anyone she'd ever met. Apart from the Doctor, of course.

And Captain Rudley: he seemed okay too.

Sarah took a handful of squidgy toffee-ish jelly things.

'Captain Rudley, now,' said the Brigadier. 'He seems a decent type. Good-looking young fellow, too. Wouldn't you agree, Sarah?'

'What? Oh, yes. Sure,' she mumbled, with her mouth full of sweets – and realized to her horror that she was blushing.

Sarah and the Brigadier were not the only ones discussing the captain.

'Well?' snapped Tragan to the face on the screen let into the mauve streaked marble wall. 'What have you found out?'

The hands holding the computer print-out were trembling. 'Rudley. Captain Waldo Rudley of the Presidential Guard.' The voice was trembling as well. 'Father: Carpal Rudley, lower upper-middle class. Temple Guardian until the Dissolution. Deceased. Mother – '

The lumps on Tragan's face swelled alarmingly. 'Not his entire history, idiot. Is there anything against him?'

The voice shook even more. 'Not that I can see, Vice-Chairman. Oh yes, promotion to lieutenant nearly blocked for a remark seemingly critical of Government policy on bond-servants. Er, that's all.'

'I knew it!' Tragan said triumphantly. 'Anti-authority. A crypto-rebel.' The lumps flushed a deep heliotrope.

'Right, Dogar,' he went on. 'Find out where he's going, what his schedule is. Full surveillance. Do you understand?'

'Yes, Vice-Chairman,' said Dogar.

'Sooner or later he'll make a slip. I shall enjoy teaching the arrogant young whipper-snapper a lesson.'

Tragan switched off the screen and leaned back in his chair. He heaved a deep sigh and closed his eyes. His skin faded to a pale lilac; and the movement of his face was no more than might be occasioned by a balmy summer breeze wafting across the calm surface of a slime-covered stagnant pond.

Chapter Sixteen

Sarah had no idea how it was that Tragan had managed to get her back into his clutches. Her head was swimming as though she'd been drugged, or perhaps was recovering from a blow.

He was dragging her along a narrow path – a path which seemed to stretch to a far horizon. All around the carnivorous plants were swaying and snapping to get at her.

But now at her feet yawned the mouth of a deep pit, from which echoed and re-echoed the ghastly howls of the creatures from the spaceship.

She turned in terror, to find the staring eyes, set deep in folds of flowing flesh, only inches from her own.

She started back – and as she plunged down into the blackness, she could hear the voice of a rescuer, come too late, calling to her desperately, 'Sarah! Sarah!'

She opened her mouth to scream but no sound would come. This was it. She was going to die.

With a jolt, she landed; the thudding of her heart melded with a knocking. The voice came again.

'Sarah? Sarah! Are you awake?'

She lay for a moment, still possessed by the horror of her dream; and then it faded.

'Sarah?'

'Yes, I'm awake,' she managed to say.

'You asked me to give you a shout when it was nearly time to go to this do of Captain Rudley's,' went on Jeremy's voice.

'Shan't be long,' she said.

By the time she'd had a shower (needle jets coming from every angle; a cleanser and a pepper-upper, she decided, for the mind and spirit as much as for the body) and dressed in the fresh, clean clothes she found laid out for her, her own having vanished during her sleep, she was a new woman.

A new woman? she thought, as she turned in front of the mirror, frankly admiring the straw-coloured high-necked shirt and narrow slacks and the way they set off the lines of her carefully slim figure. A New Woman? There's an old cliché turned into a new cliché for you. And if I am a New Woman, how come my subconscious cast me in the role of the victim? How come I didn't turn round and kick him in the goolies? If he's got any.

Postponing the effort of self-analysis to another occasion, she shrugged ruefully, gave a final push at the swing of her short hair and went to join Jeremy, who also proved to have changed his clothes. A short chalk-green tunic, which came down to mid-thigh, allowed his skinny bare legs, with championship-level knobbly knees to emerge like a hen's below her skirt of feathers.

'Do I look all right?' he said. 'To be honest, I feel a bit of a charlie.'

'Mm. Tasty,' she answered. 'That tunic makes you look like a Greek god. Well, a Greek something or other. Didn't they give you any trousers?'

'Not that I could see.'

It must have been Sarah's expression that made him decide to have another look. She sat down to wait.

Their suite, while lacking the grandiosity of the quarters of the supposed ambassadors next door, was in no way less comfortable. In a way it was almost too comfortable. The pastel colours – amber, a smoky tan, jade green – of the decoration and the furnishing; the thickness of the carpet; the softness and the reclining shape of the chairs; all were so relaxing in their effect that it would be difficult not to go straight back to sleep, Sarah decided. She looked round for something a bit more energizing.

She hauled herself out of the seductive embrace of the

armchair and wandered over to the window, realizing with a small shock that it did not show the park of the Presidential Palace as might have been expected, but a lake surrounded by mountains.

There was a row of buttons at the side of the window. Sarah tentatively poked her finger at the first. Sure enough, the window opened. She leaned out. Far down the water a small boat drifted. She could smell the trees, almost like the fresh smell of pine, and hear the lapping of the wavelets below.

But how could this be? The guest house was surrounded by an acre or two of green parkland, in the middle of a large city. For a moment, Sarah thought she must still be dreaming; but no, this was as real as the view of Hampstead Heath from her flat. Had they been moved while they slept?

She pressed the next button to close the window. But instead the view changed, as if she had changed a transparency while she was boring somebody with her holiday shots. Now she was gazing across a moonscape (or that's what it looked like) with a black sky filled with unfamiliar patterns of stars. A large round object, like a soft balloon six foot across, was rolling over the surface towards her. She took a step backwards as it arrived just outside the window, stared into the room with two plate-sized eyes, and rolled away again.

Of course! It was the same as the Kamelius setup. However they did it, they were able to program backgrounds so natural that they were indistinguishable from reality. The other buttons, as Sarah soon found out, produced a crowded swimming pool; a grand boulevard leading to a massive arch; a formal garden as rectilinear as an engineer's blueprint; all offering a package deal of sight, sound and smell, subtly enhanced to create a presence more sharply real than reality itself.

'Hey, look!'

Jeremy's voice jerked her round. Considerably more presentable, now that he had some trousers on ('They were hidden behind the door,' he said defensively, catching her glance) he was standing by a couple of reclining couches equipped with control panels on the arms and headsets like crash helmets.

'Like the thingy the Brig was trying in Space World,' Jeremy went on.

'You're right,' said Sarah, crossing to him. 'ER. Experienced Reality. I was quite peeved I didn't get a go. Come on.' She climbed onto one of the couches and plonked the headset over her cap of shining hair, where it automatically tightened to a snug but acceptable fit.

'Do you think we should?' said Jeremy. 'The Doctor did say it was dangerous.'

'No, no,' Sarah said. 'He was talking about the long term effects on society.' She inspected the push buttons on the arm of the couch. Standing apart was a solitary green button. She pushed it; nothing happened. She tried again, pressing the first one in the top row.

'Blimey O'Riley!' she exclaimed.

'What?'

She could barely hear him. She was standing with a group on the side of a mountain. The sun on her face countered the crispness of the breeze and the snow crunched under her feet as she took a step forward. 'Try the first channel,' she forced herself to say.

She was watching ski-jumping, like at the winter Olympics, but it was ski-jumping with a difference. The jumper was wearing a single ski – a small one, like a longish skateboard – and as he (she?) jumped he stretched out his arms and grew a pair of bird-type wings. Sweeping into the sky, he turned and soared up the slope on the updraught of the wind, looped the loop, swooped down to within a few feet of Sarah's face, and up the face of the mountain again even higher than the top of the jump itself.

Sarah could just dimly hear the excited exclamations stemming from Jeremy. It recalled her briefly to her real situation, and reminded her of the little green button. With an immense effort, she could feel her body on the couch; the sensations were superimposed on the present reality of the mountainside like a reflection on the surface of a bubble.

She pressed the green button.

The ground fell away from beneath her feet; her arms had become wings; and she was sailing through the sky above the snow-covered slope. She could feel the wind pushing at her cheeks, and through the goggles she was wearing she could see deep into the valley below. But then – right ahead – the next jumper in turn was soaring up towards her. They were inevitably going to collide.

At the very last moment, feeling the power in her body, revelling in the practised skill residing in her muscles, she swung like a matador turning from the charging death of the bull's horns and soared up again, above the gaping groups of onlookers, above the strange gaunt trees, high above the snow covered crags of the mountain peak itself.

She could feel a crow of delight, a laugh of glee, bubbling up from inside her; but when it burst forth, the sound she heard was not her own voice, but the deep voice of a man.

So whose feelings was she experiencing? The flyer's? Or her own?

Dismissing the thought to concentrate on landing – halfway down the mountain, where the slope had gentled to the near-horizontal – she came to a swishing stop, raised her hands to pull off her goggles, and pulled the headset off instead.

'I did it! I landed without falling over!' Jeremy's voice was halfway between a squeak and a gasp. He pulled his own headset off and blinked at Sarah, distracted but elated. 'That was the most exciting thing I've done since Nanny let me go on the big slide when I was three!'

Sarah grinned at him. 'Takes your breath away, doesn't it?'

Jeremy gave a puzzled frown. 'I didn't see you there,' he said.

'Well, of course you didn't. We were both experiencing the same thing: experiencing what the original skier did.'

'Mm. Yes, I see.' His face cleared and he said in mock

defiance, 'Well, I'm jolly well going to have another go!' He pulled on his helmet and stabbed a button at random.

Sarah sat for a moment, remembering the strangeness of feeling a man's voice coming out of her mouth. And yet, at that moment, she had felt that she was wanting to laugh with joy. So whose laugh was it?

Her thought was interrupted by Jeremy's voice. 'Not nearly so exciting, this one,' he was saying. 'I'm just sitting in front of a big campfire warming my toes. I've got bare feet.' His voice rose a couple of tones. 'In fact not just my feet; I seem to be quite naked; and there's a girl and she's ... Oh my goodness me! No, don't do that! Oh!'

He pulled the helmet from his head. 'Well, really!' he said.

'Jeremy! I do believe you're blushing,' said Sarah.

'I mean to say,' replied Jeremy, putting the headset down decisively. 'Going a bit far!'

Trying not to laugh, she donned her own helmet. 'Now then, seven's always been my lucky number, so...' She pressed the seventh button in the seventh row.

She found herself crouching down, creeping through a forest – or a jungle, more like, she said to herself. She felt her booted feet pushing through the tangled undergrowth and had to duck every now and then to avoid a low branch, or a hanging creeper. A heavy stench of decay was in her nostrils and in her ears a chattering wittering murmuring continuo which backed the solo shrieks of some alien bird.

She'd stopped now and was peering ahead as if she were looking for something. The heaviness in her hands turned out to be the substantial weight of a gun – a gun like a fat stubby rifle. She must be stalking some sort of animal, like the lairds and people stalking stags in the Highlands; all that stuff.

The crack of a breaking branch made her look to her right, and start towards the movement she made out in the mass of leaves. Then she saw him: a man dressed very much as she seemed to be, with a leather jacket and high laced boots. Sarah could see the shine of sweat on his face, and a net of scratches, red raw, on the backs of his hands.

Was he her quarry? But even as she repelled the thought, with an unspoken *No!* – or did she say it aloud? – the man looked straight at her, turned and stumbled away; and she went after him.

'What is it? What's going on?'

As she heard Jeremy's distant question, she realized what the answer must be. 'It must be one of those battle game things,' she told him. 'You know, where they fire blobs of paint at one another.'

The other player was out in the open now, in clear view, so she raised the gun and fired – whoops dearie, careful now, it had quite a kick! – and sure enough, a splash of red paint appeared in the middle of his back. Feeling quite cockahoop at the accuracy of her markmanship (but it wasn't hers really, was it?), she burst out into the clearing and ran over to the man who had fallen to the ground, pretending to be –

But he wasn't pretending at all. He was screaming; screaming the bubbling wordless scream of a man who has had half his back blown away.

The worst of it wasn't the fact that Sarah found herself lifting the gun, aiming it carefully at the base of his skull, where it joined the neck, and pulling the trigger. The worst of it was that, even while the rest of her was fighting to get away, to escape, to wrench the helmet from her head and regain her hold on the real world, a part of her was relishing the task of finishing him off – embracing with fierce satisfaction the joy of the hunter at the final slaughter of his prey.

Chapter Seventeen

'I've been trying to tell her that it wasn't real,' Jeremy said to Captain Rudley. 'It was just a sort of film thingy, wasn't it? Special effects and all. Tomato ketchup and stuff.'

Waldo Rudley had arrived to find a shaking Sarah and a flustered Jeremy desperately doing his best to comfort her in her distress.

'It was real, I tell you – and I killed him. I deliberately lifted the gun and...' The sound of the man's screams was still with her; the sight of his terminal panic, so cruelly cut short; her glee as she pulled the trigger... She shuddered violently. 'It was real all right,' she said.

'I'm afraid it was,' said the Captain. 'Oh, you didn't kill him. But he was killed when the recording was made.'

'That's sick. It's really sick.'

'I'm sorry, I should have warned you. You don't have public executions on Earth?'

'Where we come from we don't have the death penalty at all,' she said. She was hugging her arms close to herself, trying to control the shaking of her body. Or was it from a longing to be held: to be comforted like a child waking from a nightmare?

There was a knock on the door, and a servant, carrying clean bed-linen over her arm, came in and, with a deferential murmur, disappeared into Sarah's bedroom.

'Was he a murderer?' said Sarah. 'What had he done?'

'He would have been plotting against the Government – or the Corporation. If he'd been an active terrorist, he wouldn't even have been given that chance.'

'What chance did he have?' said Sarah bitterly.

'Oh, they have been known to get away,' he replied. 'But those aren't the hunts which are put onto the public networks. There must be a kill.'

'And people switch on for that?' said Jeremy, appalled.

'More than any other channel,' said Rudley.

'Then they should jolly well be ashamed of themselves. Don't you think so, Captain Rudley?' said Jeremy.

Sarah said nothing. How could she judge them without being a plain hypocrite? Even with her guts still twisting with the horror of her experience, she could feel the guilty buzz of satisfaction lingering yet.

'Don't you think it's rotten too?' persisted Jeremy, when Waldo didn't answer. But he still had no direct reply. Instead, Waldo glanced at the bedroom door, held a finger to his lips and gave a little shake of his head.

'I hope you still feel like going to the party,' he said.

'I think it's just what we need,' Sarah said.

Though the Brigadier had been pleased to fill the empty spaces with something more substantial than the Doctor's food pills, he hadn't really appreciated the cornucopia of choice they had been offered at lunch time. Always suspicious of the way those unlucky enough not to be British mucked about with their food, he had avoided most of the exotic dishes and sought out the Parakonian equivalent of a ham sandwich, or steak and chips: simple meat and vegetables, backed up with some hefty hunks of bread.

So he was looking forward to the President's dinner with a certain gloom. Bound to be a lot of foreign fol-de-riddle, he thought; hidden under a lot of sticky sauces, probably. He remembered the unfortunate incident of the sheeps' eyes at the last Middle East peace conference he'd attended, just before he joined UNIT; he thought of the bloodshot eyes of the Crab-Clawed Kamelius; he shuddered.

In the event, however, he found himself sitting down to a table which in all respects could have been a table at his club. Instead of the eating tongs or hinged chopsticks the Doctor had proposed as likely, they were using perfectly normal cutlery – knives, forks and spoons of gleaming silver – and drinking from crystal cut glass; and the food was very much what he would have chosen himself: smoked salmon (surely not) which melted in the mouth, followed by roast beef (eh?) cooked on the spit it would seem, a sublime apple tart and a cheese more Stiltonesque than Leicestershire had ever seen.

Having been brought up to believe that it was not the done thing to comment on the food one was given, he was surprised to find that the Doctor had no such qualms.

'I must congratulate you, President,' he said, 'on the pains you have taken to make us feel at home. We have been told that your emissaries have been visiting us on Earth for over thirty years; their meticulous work is evident in every mouthful we've eaten. To have produced such a superb meal which is not only Earth style but also English is – subtle.'

Subtle? What's the man talking about? thought the Brigadier. But the President (who had nibbled a token amount of each dish and occasionally sipped a glass of water) understood at once. He laughed a creaky laugh. 'We make no secret of our methods,' he said. 'To honour a guest in this way is not incompatible with our commercial intentions. But why should we be ashamed of that? To conclude a successful negotiation with Earth would be to our advantage, certainly, but Earth herself would also be immeasurably the gainer.'

The Doctor glanced at the Brigadier, who was pouring himself a glass of port. He looked up. The dark haired woman whom the President had called Onya, who had been playing the part of butler, was ushering the remaining servants from the room. Apart from Onya herself and the green-uniformed guards at the door, they were alone. Ah, the Brigadier thought, time to get down to business. He cleared his throat to give himself time to surface from the mellow befuddlement induced by the succession of excellent wines he had drunk.

'Yes, well,' he said. 'Forgive me, sir, but would you mind explaining exactly how we should all benefit from your, er, philanthropy?' Blast, he thought; sounded sarcastic, gone too far.

The President frowned. 'I understood that the discussions at the United Nations were progressing well,' he said.

'Yes. Yes, they are. It's just that, er...'

The Doctor came smoothly to his rescue. 'We have been promised a paradise, President,' he said. 'But I must admit, we're a little short on detail. Background information, you might call it.'

The President relaxed. He leant back in his wheelchair and smiled. 'I'm proud to say that it was my grandfather who brought back the rapine-seed in the first place,' he said. 'He was a trader, space-hopping for new markets and new products. He spotted the potential of rapine straightaway.'

Rapine? What the devil was rapine? Had he missed something the old goat had said?

'And it's on, er, rapine that the paradise is built?' asked the Doctor.

Good. The Doctor was equally foxed.

The President said, 'Exactly.'

The Doctor said, 'I see.'

The Brigadier thought, blowed if I do. He passed the port to the Doctor. The Doctor, whose glass was full, passed it straight on to the President. The President passed it back to the Brigadier; and the Brigadier topped up his glass. 'I'm sorry,' he said, 'but I don't understand.'

'Let me show you something,' said the President. With a slight movement of his hand, he adjusted a control on the arm of his wheelchair. It turned; and he rolled across the broad expanse of polished wood towards the window. The Brigadier hastily put down his glass and followed, accompanied by the Doctor.

'Tell me, Brigadier,' said the President, as he activated another control which drew back the heavy green curtains, 'tell me. Did you enjoy your dinner?'

Good grief! So etiquette was to be utterly thrown overboard, was it? What else could he say but 'Yes, it was delicious'? But then, it *was* delicious, wasn't it?

'It was delicious,' he said.

'Was the meat to your liking? And the vegetables? And the wines?'

'Excellent. Couldn't be bettered. Only one word, er, delicious. Yes, delicious.'

The Doctor, seemingly more amused than anything at the Brigadier's discomfiture, was looking out of the window at the floodlit grounds of the palace and the myriad lights of the city beyond. Dominated by two immense lollipop-shaped towers at the hub, the lower buildings spread radially to the skyline, where an irregular rim of high-rise blocks completed the wheel.

'Are the factories the large buildings in the distance?' he asked.

Factories? Who said anything about factories? The Brigadier looked back at the President in some bewilderment. The President smiled. 'That's right, Doctor,' he replied. 'The largest you can see – the one to the right – that's where the meat you were eating tonight was manufactured.'

'Manufactured?' said the Brigadier.

'Yes. Manufactured; from rapine. And the building with the green sign to the right of it is where they made the vegetables, and the fruit for your tart. Also from the rapine plant. The wine comes from another town, in a warmer country, where they once grew the fruit from which we used to ferment our drinks – we like to keep these old associations alive – but it was made from rapine as well.' He laughed. 'I have to admit one failure. The walnuts are imported from Earth. Apart from that, everything you have had came from rapine.'

'That's incredible,' said the Brigadier.

'The generosity of the plant *is* incredible,' replied the President, wheeling himself back to the table.

The Brigadier sipped his port with a new awareness. But it still tasted like the old crusted vintage his grandfather had been so proud of. Made from some sort of field crop? Never.

But the President had not finished. He went on to state categorically that there was nothing that a normal civilized society might use that could not be manufactured or synthesized from rapine.

'Nothing, President?'

'Nothing, Doctor.'

The sugars and proteins in the fruit, the foliage and the roots (together with the oil from the seed, which could also be used for fuel) fed them; and the various parts of the plant were the raw material for a range of products which covered every need – from a woman's clothes to a jet engine.

'You mean you've even replaced metal?' said the Brigadier, even more incredulously. 'I'd like to see that.'

'You have,' answered the President, evidently enjoying himself.

'Eh?'

'The knives and forks? So carefully made to match your Earth pattern?'

The Doctor laughed. 'Don't let it worry you, Lethbridge-Stewart,' he said. 'I would hazard a guess that everything in this room is ultimately derived from rapine: the chairs we're sitting on; the rugs; the curtains; the lighting fitments; everything. Am I right, President?'

'Very nearly. And all this from a plant that will grow in any climate, on any type of fertile soil, and produce harvest after abundant harvest.'

The Doctor tilted his head and rubbed the back of his forefinger along the side of his chin. 'Forgive me,' he said, 'but you sound like a salesman trying to persuade a doubtful customer!'

The President laughed his wheezy laugh once more. 'Very perspicacious of you, Doctor. That's exactly what I was for thirty years and more. An interplanetary salesman.' He leaned forward in his wheelchair. 'But I wasn't selling rapine. I was selling dreams. I was selling riches.'

He was no longer laughing. His expression was utterly serious and his voice urgent and intense.

'I was selling paradise,' he said.

By the time they were settling into Waldo's flycar, Sarah was feeling quite a lot better. He had been so concerned for her, seeming to understand exactly how she felt even before she told him, that somehow she felt the burden of guilt was being shared. He'd been through it himself.

'That's the very reason I won't switch through to those channels,' he'd said, as the moving walkway carried them to the flycar-park. 'You see, although they haven't found out yet how to record feelings, the recorded sensory data transferred to your brain includes all the physical components of the original emotions. You wouldn't experience the originator's fear, for instance, but you would get the fluttering in your stomach, and that would stimulate your own fear.'

'Yes, I see,' said Sarah.

'It's very difficult for the two things to be separated,' he went on, as they walked through the ranks of small flycars. 'We all have the potentiality for enjoying cruelty, I'm afraid, but in the ordinary way we inhibit it. That's why those channels are so popular. They let people do things they normally would be ashamed to do.'

'A licence to kill,' murmured Sarah.

'Yes,' said Waldo, 'and worse.'

He stopped by a small green car with the Presidential crest on the door and turned to her. He put his hands on her shoulders and turned her to him.

'So you see,' he said, 'you mustn't blame yourself for the way you felt. You couldn't help it.'

Sarah gave a shaky smile and nodded. He smiled back and turned away to open the flycar door.

But did he stay looking into her eyes a fraction longer than was necessary?

Chapter Eighteen

Albin Dogar, Sub-Controller (S) of the Entertainments Division of the Parakon Corporation, was usually left alone to get on with his job in peace. Alone, that is, apart from the five hundred and twenty-three silent figures each monitoring the output of a computer terminal – each of which, receiving the transmissions from over two thousand implants in a planetary region, was programmed to recognize overheard phrases which might be considered damaging to the corporation or treasonable to the state – and the two hundred and fifty-two with ER headsets, fingers fluttering over banks of controls as they followed the trail of those allocated particular surveillance.

An occasional routine visit from Controller (S) was to be expected, of course – when he could bear to tear himself away from his ER fantasy life buckling a swash as a space-pirate in the olden days. But that was all; unless something went wrong.

So when Vice-Chairman Tragan himself turned up, just when Dogar had decided it was safe to go home to his supper, he felt as guilty as he did when his wife walked in on him as he was indulging in a clandestine ER visit to the Outworlder Sensuorum. (The things those Shlanfurones got up to with their multi-jointed toes!)

Not that he had anything to be guilty about, he assured himself, trying to control his shaking hands. The surveillance of Captain Rudley was bang on course. He switched through to the relevant channel, which he had been checking personally throughout the evening.

'He's with two of the outworlders from Earth, Vice-

Chairman. They're on their way to a drinking party. Young people – both Parakonians and outworlders. Upper and upper-middle class. Fourteenth Sector.'

Tragan's face was rolling gently under the folds of skin. 'Are you in touch at the moment?'

'Well, no. They're in his flycar. On their way, as I said.' Dogar wiped the sweat from his forehead. 'But we have a transmitter at the party.'

'I should hope so.' The Vice-Chairman sounded almost genial. A mottle of rosy pink spots flashed briefly across his cheeks.

'A young Pellonian by the name of Rasco Heldal,' continued Dogar, encouraged. 'A very recent implant. He was in hospital last week for an infected tusk to be removed.'

'So he doesn't know he's transmitting?'

'No, sir.'

'So much the better. Warn the Fourteenth Sector patrol to stand by ready to arrest Rudley for speaking treason.'

Dogar blinked uncertainly. 'But suppose he doesn't?'

The Vice-Chairman's face rippled. 'No wonder you're stuck in middle management, Dogar,' he said. 'You really must learn to be more creative. Don't worry. Master Rudley is going to regret his little display of "lower upper-middle class" arrogance.'

The President was getting tired – and the Brigadier was getting bored. They'd got the general idea, hadn't they? Why did the Doctor have to keep on and on at the poor old codger? 'If everything is automated,' the Doctor was saying, 'nobody needs to work. Is that part of the paradise?'

'Some choose to work,' answered the President. 'We need a few to keep things turning over. It's a way of increasing one's capital; and ultimately one's status. But only the bondservants are under any obligation.' His nostrils dilated as he swallowed a yawn. The Brigadier caught a movement out of the corner of his eye: the woman Onya, keeping a careful eye on her charge.

'So you have a population largely made up of the unemployed?' the Doctor insisted.

'Of shareholders. Of consumers,' said the President wearily.

'Oh, they're on a very high dole of course. Happily unemployed, apparently. You seem to have solved capitalism's biggest problem, President.'

This roused the President almost to indignation. He explained, as vehemently as the weak old voice would let him, that on Parakon they had solved every problem. Because there was only one producer, the Corporation, wasteful competition was replaced by rational planning. Nation states – and armies – had become redundant. Because people were very happy with the way things were run, all political parties bar one had faded away.

'We have been elected, unopposed, for over forty years,' he concluded in feeble triumph.

'With the slogan, "What's good for the Corporation is good for the planet," no doubt,' said the Doctor.

He really was giving the poor old chap a roasting, thought the Brigadier. Like one of those whatever-you-say-I'm-agin-it fellows on the box. Still, he had to admit that it did all sound a bit too good to be true.

'You sound cynical, Doctor,' the President said. 'But what you say is precisely correct. As your own world will find out for itself, if you choose to join us in our prosperity.'

The Brigadier rejoined the conversation. 'You have no opposition at all, sir? There are no dissidents? Nobody who disagrees on principle?'

'Why should there be?' said the President. 'Our people have everything they could wish for.'

'Everything that money can buy,' said the Doctor, blandly.

'Exactly,' said the President, and yawned quite openly.

When the flycar took off and swooped out of the underground park into the night sky, Jeremy clung on to his seat like a little boy riding the big dipper for the first time. 'Oh. Oh. Oh!' he squeaked, eyes round and jaw dropped.

'O-o-oh!' he said again, as it left the environs of the palace and started to weave its way through the swarm of similar machines flying every which way above – and below – the city streets. At one moment so low it might as well have been an ordinary car motoring past the dazzling shop windows, at another climbing almost vertically up towards the roof tops, the flycar missed a crash by inches time after time.

'What's up?' said Waldo.

'Well, I mean, there's nobody flying this thing!'

Waldo grinned. 'No need. It's locked into the city grid. Far safer.'

Sarah, who was relishing the ride as much as Jeremy was hating it, gave herself up to the experience of the moment and let the turmoil of emotion engendered by her ER experience slide away into the past.

'How does it know which way to go?' she said.

'It's pre-programmed with the co-ordinates of all the places I visit regularly,' he replied.

'Press-button flying.'

'That's it. Starting with the first button, which brings it back home.'

'Like an old hack to the stable. Super,' said Jeremy, trying hard. His face now closely matched the greenish hue of his tunic.

As they left the busy centre, the traffic thinned out enough for the flycar to settle down to a more or less steady course. As she relaxed, Sarah found herself slipping back into her questioning mode.

'So who are these people who are giving the party?'

'Just friends.'

'Are they in the Guard too?'

'No.'

'What do they do for a living?'

Was she interviewing him? So what? She wanted to know the answers.

'Nothing at all.'

'Ah, the idle rich.'

Waldo laughed a little wryly. 'Oh, but we're all rich nowadays. We've all got shares in the Corporation.'

Sarah considered a flavourless life without the salt of work. 'Nothing to do but enjoy yourselves?'

'Super,' said Jeremy, who was beginning to turn pink again.

'I'd be bored out of my skull,' she continued.

'That's why I joined the Guard,' said Waldo. 'I wasn't clever enough to do anything else.'

Most people, he went on to explain, spent practically all of their time on the Experienced Reality couches. A man would be a skimmer champion for a while, or a woman a batterball leader or whatever. Then they'd change to something else: fall in love with some singer perhaps, and follow him or her everywhere; or spend all the time they could living the lives of an outworlder family on another planet – in a play that went on day after day and never ended.

'It happens at home,' said Sarah. 'People get hooked.'

'Hooked. Yes,' agreed Waldo. 'Like a fish that's always looking for a new bait to swallow. And the favourite bait of all is the hunt, or the execution – a guaranteed worldwide audience – when somebody accused of being a terrorist is torn to pieces and eaten alive by the Great Butcher Toad. As it happens.'

'You mean, not even a recording?' said Jeremy.

'That's disgusting,' said Sarah.

'I quite agree,' said Waldo. 'The trouble is, it's too dangerous for those of us who think so to speak out. You never know when somebody listening might have ER needles implanted. And all the time the transmissions are getting crueller – and bloodier.'

And Waldo went on to tell them about the Games.

'Combat? Hand-to-hand fighting?' said the Doctor.

'With various types of weapons, yes,' answered the President. 'The Games... are... are one of the most popular spectacles.'

Was his hesitation merely the result of tiredness, thought the Brigadier, or was he hiding something?

'Do you mean that they fight to the death, these fellows?' he said.

The President mumbled something indistinct. Onya moved forward, as though to intervene, but was waved irritably away. 'Any sport has its dangers,' he said, more intelligibly, though his speech was still slurred. 'A climber can – can fall off a mountain, after all.'

The Doctor wouldn't let him get away with it. 'I think the Brigadier was asking if the combatants are actually trying to kill each other, President,' he said.

But his opponent wouldn't be pinned down. 'I... Forgive me,' he said, 'but I think I must rest. My stamina is not... Please don't think me impolite, I... Please stay and finish the, er...' His voice trailed away.

Onya was already at his side. 'Come, President. Your guests will excuse you, I feel sure.'

This time he welcomed her attention and allowed her to wheel him away. The guards followed.

'Gladiators, by jiminy!' said the Brigadier.

'Yes,' said the Doctor. 'To keep the plebs quiet. The Romans had a word for it, or rather three words: *"panis et circenses"* – bread and circuses. It worked then; it works now.'

The crowded streets became wide empty avenues; the buildings, crammed together like a child's bricks packed into their box, gave way to elegant mansions standing in their own grounds, each as different from the surrounding alien designs as a Beverley Hills pseudo-Mexican ranch-house is from its neighbouring Tudoresque manor, or the Moorish villa next door complete with fretted windows, high-walled garden and camel-shed large enough to accommodate a couple of stretch limos.

'Rich is right!' said Sarah, as the flycar slowed to a hover and sank easily into a lucky space between a large shiny saucer-craft and what seemed to be a scooter with stumpy wings. Waldo looked up at the imposing facade of the house, glinting in the double light of the twin moons, with silver streaks striking upwards like frozen lightning, as if evaluating it for the first time.

'Yes. I suppose it is,' he said. 'It's old money. Greckle's people were landowners before the Corporation bought everybody out. Everybody wants to go to Greckle's parties.'

Jeremy scrambled out. Sarah turned to follow him but Waldo put a hand on her arm. 'Are you sure you're feeling all right?' he said.

As Sarah followed him to the grand front door, she talked to herself like a Dutch Aunt. (Good that: a cliché caught bending and given a swift kick up the bum!) Listen to me, my girl, she said to herself. You are an investigative journalist on a story. The last thing you need is an emotional involvement with a handsome hunk who isn't even a real human being.

You're so right, she agreed with herself; but as she remembered the deep brown eyes (Velvety brown? Or was that another cliché?), so filled with concern, she knew she didn't believe a word of it.

The Brigadier sipped his port. The Doctor had been right to probe. How much more was there to learn about this place? He looked up. The woman was returning; and she was full of gentle apologies.

'The President becomes very upset if he has to face some of the more disturbing aspects of modern life,' she said. 'To be honest, his mind refuses to take in the plain facts.'

The Doctor nodded. 'That's an affliction which isn't confined to the aged, by any means.'

The Brigadier looked at her as she continued her explanation. Neatly and unobtrusively dressed in a dark green suit, with her black hair pinned up in a serviceable bun, she nevertheless had an air of natural authority surprising in a servant, however senior. Who was she? And what position did she actually have in the President's household?

'We try to shield him as much as we can,' she was saying. 'He is very old – the father of his people. Their love for him is one of the few things which gives me hope for the future.'

Not a very servant-like thing to say. Hardly *comme il faut* to start interrogating your host's domestic staff, but never mind, this ought to be cleared up.

Before the Brigadier could open his mouth, the Doctor spoke. 'Forgive me, but you are?' He left the question hanging in the air.

'My name is Onya Farjen,' she replied. 'I suppose you could call me the President's housekeeper.' She turned to go. 'I'll leave you to drink your wine.'

She couldn't just fob them off like that! 'Er, there are one or two things I'd like to ask you – if you wouldn't mind,' the Brigadier said, awkwardly.

She turned back briefly. 'I've said too much already,' she replied. 'Please don't go. The President will return when he feels better.'

The Brigadier, frustrated, watched her go. 'Pretty rum sort of housekeeper, if you ask me,' he said, as the door slid shut. 'Do you really believe the old chap doesn't know what's going on?'

The Doctor grunted.

'Yes, but do you?'

'Certainly,' he said. 'He wouldn't be the first President to be kept in the dark – and he won't be the last.'

Chapter Nineteen

'Help yourselves to a little old glass of blip-juice, do! Rasco! Come and drig-drig like wild!'

Greckle – for that's who it must be, thought Sarah – grabbed the hand of a nearby guest and, silver mini-skirt twirling (Silver to match the hair framing her little round face; that wasn't a wig – but how could dye make hair shine like an old Georgian cream jug?), she drigged her way into the mass of head-banging, shoulder-banging, belly-banging driggers. The dance left a lot to the interpretation of the individual dancers, which was just as well, since many of the alien body-shapes Sarah could see would have found a more strictly formal set of movements impossible.

Rasco, Greckle's partner, for instance. How could he manage to dance so nimbly, if a trifle thumpily, on feet like that? What had the Doctor said? Parallel evolution? Sarah had had a maths mistress who was known as Porker, but Rasco would have won hooves down in a wart-hog look-alike contest. And the creature – person rather; one mustn't be species-ist! – who was swaying about on twelve feathery tentacles might have been happier with an old-fashioned waltz than with the floor-shaking drigger-drig-drig-drigger-drigger-drig thud of the off-the-beat drig-drig beat.

Nevertheless, the majority of the guests were young, beautiful and Parakonian. Feeling overdressed in her trousers – the amount of skin on view, barely tempered by exiguous but exotic costumes, wouldn't have been out of place on a surfers' beach – Sarah managed to make her way to the drinks table, where Jeremy was accepting from a servant a surprisingly small glass of liquid scooped from a bowl which bubbled and swirled like a mini-maelstrom.

'Hey, hey, hey!' he said when he caught sight of her. 'This is far out, man!'

'Oh, for heaven's sake, Jeremy,' she said, 'where did you learn that? From your grandpa?'

'No, but I mean . . .! Just look at the walls, all sort of coming and going – and rainbows! Like the inside of a waterfall!'

'That's exactly what it is,' said Waldo.

A party inside a waterfall? 'Indoors?' said Sarah.

'If that's what you want,' he answered. 'Hang on, I'll show you.

'Hey, Greckle!' he called out as his hostess bumped into view.

'What is it, my little old toy soldier, my soldier toy, my soldier boy?' she called back.

'Have you got an ambience pluralizer?'

'Insult me, then,' replied Greckle in mock dudgeon. 'As if I didn't sell the last share of my poor old widowed mother's inheritance!'

Waldo grinned. 'They're not cheap to hire,' he explained to Sarah.

'Where is it?' he went on to Greckle.

'It lurks behind the drinks, doesn't it? Like a virgin at a blip-do.' Greckle and Rasco were swallowed up anew in the jerking throng of driggers.

Waldo laughed. 'That's something I can't wait to see,' he called after her, and went round behind the table, where a servant who had heard the exchange was removing a fringed silver shawl which was draped over a black box.

'This thingy-juice is deeliciosus, Sarah. You ought to try some,' said Jeremy, happily helping himself to a refill.

Waldo looked up from the control panel of the apparatus. 'I'd go easy with that stuff if I were you, Jeremy.

That's how it gets its name. It sneaks up from behind and blips you.'

He consulted a list attached to the top of the box. 'Here we go,' he said, and pushed a pair of buttons. There were a few ironic cheers from the party, but nobody stopped dancing.

'Good gracious!' said Sarah.

'We're in a sort of cathedral thingy,' said Jeremy.

They were too. The falling water, the wispy clouds of vapour, the rainbows; all had melted away, to be replaced by majestic columns and a high vaulted roof. Tall, narrow windows of royal reds and yellows and blues let in shafts of heavenly – almost holy – sunlight, even though it was night outside.

'Holding parties in old temples was quite the thing for a while, when they were first sold off,' said Waldo. 'But then nobody cared, so it fell a bit flat.' He pressed another couple of buttons.

At once they were in a large clearing in a forest. There was a smell of wet leaves, and even over the heavy music the sound of jungle creatures could be heard.

Of course! It was the same as the view from the window in the apartment; and for that matter... 'I get it,' said Jeremy. 'It's like the desert at Space World. Sort of projected.'

'That's right,' said Waldo. 'Recorded, like Experienced Reality, and projected into our brains.' He pressed two more buttons.

This time they found themselves, under a grey threatening sky, on the heaving deck of a ship at sea. Sarah could even feel the spray blown onto her face and savour its strange taste on her lips – yet when she put up her hand, her skin was dry.

There were shouts of protest all round, led by Greckle herself: 'Enough, enough, she cried, all humptified and thrum! Drig-drigging on a boat deck? At boats I draw the line!' She snapped her fingers and the music stopped, leaving no sound but the howling of the wind and the expostulations of the guests.

'You want us to be seasick, then?' she said, coming over to Waldo, with her partner clumping along behind her. Her teasing tones were belied by her expression.

'Sorry,' said Waldo and hastily pressed two more buttons.

At once Greckle's little-girl face lit up. 'Better,' she said. 'Oh, inordinately better. Oh, consummately better!'

Sarah looked around in astonishment. The lighting had dropped to a sensuous red. The new low ceiling and plush crimson walls were covered with elaborately carved shapes which managed to be at once abstract and plainly erotic.

Greckle moved close to Waldo. 'Thank you, Waldo Rudley,' she said huskily. 'A moon-brothel just suits my mood. It makes my skin feel all sliggly-hoo.' She moved even closer. 'All over,' she said.

Well, really! thought Sarah Jane. In front of everybody, too!

Waldo took a step to the side and walked round her. 'Take a few deep breaths,' he said in a hearty voice. 'It'll soon go away.'

Greckle was unabashed. 'Brrrr!' she said, pretending to shiver. 'You're as c-c-c-cold as an ice-lizard, you are. Never mind. We're going to watch the semi-finals of the Games later. I've had the pluralizer hooked up to the stadium transmission. That'll heat you up.'

'Why?'

'Why? Because it's exciting, that's why.'

Jeremy looked up as he took his third glass of blip. 'Wha' games are those?' he said in a slightly out-of-focus voice.

'The games I told you about.'

'The killing games?'

'Yes,' said Waldo, grimly. 'The killing games.'

Oh Lor', thought Sarah. Did they have to stay? The prospect of watching people hacking each other to death quite took away whatever party spirit she had managed to conjure up.

'And what's wrong with killing games?' said a voice, a deep voice – an impossibly deep voice.

Waldo turned. 'Oh, I might have known you'd want to join in,' he said. 'Sarah, Jeremy, this is an old sparring partner of mine: Rasco Heldal.'

Before either of them could say 'Hi' – or perhaps 'How do you do' – the heavy porcine face frowned and spoke again. 'I said, what's wrong with killing games?'

Sub-Controller Dogar took his pleasures quietly. He was a watcher by nature; an observer, he would have called himself, even if an uglier, out-of-fashion word sometimes brushed across his thoughts.

He certainly would never have chosen to go to a blip party, though he sometimes had a sneaking envy of the young; nobody seemed to take any notice of the Twelve Commandments these days; they just did what they felt like – but if he'd found himself at one, the last thing he would have done would have been to join in the drig-drig.

True, he experienced a faint sense of physical release as he felt the rhythmic spasms of Rasco Heldal's muscular body, but even at the reduced level used for surveillance, the volume of the music – if that's what they called it – and the relentlessness of the jolting soon made him feel quite nauseated.

Vice-Chairman Tragan had removed his own headset as soon as Greckle hauled Heldal onto the dance floor. He sat watching with his pale mauve eyes, waiting for a signal from Dogar.

Thankfully, the dancing stopped at last. Dogar, listening hard for Rudley's voice, heard him say, 'Killing games . . .' in a disapproving way; and as he found himself speaking in turn, in a heavy booming voice, directly to the Captain. He waved frantically at the Vice-Chairman, who at once donned his helmet. By this time, Heldal was saying for a second time, 'What's wrong with killing games?' Dogar waited tensely for Rudley's answer.

'I don't like them, that's all,' he said.

Dogar spoke with the nervous urgency of the inefficient. 'Is that enough? Shall I send in the patrol?'

'No, no,' Tragan answered impatiently. 'That's just an expression of feeling. That's not nearly enough. Yet. Ssh!'

Rudley's remark had occasioned a chorus of protest, not least from his hostess. 'But the Games are a flame-out!' she said. 'Everybody hots at the Games!'

'That's one of the things I detest about them,' answered Rudley, 'what they do to us – filling us with hate and lust.'

The Vice-Chairman's face erupted in a surge of bumps. 'His father. A Temple Guardian, didn't you say?'

Dogar nodded. 'Dead now.'

'Typical Temple cant,' said Tragan.

'I certainly hate that Jenhegger,' said Greckle. 'I hope the champion rips his liver out.'

Sarah could hardly believe the tide of viciousness that all in a moment rose from the company. With the music stopped, the raised voices had attracted the attention of a large number of the partygoers, who seemed to be divided equally between the supporters of the unbeaten champion and his challenger in the semi-final, Jenhegger. She watched with horror the snarling, antagonistic faces round her. Never mind about watching the mayhem at the Games, they were ready to tear each other apart.

'There you are, you see,' said Waldo. 'You actually want to see their guts spilling onto the sand. What's wrong with you all?'

'Nobody asks them to fight. It's their own choice,' said Heldal.

'You think so?' said Waldo. 'Bondservants promised their freedom? Lower-lower class morons bribed with a bundle of shares? Criminals threatened with the hunt? What sort of choices are those?'

Greckle glanced round her party, which seemed to have come to a standstill. She changed her tone. 'But, sweet little old Waldo, think of the money the Corporation makes! The last Games alone upped our dividend by nearly a quarter!'

Waldo seemed even more disgusted. 'You think it's right that the Corporation should kill people just for the sake of a bit of extra profit?' he said.

'That's better. That's a lot better,' said Tragan. 'Is the patrol standing by?'

'Outside their door, Vice-Chairman.'

'Of course it's right,' Heldal was growling. 'It's a perfect example of how the market works.'

Waldo looked as if he would explode, but Heldal bulldozed on: 'The fighters sell their skill, the Corporation sells the show, the audience get what they want, and everybody's better off into the bargain. What's wrong with that?'

Waldo was now really angry. 'I'll tell you what's wrong with it,' he said. 'It turns people into things. That's what's wrong with it!'

Greckle giggled nervously. 'You'll be telling us it's a sin next,' she said.

'It *is* a sin!' Waldo said passionately. 'It's a sin against life. It's a sin against the spirit. The Government ought to stop it, but they're in it up to their necks!'

'Got him!' said Tragan.

'Go, go, go!' Dogar shouted into his transmitter.

The appalled reaction at the party was violently interrupted, as the door flew open to admit four purple-uniformed patrolmen, two of whom, to Sarah's horror, were holding back on straining leashes the creatures (or their doubles) she had last seen on the spaceship.

The crowd fell silent, their instinctive recoil of fear stopped by the command of the patrol leader: 'Stand still! Everybody!' With a snap of his fingers, he quietened the snarling beasts.

He strode to the central group, his boots sounding a menacing echo as he crossed the empty dance floor. 'Which is Rudley?' he said.

Waldo stepped forward. 'I am Waldo Rudley,' he said.

'Waldo Rudley, you are under arrest.'

'What? Whatever for?'

'Gross violation of the Treason Act.'

'This is ridiculous. I'm Captain of the Presidential Guard.'

Was there a glimmer of satisfaction as the patrol leader replied? 'The law knows no favourites,' he said. 'You've been speaking treason. You are under arrest.'

Sarah could hold back no longer. 'But all he said was – '

'Silence!'

Greckle breathed in Sarah's ear, 'Keep quiet, or they'll take you too.'

As Waldo was marched away, he called back, saying, 'Listen everybody! Things don't have to be like this. It's not too – ' but his voice was stopped by a vicious blow.

As the door closed, Sarah turned to Greckle. 'What happens now?' she said. 'Where do they take him?' But Greckle behaved as if she hadn't said a word. Turning away, she called out, 'Music please, Momy!' and then, raising her voice over the chatter, she went on, 'Now come on, everybody, there's obbles of blip-juice left. I want everyone out there, drigging themselves blatt!'

The drig music started again, as insistently as before, but with a more sensual swing, in tune with the moon-brothel background. The guests started to move to the off-beat rhythm and in no time the party had thankfully resumed, as if the irritating hiatus had never occurred.

'But we've got to do something!' shouted Sarah over the din.

'What is there to do? He asked for it and he got it,' said Heldal.

'But he only said – '

Sarah was interrupted by the shrill, almost hysterical voice of Greckle: 'Stop it, stop it, stop it! You'll have them back again! I won't have my party spoiled by that odious young man!' She became aware of the glances of the nearby guests and visibly controlled herself. 'Grab yourself a glass of blip and put that webbler to sleep-oh,' she said in more normal tones.

'Come on, Rasco. Drig-time!' she added, pushing the heavy bulk of her partner onto the red-lit dance floor.

As Heldal abandoned himself to the mind-numbing sensual beat, he called back to Sarah his final thought on the matter. It might have been drowned in the cacophony of the drig-drig, but Sarah heard it as clearly as if it were resonating through the silent caverns of one of the alien moons.

'Forget him,' she heard Heldal say. 'He's dead.'

Chapter Twenty

'He's what? Speak up, Tragan!'

Albin Dogar couldn't help a small shudder of panic which overlayed his fear of the Vice-Chairman as he heard the plummy tones of Chairman Freeth himself, albeit distorted by their storm-tossed flight through space.

'I said that the President invited them both to dinner,' replied Tragan, his face roughened by minute purple pimples.

'And you did nothing to stop them going?'

'How would you expect me to do that? Are you ready to show our hand?'

'No, no, of course not,' said Freeth, 'But this is terrible news. They might tell him anything at all. You must do something. Don't wait until I have landed. Do something *now*.'

The Sub-Controller watched, appalled but fascinated, as Tragan's face started to bubble.

'By all means,' said the Vice-Chairman. 'What would you suggest?'

Freeth's voice hardened. 'You are in charge of security, Tragan. Do your job.'

The bubbling violently increased.

'And Tragan, before anything else, in case we have to advance our plans, neutralize the Presidential Guard. But legally. Do you hear me? It must be done legally. Get rid of that meddler Rudley. They're nothing without him.'

The bubbling was dying down. A rosy flush was sweeping Tragan's skin. 'That has already been attended to, Chairman,' he said.

'So you can do something right. The moon *is* made of green cheese!' The rich chuckle was lost in a burst of static.

'I beg your pardon?'

'Never mind. Then all you have to do is to limit the damage occasioned by your earlier bungling. I suggest you get on with it.'

Tragan's eyes were cold and unmoving in his erupting face. 'I have your permission to do whatever is necessary?'

Was there a longer pause than the usual transmission gap before the Chairman answered? 'Very well,' he said, and switched off.

Dogar watched fearfully, lest he should be the surrogate target of the Vice-Chairman's wrath. But to his surprise, Tragan's face smoothed to a gentle ripple. He rose to his feet, stretched and said in his flattest voice, 'Good. Very good. It's quite time this charade was put to an end.'

The Sub-Controller watched him to the door and sighed with relief. He could safely leave the rest of the night to the Senior Supervisor. At last he could go home.

His satisfaction vanished as he pictured his wife waiting for him. His bowels turned to water again. She'd never believe his excuse. She never did.

The old boy toddling off like that at least gave them a chance to regroup, discuss tactics and all that sort of thing, thought the Brigadier, firmly pushing away the almost empty decanter. Got to keep a clear head, he thought muzzily.

'Even on their own terms,' the Doctor was saying, 'there's one thing missing from the paradise equation, Lethbridge-Stewart.'

'A good Highland malt?'

The Doctor ignored his attempted humour. 'It could be expressed in several different ways,' he went on. 'Nothing for nothing and precious little for sixpence, as King Lear very nearly said; there's no such thing as a free lunch, as he might have said if he'd thought of it; or the higher the fewer.'

The Brigadier sighed. 'You've lost me,' he said.

'How can they keep taking all these riches from the soil if they never put anything back? The more they take, the less there'll be. The equation doesn't balance.'

Fair enough. But what had that got to do with the price of walnuts? thought the Brigadier, taking one and cracking it. 'There's only one person who can find out the answers and still be safe,' the Doctor said, 'and that's the President himself. It seems to be quite clear that he's been kept in the dark. It's time that stopped. We must tell him the whole story.'

'Well done, Doctor!' said a flat voice behind them. They turned. 'An excellent scheme. What a shame you didn't think of it earlier.'

The voice seemed familiar – but the face! Good grief, it was like a – an overripe plum – a stranded jelly fish – a rotting...

'Mr Tragan, isn't it?' said the Doctor. 'What a pleasant surprise.'

'No, no. Don't move,' said Tragan, stepping forward into the pool of light round the dining table. He produced a gun like an automatic with an extended barrel and curiously shaped chambers like the whorls of a sea shell grouped round the stock.

'I think we'd better listen to him, Lethbridge-Stewart,' the Doctor said. 'That's a paralysing stun gun. It doesn't kill you, or even make you unconscious. Just paralyses you for a very long time.'

'A very long time,' agreed Tragan. 'The rest of your life, in fact. But then, in your case, that's probably quite a short time, isn't it?'

'If you kill us,' said the Doctor quietly, 'you'll never manage to keep it quiet.'

'You think not?' said Tragan pleasantly, his face a rippling pink. 'I don't agree. Provided we, er, terminate the contracts of all four of you, so to speak. The United Nations Mission would of course leave a polite note of regret for its sudden departure. And your friends on Earth – would they send a search party to Parakon?'

The blighter was enjoying himself!

'Well, whatever you mean to do,' said the Doctor, 'may I suggest you get on with it?'

'You mustn't be in such a hurry,' said the Vice-Chairman reprovingly. 'We shall now return to your suite and wait for your companions. They're on their way. And then, then we shall have to come to a conclusion. Or some of us will.'

The Doctor looked past Tragan. He stood up. 'I hope you're feeling better, sir,' he said, pitching his voice up.

Tragan laughed. 'You forget I was a policeman, Doctor. You'll have to do better than that.'

A wheezy old voice came from the darkness: 'Thank you, I am. Will you ever forgive my discourtesy?'

Tragan spun round, whipping the gun behind his back.

'Vice-Chairman Tragan?' said the President in displeased surprise. 'What are you doing here?'

Before Tragan could answer, the Doctor stepped forward. 'Mr Tragan had a message for us,' he said. 'But if you will forgive me, I'm very pleased that he's here, as he can hear what I have to say to you.'

The President, who was followed by his two guards and, discreetly behind, Onya Farjen, wheeled himself forward to the head of the table and gestured to his guests to resume their seats.

'It may take a little while,' said the Doctor, 'and it's of the utmost importance that you understand clearly.'

'How very mysterious,' said the President.

Tragan, who had managed to conceal his gun, stepped forward. 'I don't think it would be advisable to – '

The President spoke sharply. 'Vice-Chairman! You forget yourself, I think.'

But Tragan was not to be put off. 'I'm sorry, sir,' he said, 'but this man has already – '

Now the old man was really angry. 'This man, as you call him, is the honoured guest of your president, and the ambassador of a mighty world. I will hear no more from you.' He turned enquiringly to the Doctor.

Well done that man, thought the Brigadier, as the Doctor paused as if to marshall his thoughts.

'It relates to certain events that took place before we left Earth,' he started to say, only to be stopped again.

'Forgive me for interrupting,' said a fruity voice.

Freeth, by jiminy!

The President's withered face was beaming. 'Never an interruption!' he said. 'It does my old heart good to see you back. Doctor! Brigadier! May I introduce the Chairman of the Parakon Corporation: my son, Balog Freeth.'

What!?

'We've already had the pleasure of Mr Freeth's acquaintance,' said the Doctor calmly. 'Your son, you say?'

'Why yes,' answered the President. 'He took over from me when I resigned to run for President. Would I have trusted my corporation to a stranger?' He turned back to Freeth. 'Sit down, my boy. Pour yourself a glass. The Doctor is about to tell us a story. I must say he has me thoroughly intrigued.'

Freeth stayed quite still, a slight smile curving his thick lips, his little eyes between the folds of flesh flicking to and fro.

There was a silence. The Brigadier looked at Tragan; was he smiling too? It was impossible to tell.

The Doctor said, 'I think the moment has passed, sir. If you will forgive me, I'll leave it to another time.'

The President raised an eyebrow. 'As you will,' he said courteously. 'I shall have to contain my disappointment as patiently as I can.'

After exchanging a few more polite, diplomatic, empty platitudes, the Doctor and the Brigadier were allowed to retire, having expressed the enormous sense of privilege and eager anticipation they felt at the thought of meeting the Chancellor and other Ministers of the Government the next morning.

As they left, Tragan made to follow, only to be stopped by the President's voice, made firm by its sternness. 'Not you, Vice-Chairman,' he said. 'Before you go, I should like to hear what message can be so urgent that you consider it gives you permission to invade my private quarters...' His voice was cut off by the closing of the door behind them.

'We can't stay here now,' the Brigadier said out of the side of his mouth, as he strode down the corridor after the guard escorting them to the front door of the palace.

'Certainly not,' replied the Doctor, in like manner. 'But we can't leave without Sarah and Jeremy. Tragan said they were on their way back. Let's hope he was right.'

At this moment the pair in question were hanging on to the edges of their seats as Waldo's flycar swooped down towards its home park. In spite of Jeremy's fears that it might drop out of the sky ('I mean! We don't really know how to work it, and it hasn't got any wings or jet-thingies or *anything*!'), it had responded immaculately to Sarah's finger pressing on its home button.

So it was that when they arrived at a run at the entrance to the Ambassadorial suite, they met the others running the other way.

'Sarah! Thank goodness!' said the Doctor. 'Come on, there's no time to lose!' Taking no notice of her urgent pleas for him to stop and listen to her, he set off with the Brigadier back the way they'd come.

'Hey, wait for me!' cried Jeremy, as Sarah raced in pursuit.

'Where are we going?' she gasped, as she caught up with the Brigadier.

'The TARDIS. We've got to get away.'

'But we can't do that. They're going to kill Waldo!'

'What? Captain Rudley? When? How?'

'Execute him – hunt him. Oh, I don't know. What does it matter? We've got to stop them! Doctor! Please!'

But the Doctor was disappearing through the door that led to the outside. Sarah dived after him, closely followed by the Brigadier. But as the Doctor ran the last few yards towards the TARDIS, which was waiting patiently in the middle of the courtyard, a figure appeared from behind it.

'You didn't really think we'd be so stupid as to leave your ship unguarded, did you?' said Tragan, his face turbulent; and as Jeremy crashed through the door behind them Sarah became aware that other figures, in purple uniforms and holding strangely shaped guns, were appearing from every side.

The massive bulk of Chairman Freeth rolled into view. 'We meet again, Doctor,' he said. There was a crack as he squeezed two walnuts together in his little podgy hand.

'Just in time to say goodbye,' he went on. 'And we've hardly had an opportunity to get to know each other. To misquote a little, I think this could be the end of a beautiful friendship.'

'What are you going to do?' said the Doctor.

'Oh, come now, Doctor,' he said, poking an exploratory finger amongst the broken shells. 'You know very well what I'm going to do.' He looked up. 'The only question is, "How?"'

He put half a walnut into his mouth and chomped it up.

Chapter Twenty-One

'Can't think what they're waiting for,' said the Brigadier.

Jeremy was finding it difficult to concentrate. Although the disorientating effects of the blip-juice were starting to wear off, they were being replaced by a throb-throb-throbber-throb behind the eyes which felt as if there were a drig-ball in progress inside his head.

Having been hustled from the courtyard back to the suite, they had been locked in, with a guard outside the door and a promise from Freeth that he would return.

'Now, you won't go away, will you?' he'd said, winsomely. 'Do forgive me for deserting you. I'm sure you'll find some way of amusing yourselves.'

Quite a decent chap really, thought Jeremy. Not like that other gink with the wobbly blue face.

'It's quite clear that they're frightened of the power that the President still has,' said the Doctor in reply to the Brigadier. 'Freeth has to convince his father that we've left Parakon before he can do anything final. It's probably too late tonight, so I expect we've got a few hours.'

Sarah seemed to be in a bit of a state, thought Jeremy. 'Doctor, please!' she said. 'We've got to do something about Captain Rudley. They're going to kill him!'

Oh, Lor'. Yes, of course, Waldo. Forgotten about him.

'They're going to dispose of all of us,' replied the Doctor.

What? What! Whatever for?

'Why?' said Jeremy, pressing a hand to his forehead to steady the beat.

'We have it in our power to stop the Parakon

Corporation operating on Earth. They're not going to give up a treaty worth billions without a murmur,' answered the Doctor. As he spoke, he was inspecting the windows, which were similar to the ones in the other suite, showing the view of the lake.

'Not even real windows,' he said. 'In any case, we're on the fourth floor and, as I remember, it's a sheer drop. Have a look round, all of you. See if there's another way out: a fire escape, a ventilator shaft, anything.'

They scattered into the surprisingly large number of rooms. Jeremy found himself in a sort of sub-suite, like a little flatlet. Probably intended for a valet or ladies' maid or whoever, thought Jeremy, as he ferreted through the cupboards.

A quick search revealed nothing helpful. He sat down on the bed. If he held his head very still, it settled to a steady ache which was almost tolerable.

He heard the murmur of voices. Evidently the others had had no more success than he had. 'We shall have to think of something else,' he heard the Doctor saying.

'For instance?' That was the Brigadier.

'Well, we could . . .' The Doctor's voice trailed away.

'Yes?' said Sarah.

'If we . . .' the Doctor started again; and stopped again.

'What?' The Brig.

A minor explosion from the Doctor: 'Look, it's all very well gazing up at me like spaniel puppies waiting for a lump of sugar. Everybody's blessed with a modicum of cerebral tissue, after all.'

Eh?

'Now, come on! Think!'

Good idea. Trust the Doctor. If they all had a bit of a think . . . Jeremy lay back onto the bed and closed his eyes in order to concentrate better.

Now then, to assess the position: they were locked in upstairs with the TARDIS downstairs; though come to think of it, there didn't seem to be any stairs. Only lifts. The fourth floor was connected to the ground floor by one set of lifts, and the ground floor was connected to the knee-bone and the knee-bone was connected to the leg-bone...

Night-night, Jeremy.

The chamber in which Waldo Rudley was incarcerated was not the traditional dungeon of the fairytales or even the bleak brick cell of a long-term prison. Having other methods – more efficient and more permanent – of dealing with their delinquents, the Parakonian security forces were content to contain their temporary prisoners in rooms not unlike those of a cheap rooming house. True, there were bars on the windows and manacles chained to the wall ready for the potentially violent, but the decorations were clean and simple and the furnishings adequately comfortable.

There were even pictures on the wall – firmly screwed down and with unbreakable glass. These depicted in garish colour, with an egregious use of red, the various fates which might be in store for the current tenant.

The temperature was always that of a mild spring day and the food was reasonable, although most of it was apt to end up in the dustbin.

'You'll waste away,' said Tragan, looking at Waldo's untouched breakfast. 'That'll never do.'

'Fattening me up for the kill, are you?' said Waldo, who was sitting on the bed.

'Crude but accurate. Funny how these old expressions linger, isn't it?' Tragan's face was a delicate mauve; the warts and boils moved gently up and down like scum on the surface of a polluted sea.

'I demand to see the President,' said Waldo. 'I have that right, at least.'

'No, no,' replied the Vice-Chairman. 'You have no rights. You forfeited all rights when you chose to incite your fellow guests to treason.'

'But that's ridiculous. We were just having a discussion.'

'You seem to forget that we have a full ER recording of your offence,' said Tragan patiently, as if explaining to a slow but willing child. 'Everything will be conducted according to the due process of law. That recording will be played immediately before the transmission of the carrying out of your sentence, so that justice may be seen to be done.'

Waldo laughed bitterly. 'You mean, to frighten everybody into behaving themselves.'

'You're uncommonly bright for a military man, Captain Rudley.'

'And what is my sentence?'

This question launched the Vice-Chairman into quite a lengthy disquisition on the various possibilities. His own preference, it seemed, would be to see the Captain slowly dismembered by a curious kranjal ape, or chewed to death by a swarm of soldier chais, either of which could eventuate while he was being hunted; more certain destinies, such as the old-fashioned mincing machine, could be easily arranged should he refuse the hunt; and of course – and here the Vice-Chairman displayed a certain reluctance – the law granted him the privilege of choosing to volunteer as a combatant in the Games.

'Kill or be killed,' said Waldo.

'You are being offered a strong chance of survival,' said Tragan disapprovingly. 'Some last for years. The present favourite for the final, this Jenhegger, for example.'

'So he won last night, did he? That makes seventy-three he's finished off.' He stood up and walked to the window, looking out at the high blue sky.

'Murder as a way of life somehow doesn't appeal,' he went on. 'I may be a fool but I'm not a hypocrite.'

Tragan gazed at the hated back. 'Death before dishonour,' he said. 'How very noble.'

'Jeremy. Jeremy! Wake up!'

Jeremy opened his eyes. He sat up and stretched.

'I wasn't asleep,' he said to Sarah, who was standing in the doorway. 'I just shut my eyes for a moment. Helps me to think, you see.'

'Oh, Jeremy,' she said. 'It's morning. You've been asleep for hours.'

'Oh.' He got off the bed and walked over to her. 'Do you think they'll bring us some breakfast?'

He caught sight of her expression as she turned back into the main room of the suite. Huh! Elder sister stuff again! All very well, but he didn't get anything at the party – except that blip-juice, of course. He winced, and then found it was unnecessary. The pain had gone, thank goodness. But he certainly was rattling inside.

'We've got more to worry about than cornflakes,' Sarah said. She lowered her voice and glanced across the other side of the room, where the Doctor was standing, looking out at the lake that wasn't there. 'I don't think he's been asleep all night,' she said. 'He's just been walking up and down, up and down like a . . . a . . .'

'Like a caged lion,' supplied Jeremy.

'Spoken like a true journalist,' she said, to his surprise. She wasn't usually so complimentary.

'Still,' she went on, 'they say a cliché is a cliché because it works. Yes. Just like a caged lion. A very unhappy caged lion.'

The Doctor swung round and moved over towards the door as though listening. The Brigadier rose from his easy chair and cocked his head. Yes, quite right. There was a noise: the sound of voices – and the clink of crockery. Breakfast?

The door slid open and a guard appeared, gun in hand. 'Right, you lot. Get back! Back!' As soon as he was satisfied, he turned and gave a jerk of his head.

Onya Farjen appeared pushing a sort of trolley, followed by another guard, who turned his back on the room, his gun ready. The food on the trolley, while by no means equalling the feast of yesterday, was a substantial collation for a prison breakfast. Jeremy could almost imagine that he could smell fried bacon. He could feel the saliva gathering in his mouth. It was true, then. Your mouth really did water!

'Listen here,' the first guard was saying. 'You stay back until I've closed the door again. Then you can stuff yourselves silly, for all I care. Got it?'

'How could we resist such an elegant invitation?' said the Doctor.

Onya, who had wheeled the trolley well into the room, almost to the window, looked up with a worried expression. 'Guard!' she said sharply. 'Look at this.'

What had she found? Had the Doctor been up to something? Surely she wouldn't give him away?

'What is it?' said the first guard.

'Come and see,' she said. Whatever it was, it was important – an amazing discovery, clearly.

The guard, casting suspicious glances around, came slowly over to her. 'I can't see anything,' he said.

'No, no,' she said impatiently. 'Down there.' She pointed to the angle of the wall under the window. The guard bent down and peered at the floor.

With a sharp controlled jab, not moving her hand more than six inches, Onya struck the bending man on the back of the neck; he collapsed, soundlessly.

'Oh dear,' said Onya. 'Are you all right?' She turned to the door and called to the other security man. 'Yed! I think he's fainted!' The man moved into the doorway, staring uncertainly across the room.

'Hai!' The Doctor was if anything even faster than Onya had been. Yed went flying into an aerial somersault which would have been quite a feat if he had been conscious of what he was doing. But he wasn't. He landed in a crumpled heap by Jeremy and Sarah.

'I say,' said Jeremy.

'Oh, very neat, Doctor,' said Onya. 'I couldn't have done it better myself.'

'Who *are* you?' said the Brigadier.

'No time for explanations now. Come on, fast as you like,' said Onya, leading the way out of the suite at a fast clip.

Another sister, thought Jeremy, and set off after them all, with a bitter farewell glance at the loaded trolley.

It was the breakfast trolley – and the fact that the food

on it was still hot – which told Freeth that the escape had taken place minutes rather than hours ago.

In spite of the Chairman's strictures on the efficiency of his security, Tragan's emergency system snapped into action. By the time the fugitives had reached the flycar-park, via the staff exit, the alarm bells were sounding – and even as Onya ushered them urgently into a small blue flycar, almost pushing the trailing Jeremy, a guard appeared at the far end of the walkway. Without even pausing to challenge them, he raised his weapon and fired.

With a cry of pain, Onya fell into the car. 'He got my shoulder,' she gasped; and as the Brigadier helped her into a seat, it was apparent that her right arm was hanging uselessly by her side.

From the seat Sarah had scrambled into, she could see the guard running towards the car, with another close behind. It looked as if the escape was over almost before it had begun. But even as the thought crossed her mind, the strange whine of the engine (Propulsion unit? Whatever.) interrupted it.

'Don't worry,' said the Doctor, his hands fastening onto the controls. I can fly it. Here we go.' And even faster than in Waldo's car, they shot out into the sunlight.

'All units. All units. Apprehend fugitives leaving the area of the Presidential Palace.' The thin distorted voice came from a speaker concealed in the control panel.

'It's tuned to the frequency of the security patrols,' said Onya.

'And there's one now,' she added as the wail of a distant siren replaced the fading alarm bells.

By this time they had left the Palace grounds and were flying over the streets of the city. The crescendo of the siren was joined by others converging on the park.

Before Sarah could turn her head to look for the tell-tale purple of the security cars, the Doctor spoke again. 'I'll soon lose them,' he said. 'Hang on to your hats.'

It was like being in a rocket launch – like in all those old movies. Sarah felt herself slammed into the back of her seat with her head pinned to the neckrest. Whether

her face actually distorted with the G-force – that was what they called it, wasn't it? – she had no idea. It certainly felt like it; particularly when, with gut-twisting effect, the Doctor weaved his way through the seemingly snail-slow traffic meandering above the streets.

In seconds – or minutes, perhaps; time seemed to belong to another world – they had left behind the crowded blocks of shops and houses and were flying amongst the towering factories on the outskirts of the city. They slowed down to the speed of a record breaking racing car.

'Mind if we go back to get my stomach?' said Sarah.

'I know what you mean,' said the Doctor. 'I must admit, I didn't expect quite that speed.'

'There's supposed to be a limiter,' said Onya. 'But I removed the governor.'

'What a woman!' said the Brigadier.

'Isn't there a risk of positive feedback in the helical particle-generator?' said the Doctor.

'Not if you – ' Onya started to reply. She looked at the Doctor with astonishment. 'You know these cars?' she said.

'Have you been here before, Doctor?' said the Brigadier. 'Why didn't you say?'

'No, no,' he answered. 'They're very like the skimmers we used to fly when I was a boy on Gallifrey. You never forget how to ride a bicycle, do you? Now then, where to?'

Chapter Twenty-Two

'You've lost them?'

'We were just too late, Chairman Freeth.'

'Then find them, Tragan!'

'They were in an ordinary small flycar like any one of thousands. How would you suggest I set about it?'

His only answer was a strangled cry of fury.

Onya Farjen was very sorry to hear the news of Waldo's arrest. He was always a headstrong young man, she thought. Still, as she pointed out to Sarah, he was in no immediate danger. The authorities always did things according to the rules, whether the rules were laid down in the statute book or merely the custom of years. It would take time to organize the hunt. Then there might be a chance of saving him – and only then.

'How?' said Sarah.

'You'll see,' said Onya.

The Doctor, who had set the flycar to automatic on a course given him by Onya, looked up. 'How's the arm?' he said.

'I still can't move it,' she said. 'But the feeling is beginning to come back. It's lucky he was at extreme range. It'll take a few days, but I'll recover.'

'That sounds like the voice of experience,' said the Brigadier.

'I must admit, it's not the first time I've been hit.' Her mind flickered over the memories.

'The housekeepers on Parakon seem to lead surprisingly full lives,' said the Doctor. 'That was as pretty a piece of unarmed combat back there as I've seen in years.'

Onya heard the compliment with a wry internal smile. To be forced into violence at all was in itself a failure – or that's what old Darshee would have said, even as he taught her the skilful use of violence.

'Thank you, Doctor,' she said. 'I must say the same to you.'

'A similar discipline, I suspect,' he replied. 'I call it Venusian Aikido. It's been most helpful to me over the years, but I always regret having to use it. In a sense, I feel I've failed.'

Who was this man?

Her thought was evidently reciprocated by the Brigadier. 'If you'll forgive me,' he was saying, 'who are you? And where are you taking us? You're not really the President's servant, are you?'

Was she? Or had she just been using the position as a front? That too, of course, but... 'I have loved him and protected him,' she said. 'And now I shall never be able to return.'

'I'm taking you to my real home,' she added, in answer to the Brigadier's second question. 'As for who I am – '

'Wowie-zowie!' interrupted Jeremy, who'd been looking out of the window, not listening to the conversation. 'Look at that! It must be the size of a rugger pitch!'

Onya followed his gaze: a space freighter landing. 'Yes, the Interplanetary Freighter Docks are scattered all round the perimeter of the city – of every city.'

'That thing's a freighter?' said Sarah. 'You mean it's full of goods of some sort?'

Onya nodded. 'Raw material coming in for processing.'

'Rapine?' asked the Doctor.

'Exactly. And going back, everything Parakon can manufacture from it. They say that there's a Corporation freighter either landing or taking off from somewhere on the planet for every twenty breaths you take. And I say those freighters are killing us, as surely as the Corporation killed the land below us.'

They all looked down.

'It looks like sea,' said the Brigadier. 'Are we flying over the ocean? No, hang on,' he said. 'It looks just like . . . I remember once, when I was flying from Kathmandu to Patna, from the air the edge of the *Terai* – the jungle – looked just like a coastline. That's not the sea.'

'Kathmandu, Lethbridge-Stewart?' said the Doctor. 'Backpacking, were you? Dropping out and tuning in? You must have looked rather fetching in a kaftan.'

'Undercover,' said the Brigadier shortly. He turned back to Onya. 'It's desert.'

She looked at the Doctor. She suspected that he'd come to this conclusion long before. He saw her looking at him. 'A gigantic dustbowl, isn't it?' he said. 'Does anything grow on Parakon any more?'

'Practically nothing,' she answered. 'All the accessible fertile land was turned over entirely to rapine. You can see the result.'

'But that's terrible,' said Sarah.

'There are a few patches of wilderness left, where the terrain made it difficult to farm. That's where we're going now, to the largest. It's known as the Lackan, the place of no hope.'

'Oh cheers,' Jeremy muttered in Sarah's ear. 'That's all we need!'

Onya ignored him. 'I heard the President say that Parakon is a paradise; it's more like a hell,' she said. 'Oh, it used to be a paradise in earlier times; a lush green paradise where the people hunted and grew their crops, giving their thanks to the earth and the sky – living real lives, not lives of illusion and fantasy.'

'Oh, the Golden Age,' said the Doctor drily. 'In every culture I've ever met, they've had a legend of an ancient Golden Age. And there's usually no lack of guides claiming to know the way back.'

'This is not legend, Doctor. It's fact. I'm not talking about a dream world with no pain. To seek that is to be trapped in the more insidious fantasy of all. I'm talking of a world full of pain – but it was real pain, to be suffered and borne, knowing it would be balanced by joy in the spirit.'

'I'm sorry,' said the Doctor.

'Please,' she said. It didn't matter; why should she take offence? It was far more important that they should understand.

'The President told you that rapine is a generous plant. Rapine is greed. It takes the best from the earth and puts nothing back.

'It's taught us all how to be greedy too, until our cravings have become the whole of our lives, and our spirit is dying from lack of joy...'

She stopped short. When she spoke again, it was almost to herself.

'... and I can't tell if my heart is breaking for the sorrow of it – or being torn apart by rage.'

For a while, the only sound was the faint hum of the flycar as it made its way over the endless waste below. The silence was broken by the Doctor quietly echoing the earlier question of the Brigadier.

'Who are you, Onya Farjen?' he asked.

'Who is she? Where does she come from?'

In the very nature of things, Freeth's expression could never be described as thin-lipped, but his mouth had tightened to a downcurved grimace which made his feelings quite evident.

'That is precisely what I am checking at the moment,' replied his Vice-Chairman, surveying with dead eyes the data coming up on the screen before him.

Freeth sucked at a gap between his teeth. 'To be outwitted by a housekeeper! And these are the men to whom you entrusted our entire future. I must admit that I am the tiniest bit put out.'

'They have been suitably disciplined.'

'I should hope so.'

A more vigorous suck having proved fruitless, a plump finger was poked into Freeth's mouth and the tiny nail successfully extracted the recalcitrant bit of food. Having inspected it closely, he reinserted it into the maw and, with plain enjoyment, refinished his breakfast.

'Here we are,' said Tragan, the back of his neck fading from royal purple to lilac. 'Onya Farjen: bondservant to the President. Previous employer, Katyan Glessey, deceased. Highly recommended. Previous records unavailable.'

'Unavailable!' said Freeth, peering at the screen.

'Destroyed in the Temple Dissolution riots. You remember the fire at Parakon House?'

'How could I forget it? I lost two cases of pre-rapine vintage wine.'

'So that's that,' said Tragan, switching off.

'Our only lead is this Katyan Glessey. Correct?'

'So it would seem.'

'And she's dead.'

Tragan's face was quivering dangerously. 'We shall have to wait for them to show their hand.'

'You are proposing to abandon the search?'

'Of course not. I shall put my best men on to it.'

'Now, there's a comfort,' said Freeth.

'Who am I?' Onya recalled the timeless days she had spent with that question stuck in her mind like a lump of hastily swallowed, undigested, unwanted food in a rebellious stomach. True there was a fierce hunger; but not so much for an answer (answers came tumbling in, each more unsatisfactory than the last), more to be rid of the question.

The Doctor and the Brigadier would be happy with a simpler answer than those with which she had tried to satisfy Darshee; and yet, after all, what could be simpler than the answer he had accepted at last, with his familiar giggle joining her own uncontainable laughter at its absurdity!

The name Katyan Glessey was no more real than the name Onya Farjen, which had been plucked out of the air (and Onya smiled at the expression) by her teacher on that very same day; or maybe it was just as real. She had been Katyan Glessey for all of her life, after all, and that stretched infinitely backwards into the darkness of the pre-memory void.

One day she had awoken with the shocking realization that it would be intolerable to be Katyan any more. Katyan's life as a research biologist dedicated to the manipulation of the molecular structures in the heart of the rapine cell, with the object of making it ever more productive, ever more versatile; this life had for many years been as absorbing to her as a vivid, exultant dream. Perhaps it was inevitable that she would wake up.

'Ordinary life seemed to be nothing but an irritating interruption,' she told them. 'But then, I fell in love. Caldon used to make me laugh; I used to tell him that that was the only reason I put up with him. He didn't work. He didn't do anything much. He loved talking – and thinking. Dangerous things to do on Parakon.'

She stopped talking. She put up her hand and touched her cheek. She was surprised to find that there was no tear to wipe away.

'What happened?' asked Sarah gently.

'He disappeared – and so did a number of his friends. Three of them. I suppose they thought it would be too dangerous to put them on show. They might have said the wrong thing.

'I was frightened for my own life. At the very least they might have taken my job away from me and I couldn't bear the thought of that. I kept very quiet and hid myself behind the work.

'But all the time, I could hear his voice; I could hear his laughter; and I came to realize what it had been hiding. Little by little I too came to understand the horror of what we were doing, of what I was doing; and the time came when I couldn't face it any longer. But I didn't know where to turn. I felt polluted, defiled. I was slowly going mad.'

'What did you do?' asked the Doctor.

'I ran away.'

Literally running; first standing in her lab as still as a carved figure, as if the slightest movement would awaken the demons of thought; then finding herself running a tearing race through the corridors of the research building – through the corridors of her mind – desperate to outpace the snapping, snarling pack which sought to destroy her.

It was the running which very nearly betrayed her. Only the guilty ran on Parakon. Stopped by a security man as she left the building, thrusting her pass at him, gasping out an excuse: '... late for a meeting, a meeting with my Controller; please, please, please! I shall be late!'

She had then forced herself to walk, albeit with a little skipping run every few yards, until she fell into the seat of her flycar, sobbing for her breath, and took off – flying high, high, high to distance herself from the vileness she had left behind.

Flying in a desperate automatism for a time out of time, she at last calmed down enough to be able to look about her. She had left the city far behind. The circling horizon contained nothing but the dull yellow-brown of desert.

An empty sky; an empty land. But still her mind wasn't empty. The insistent images, the nagging voices that she was trying so hard to escape were still there. She increased her speed to the maximum. The low hum rose to a panic-stricken shriek. But still it wasn't fast enough; and she had no idea where she was.

She was flying south; at least she knew that. Her memory told her that the ravished earth extended to the faraway coast without a break. But now, almost dead ahead, she could see a large patch of green. The Lackan; what else could it be?

She swung the craft towards it, yearning for it as if she were lost in a desert and thirsting for water; as if in its greenness might lie the quietness she craved. As the flycar hurtled down, she fought with the controls, trying to hold it back as fiercely as she had tried to contain the turmoil of her thoughts, and with as little success.

The screaming of the drive in full reverse thrust, the screaming in her mind, the sound of her own voice scream-

ing; the compassionate greenness of the Lackan opening to her view; and at last, the benison of peace as the screaming stopped.

'Look,' she said, 'there it is. That's where we're going.'

The Doctor moved to the controls and altered course towards it. The green was growing visibly as they approached it.

'I have come to love the Lackan,' Onya continued. 'Whenever I come back to it, it feels as if I were going out of a dark room filled with choking smoke into the fresh air, into the sunlight. Oh, I know the forest is dangerous, full of horrible creatures – after all, the Lackan is where they hold the hunts for ER.'

'The place of no hope,' said the Brigadier.

'Exactly. But at least it's real and – and as it was meant to be.'

Now they could distinguish the individual trees and the clearings at the edge like little beaches.

'It looks like an island,' said Jeremy.

'Yes,' said Sarah. 'A green island in a dead sea.'

Chapter Twenty-Three

'You say that this is your real home?' the Brigadier said as they flew towards the Lackan. 'A jungle full of wild beasts?'

Onya laughed. 'Not quite,' she said. 'In the middle, with rocky hills all round – it would be too much to call them mountains – there's a high valley which is just as Parakon used to be long ago – oh, long before rapine; before there was any such thing as industry. And the only one of the original tribes never to have been conquered are living their lives there as they have done from the beginning. They call it "Kimonya" – Skyland. That's my home.'

'So,' said the Doctor, 'I make for the centre.'

'No, we can't take the chance of leading the Corporation there. You see, I'm not the only one to run away. There's well over three hundred of us by now. I'm afraid we have to hide the car and go in on foot.

'I'll take her down to the periphery, then.'

Onya nodded. 'If you keep on this course, you'll see a slightly bigger clearing, surrounded by fruit trees.'

Sarah said, 'Breakfast at last. Eh, Jeremy?'

Jeremy said, 'My stomach's forgotten the meaning of the word.'

The voices were different now: hushed and gentle, coming near and going far, to be heard though the tides of pain which also ebbed and flowed through her body and her mind.

There was touch too; the gentle soothing of female fingers and the dry firm male pressure on her brow – or were they the touch of the same cool hand?

And what of the faces? How could Katyan see once more and love anew the sweet lost face of her mother and yet know it too as the crumpled face of a stranger?

Then one morning when she opened her eyes, she saw herself to be in a room – a hut? – with unpainted wooden walls. A beam of sunlight was pushing its way past a roughly woven curtain, half looped back from an unglazed window, little more than an oblong hole. She seemed to be lying on a pile of skins and furs, which held her body in a soft embrace, as though to reassure her that, yes, her pain was gone.

On the other side of the small room, she could see the back of a small figure, a boy – or could it be a girl? – sitting cross-legged, gazing out of the open door.

Where was she?

As though in response to her thought (or had she spoken?), the figure leapt to its feet and with the spring of youth in its step almost ran to her side.

'You are awake, my daughter,' said the little old man in a light, smiling voice.

'I . . . I . . .' She couldn't find the words.

'You have been away from us for a long time. Several times we thought we had lost you to the demons you have been fighting. But now you are back, and you are safe.'

Safe.

As she tried to repeat the word, it grew in her throat and filled her whole being. The tears which had never come when Caldon had been taken, nor since, were running down her face. She turned her head away and wept as she had not wept for many years.

She felt a light touch on her shoulder, and heard the murmur of his voice. 'Weep, my daughter. Grieve for all that you have lost. For only by losing will you find.'

In a while, the racking, tearing sobs died away, leaving only the hiccuping gasps she recognized from childhood. With a long shuddering sigh, she accepted with relief that the storm had blown away.

She turned her head. The little man was back by the door, sitting as before, gazing out into the sunlight.

Why did she feel that she had come home?

She fell asleep.

Jeremy was at last getting some breakfast. With the juice from the golden, sweet, sharp fruit spilling from every bite, he was at last able to quieten the demands of his importunate innards. He'd eaten two already; he swallowed the last lush piece of his third.

'Yummy, aren't they?' he said to Sarah. 'Like – like a champagne cocktail.'

'I was about to say, like a sherbert dip,' she said, pulling out her handkerchief to wipe her mouth.

He looked up at the twisted branches of the tree next to the one with the fizzy fruit. Hanging from them were rich red globes even more plumped out with the promise of succulence. He reached out a hand. 'I wonder what these are,' he said.

'No! Stop!'

He pulled back his hand as if he'd touched a live wire. Now what? More elder sister stuff?

'For Heaven's sake, Jeremy! Don't you ever listen? They only look like fruit. Those are the sort of land jellyfish things that Onya said eat you up from the inside.'

He looked up at the Jezebel spheres in their tempting robes of scarlet. 'I don't think I like this place,' he said.

Waldo Rudley lay on his bed trying to think his way through a realistic assessment of his position. Once the transmission needles had been implanted in his brain, his privacy would be gone. Although the watchers would not be able to pick up his thoughts, they would know his every action as certainly as if they were in the room with him. So if he were going to attempt an escape ...

The notion died almost before it had formed. Even if he managed to get out of his cell, maybe stealing his guard's uniform, there was no way he could bluff his way past the genetic identity scanners he would encounter at every level of the Entertainments Division HQ.

As he told Sarah, there had always been tales of unsuccessful hunts, where the quarry had escaped in the Lackan itself. But escaped to what? The life of a wild beast? There would be no way of crossing the waterless waste surrounding the forest.

He gave up the riddle and allowed himself the luxury of thinking about the outworlder girl. Never had he met a Parakonian who shared his views so completely; and as for her distress at what she had experienced... He visualized himself taking her in his arms and comforting her. He could almost feel her head resting against his chest.

He shook his head, angry with himself at the fantasy and angry with a world which could offer such a hope only to snatch it back. He would never see her again, and the absolute certainty of that knowledge was more painful than the almost certain threat of death.

Although Waldo was left with a short, sharp headache, the actual implantation of the transmission needles hardly hurt at all, in spite of the shaking hands of the technician who used the gun. Waldo felt quite sorry for him having to operate under the cold gaze of Vice-Chairman Tragan.

There would have been little point in trying to resist. Better to die with the bullet of the hunter in his back than to suffer the torturously slow ebbing of life he would have experienced as the paralysed victim of a stun gun.

Once they were left alone, Tragan explained that the hunt would, in fact, start that very day.

'You seem surprised,' he said. 'You must understand that we in the Entertainments Division pride ourselves on our efficiency. Keeping people locked up is a needless expense. Until you are dead, you appear on the wrong side of the balance sheet, you see. A recorded hunt can be entered as an asset even before it is transmitted.'

Waldo said nothing. What was there to say?

'You'll be given a small pack of rations – the same as the ones given to the hunter and his tracker in fact. The chase has been known to last for several days. You'll wear the same protective clothing, and regulation jungle boots. A large part of the enjoyment of our audience comes from the pretence that you have a chance.' He looked at Waldo sharply. 'That's why we encourage the rumours of escape in past hunts.'

'Thank you for your honesty, at least,' said Waldo.

Tragan turned back at the door. 'I think you may regret your puritanical disregard of our transmissions. You might have learnt a lot.'

'For instance?'

'For instance, the vital importance of making your night-time shelter a weeping drav bush rather than a swarm of blood-sucking trigworms. They have a very similar appearance.'

Waldo smiled.

'Yes, I am trying to scare you,' said the Vice-Chairman, with some irritation in his voice for once. 'And I have no doubt that I'm succeeding, in spite of your bravado. How's the headache, by the way?'

'It's quite gone,' replied Waldo. 'I'm sorry to disappoint you.'

'No, no,' said Tragan. 'I should hate you to *start* our little game wanting to die. That comes at the end.'

Sarah sat on a fallen tree, keeping an eye on the guzzling Jeremy, and thought about Waldo. Presumably Onya meant that it might be possible to rescue him from the hunt itself.

Was she in love? She'd been in love before, but this was somehow different. She just liked thinking about him – the way you couldn't stop thinking of a cheese and pickle sandwich when you hadn't eaten for yonks and were stuck on a story.

She grinned at the thought – and the image came up of his back view as he led her out of the clutches of Tragan.

There was no question of it. She preferred men with small bums.

Oh for Heaven's sake! Now she was not only writing

clichés, she was a walking talking cliché herself. And how superficial could you get, thinking about a bum – no matter how elegantly shaped – when its owner was in mortal danger?

Pushing her tangle of emotions to one side for consideration later, she gazed across the clearing to the small group by the camouflaged flycar. The Doctor seemed to be stroking Onya's paralysed arm – or was it more like a laying on of hands?

Pleased that her attention had been diverted, she got up and went over.

'The stungun blocked the energy flow, you see,' the Doctor was saying, 'so we have to reverse the effect.'

'Reverse the polarity of the neutron flow, eh Doctor?' said the Brigadier.

'You may mock, Lethbridge-Stewart,' answered the Doctor. 'I know as well as you do that the expression would sound like nonsense to a classical sub-atomic physicist. Well, now I'm reversing the pseudo-polarity of the metaphorical synapses in Onya's putative energy channels. And that's just as nonsensical – and just as effective.'

Sarah hadn't a clue what he was talking about.

'I haven't a clue what you're talking about,' said the Brigadier.

Good, thought Sarah. She wasn't the only simpleton around.

'Oh, but I know exactly what he means,' said Onya, with a laugh. 'It might be my old teacher talking.'

'Thank you, Doctor,' she added, flexing her arm. 'Look. It's completely better.'

'Well, bless my soul,' said the Brigadier, as Jeremy wandered up, wearing the air of worried concentration of a small boy who had just added a bag of chips to a stomach already containing two ice-lollies, a hot dog, a portion of candyfloss and a mini-pizza.

Before they could set off, Onya produced a small black box with a couple of wires coming out of it. She told them that they all had to be deactivated, in case any of them had ER transmission needles implanted in their brains.

'The needles are made of a bio-compatible organic polymer which is disposed of by the body within a relatively short time,' she said. 'This merely speeds up the process.'

'But we know quite well that we haven't been, ah, tampered with,' said the Brigadier.

'You wouldn't necessarily remember having an implantation,' replied Onya. 'But if you had, you could lead them straight to Skyland. We daren't take the risk. Have any of you been alone with Vice-Chairman Tragan or any of his people?'

'I'd rather not think about it,' said Sarah.

'Just hold these electrodes to your temples.'

'Will it hurt?'

'Not a bit.'

Sarah followed instructions. There was a faint hum from the box. She didn't feel a thing.

'Who's next?'

The Doctor moved forward, as Jeremy, with a polite 'Excuse me,' retired behind a handy bush.

The silence of the desert (only made more intense by the distant calling of the jungle birds) was marred by two alien noises: the repeated hum of the deactivator; and the sound of Jeremy throwing up.

Chapter Twenty-Four

Vice-Chairman Tragan usually visited his superior's house only on social occasions, such as one of their 'special' parties. For him to be summoned in the middle of the working day and required to make a report was unprecedented.

'Good of you to spare the time from your busy schedule,' said Freeth, who was sitting at his massive dining table, with a large napkin tied round his neck, well on the way to finishing a heaped plate of Whitstable oysters.

'No, no, don't sit down,' he went on. 'I know you'll be dying to get back to – to whatever it is you find to fill your time.' He chose the largest of the oysters that was left and gulped it down. 'You can't imagine the glee with which I learned – I was a mere stripling at the time – that these little beasts are still alive when we swallow them. I used to imagine them crying out for help as they slid down my throat – and landing with a plop in the acids of my stomach.'

He picked up a fork and stabbed it into the body of one of the oysters before him. 'Eek!' he said in a tiny voice, and giggled. He swallowed another. 'You will forgive me if I finish my lunch?'

'Of course.' Tragan's mouth was a tight slit in the midst of his tumultuous face.

'So,' the Chairman continued, 'young Waldo Rudley is e'en now winging his way to his fated destiny. Or is that a tautology – "fated destiny"? Well, never mind. Let us hope he meets his pleonastic doom.

'Unlike your recent candidates. A little hobby of yours,

is it? Letting people escape?' He dispatched another bivalve on its last journey.

Tragan was standing as stiffly as one of his own statues. Only the darkening face betrayed the fact that he was alive. 'Captain Rudley is on his way to the Lackan, yes,' he said.

Freeth took a noisy slurp from a pint of Château d'Yquem.

'You know, it's amazing what getting one's trotters into the trough and one's snout into a glass or two of slosh will do for the spirits, Tragan. I begin to feel optimistic again.'

'I'm glad to hear it.'

'I'm almost persuaded that your catastrophic inefficiency is merely an amusing – or dare I say, lovable? – little idiosyncracy.' He squinted with unamused, unloving piggy eyes at his victim. 'Almost,' he said.

'Of course, a repetition could lead to the most painful consequences,' he continued. 'And you do understand, dear boy, that when I say painful, I mean ag-o-nising. But of course you do.'

'There'll be no repetition,' said Tragan.

'Good,' said Freeth.

He ate another half dozen oysters.

'Will that be all, Chairman?' said Tragan.

'No,' said Freeth.

He ate two more.

He took another swig of wine.

He ate the last three; and sighed.

'Still,' he said, removing the napkin and delicately dabbing the corners of his thick lips, 'what harm can these wretched people do to us now? As long as we hold their ship they can't return to Earth; and as for the rest, aren't they fugitives? If they show a nose above the parapet – pop! I've always enjoyed shooting a sitting bird.'

'All the same, Chairman,' said Tragan. 'I think it would be as well to tread very delicately, until we're sure.'

Freeth nodded vigorously, his jowls wobbling. 'Oh, belt and braces, belt and braces every time.'

He belched loud and long. He smiled sweetly and spoke in a voice brimming with affection.

'That's why you're going to find them for me – and destroy them. Aren't you, Tragan my pet?'

From the start, Jeremy found it difficult to keep up. Onya led the way. Before leaving the flycar, which they had buried under a pile of branches and leaves, she had changed from her housekeeper garb into the boots and slacks more suitable for fighting a way through a jungle.

They'd been going for what seemed like hours. Jeremy could see Onya at the head of the column. She never seemed to need a rest, he thought. She just ploughed ahead, without a thought for the poor blighters at the back. Sometimes she'd pause and have a bit of a look round, or glance at a sort of compass thingy she carried, but before you could so much as catch your breath, she was off again, chopping her way through the tangle with a big heavy knife – what did they call it? A matchet, wasn't it? Like hatchet. Only matchet. That sort of thing, it was.

Apart from anything else, she'd told everyone to look out and keep together, because of all the nasties they'd got in these woods (if those giant plummy things that ate you from the tummy outwards were anything to go by, he didn't need telling) and then went racing on ahead like those fellows at school who won the Victor Ludorum and stuff – and Jeremy had always come last in those races too.

He was hot and thirsty. And then there was that bird, if it was a bird, which must have followed them all the way, just making a noise like an unoiled hinge – eeerk! eeerk! eeerk! – over and over, one every three seconds regular as Hickory Dickory; and then it would stop – and just when you were about to say 'Thank the Lord for that,' it started again: eeerk! eeerk! eeerk!

He was just about to call out for them all to slow down a bit, when it happened. He'd put on a bit of spurt to catch up, so they'd hear him, and just as he was opening his mouth to shout, something grabbed his right foot.

For a moment he was frozen. But then he let out a yell that must have been heard in Parakon City.

'What's the matter?' called the Brigadier.

'Something's . . . Something's got me by the foot!'

'Keep very still!' said the Doctor.

'I can't do anything else,' squeaked Jeremy.

The Doctor turned to the others. 'Don't move, anybody,' he said. 'Onya, have you any idea what it might be?'

Jeremy could only just hear her low reply. 'No,' she said. 'Unless it's a trap lizard. You'd have to cut its head off before a trap lizard would let go – and if it's an arrow serpent, we're all in trouble.'

Oh, help!

'He-e-e-lp!' he called in a sort of loud whisper.

'Sssh!' said the Doctor, who was moving towards him so smoothly and surely that scarcely a leaf was disturbed.

'It's all right, old fellow,' he went on, speaking on his breath, 'we'll soon have you out of there. Sssh! Sssh!'

He was now right by Jeremy. He slowly squatted until, with movements as slow and careful as a stalking cat, he could reach out and part the leaves which hid the creature from view. Jeremy screwed up his eyes. He couldn't bear to look. What if it bit his foot right off!

'All right, Jeremy,' said the Doctor in a normal voice, standing up. 'You can take it out.'

'The thing's still got me!'

'You've caught your ankle between two tree roots.'

'What?'

He looked down. Sure enough, there was his right leg jammed firmly between two high roots.

'So I have. Sorry.'

Pulling his leg backwards he extracted his foot.

'Oh Jeremy!' said Sarah.

There! No sympathy. No backing up a fellow journalist. Just the elder sister routine all over again!

'For Pete's sake, let's get a move on,' said the Doctor, moving back to Onya. 'Lethbridge-Steward, would you be so good as to bring up the rear? Then you can keep an eye on him.'

And then the Brig started ordering him about as well. 'Come on, Jeremy,' he was saying. 'On our way. Chop chop.'

Why did everybody have to be so beastly rotten to him? He'd said sorry, hadn't he?

'Sorry, everybody,' he said again as they moved off. 'I mean, I really am sorry, you know. Sorry, Onya. Sorry, Sarah. I mean, sorry and all that.'

At least he'd had a bit of a rest.

By the time they stopped for their proper rest, when the rays of the great red sun were slanting almost vertically through the high branches, Onya could see that they were all starting to flag, even the Doctor and the Brigadier. Perhaps she'd been pushing too hard, she thought. It was difficult to judge.

'About as far again to reach the eastern hills,' she said, as she distributed pieces of tipka root, with the poisonous skin scraped off. 'Then we start climbing. When we get to the top, you'll be able to see the valley. That's when I feel I've come home, to my family.'

'When I lost my teacher,' said the Doctor, 'I felt as if my father had died.'

Again she considered this man who so often seemed to mirror her own thoughts. She propped her back against a convenient slark tree (she could tell from the condition of the bones in it that the slark nest was old and abandoned) and told him – told them all – about old Darshee.

So many pictures in her head: seeing Katyan Glessey as if she were another person, as in a sense she was; knowing again the quiet welcome of the people of Skyland, the Kimonyans; living once more the endless days which allowed the grateful sun to heal the hurt in her body – and at the last, having no choice but to face the sickness in her mind.

Katyan had become a familiar sight to the Kimonyans, wandering from her tiny hut near Darshee's through the scattered wooden buildings which formed their village.

When she had first emerged from her refuge, it seemed to her that the huts were placed at random, as if a giant hand had dropped them from the sky to settle at the whim of the wind.

But as she explored the settlement, she found that each was sitting in exactly the right position; convenient to the stream perhaps, and sitting on the precise point of a gentle slope which would allow a view of the beasts in their communal corral, yet forming with its immediate neighbours a family of houses which, in its welcoming arms, offered a focus of love and security to all.

For the Kimonyans were a beautiful people. Like prepubescent children, both in stature and in the innocence of their smooth large eyed faces, they seemed incapable of building or making anything that was not beautiful to see.

The roughly hewn beams which formed the houses; the lie of the fences with the contours of the fields and the sweep of the corn; the very fall of a half-eaten haystack; all answered the curves of the wide green valley and the harsher lines of the rocky hills which enclosed it. Nothing was square or straight; to Katyan, it felt as if every line, every plane, had grown in its rightful place, as inevitably as the muscles and sinews grow in the body of a living creature.

But the more this became plain, and the more the families (and it was difficult to know where one family started and the next one stopped) took her into their homes, welcoming her as if she were a beloved daughter returned from afar, the more alien she felt – and the more she withdrew into the solitude of her little house, as if her very presence would defile Kimonya.

It never seemed that the young-old man who was called the father of the tribe set out to be her teacher.

He would appear apparently at random, but always when she was in need; and disappear long before she felt his presence irksome. A word or two of comfort, or of loving mockery; an overtly simple story which turned out to be enormously complex – and then even simpler than had first appeared; a light suggestion of a game she might like to play; such things became the nourishment she needed on the spiritual journey she had unwittingly undertaken.

So, travelling alone but always knowing there was a hand waiting to catch her should she fall, she braved the darkness, fought the Katyan demons and annihilated them – only to find herself teetering on the edge of an abyss of emptiness. Darshee's hand reached out to her – and pushed her into the void.

But who was falling? Not Katyan Glessey. She had perished with the demons. And how could she be falling if there was nowhere left to go? And suddenly the darkness was shining with the radiance of the sun – and there was nowhere left to go.

'... there was nowhere left to go,' said Onya.

She looked at her four listeners. On only one of the faces did she see any understanding of what she was saying. How could she explain what she meant?

'He showed me how to... to untie the knots in my mind,' she said. 'How to let the clouds melt away so that I could see the sky again.'

Words!

'And so he called me Onya Farjen: Sky Born, or Born of the Sky.'

There was silence; and then Sarah breathed, 'Look! Look at that butterfly!'

The insect, a handsbreadth across, was fluttering above Onya's head. The Doctor put out a gentle hand and plucked it from the air, placing it on his left hand, where it lay, silver-blue wings outspread. He stroked its back with the middle finger of his right hand, and then he tossed it into the air, where it flew in a wide zig-zag up into the canopy of trees and out into the sun.

Onya laughed. 'Come on,' she said, 'we must be going.'

Jeremy groaned. 'Must we?' he said.

Chapter Twenty-Five

Haban Rance stood in the doorway of the long hut wiping the sweat from his craggy face and surveying the chattering crowd of men and women in the club area.

Like many of them, he had just come from completing his shift of manual labour in the irrigated fields that Kaido, the chief of the Kimonyans, had given to the newcomers to grow their food and graze their herds.

They seemed happy enough at the moment, he thought. No sign of the undercurrents of discontent which seemed to grow stronger as the group enlarged.

At the last meeting, he had managed to bring out into the open the resentment many felt towards those who weren't doing their share. New sanctions had been imposed, but it wasn't enough. The sooner they all saw some action, the better.

'Rance! Rance!'

He lifted a hand to acknowledge the call and threaded his way through to get himself a drink before investigating it. That was another thing, he thought as he took a swig: too much sap wine. The Kimonyans drank it only at feasts, and then rarely to excess. Often, the newcomers who were missing from their work were incapable of rising from their beds.

'What is it, Medan?' he asked, as he made his way through the work area past the rows of benches where people were mending, or making, or adapting all sorts and shapes of electronic apparatus.

Medan looked up from his screen and took off his

headset. 'That lazy tyke Ungar hasn't relieved me. I'm not going to end up doing a double watch again.'

'What's got into you today?'

'I've got a sore head, I need a drink and I'm missing my wife. Next question?'

The vehemence in his voice made a number of nearby heads turn from their task of monitoring the multitudinous Parakonian transmissions and communication links.

'Cool down,' said Rance. 'I'll take over until he comes.'

Taking Medan's place, he lifted the headset. 'Anything to report?' he said.

'Not a lot. Spot of interference in the ER matrix. Right in the middle of the Lackan.'

'God help us, not another hunt?'

'No, there's no transmission, just a –' Medan stopped and nodded towards the screen. 'There it is again.'

Rance recognized the trace immediately. 'That's the direction finder. It must be Onya with a new bunch of guests.'

'We'll run out of huts the way she's going on,' said Medan, sloping off towards the drinks.

What a miserable son of a Pivlon hog! Did nothing ever make him happy? Still, thought Rance, remembering his earlier thoughts, in a way he was right. The settlement was getting uncontrollable. If it got any bigger –

His thoughts were interrupted by Medan's raised voice from halfway down the hut uttering threats, seemingly ignored by their intended target.

It was Ungar arriving at last, unshaven and bleary. Rance relinquished the chair. 'It's not good enough, you know. If we don't all pull our weight – '

'Yeah, yeah, I'm sorry, right? I'm just a few minutes late, that's all. I haven't killed the sacred pig or something.'

'Well, get on with it. Keep an eye on that frequency, and stay awake this time.'

Better let Kaido know that their precious Mamonya was on her way, thought Rance. He wondered yet again how it could be that Onya was regarded as the ritual mother of the Kimonyan tribe. Then again, what did it matter? It served its purpose. He noticed as he passed that Medan was already downing his second drink.

As he crossed the bridge, he became aware of an air of excitement in the Kimonyan village. Little groups of people were talking loudly, waving their hands in the air. There was a lot of laughter. Others were running from hut to hut, as if carrying great news.

A small bunch had clustered round the slightly taller figure of Kaido, who was as clearly delighted as the rest. He seemed to be issuing instructions.

'Kaido!' called Rance. 'What's going on?'

Kaido turned, his small brown face beaming, and said in his deep voice, 'Big feast tonight. We are killing our fattest deer. Mamonya's coming!'

With a polite smile and nod, he turned back.

'I'll never get to the bottom of these people,' said Haban Rance to himself. 'How the hell did he know that?'

The Brigadier was doing his best to disguise his panting as controlled deep breathing. He was a little taken aback to discover how out of condition he was. Now that they had traversed the main part of the forest and had started a fairly stiff climb up the barer hillside, the strong steady pace Onya had been setting since lunchtime was proving somewhat hard, especially on the thigh muscles.

He made a mental resolution that when they got back home – if they ever did; a problematical proposition at best – he would resume the morning jog which had served him so well in the past.

Apart from anything else, he had to set a good example to the men. Even in the present bizarre situation, he could hardly cry 'pax' before the boy did; and he seemed to have settled down into a sullen trudge that could go on for miles.

'Ouch!' said Jeremy, nearly falling over.

'Now what?' said the Brigadier.

'Twisted my ankle.'

'Well, for Heaven's sake be more careful. We don't want to have to carry you.'

'Not my fault. It's all these rocks. I can't keep up *and* look where I'm going.'

The others were disappearing into a small thicket. 'Hang on a minute!' called the Brigadier. He was quite glad of the excuse, to tell the truth. 'All right?' he said to Jeremy, who was wiggling his foot experimentally.

'I'm sorry,' said Onya when they caught up. 'I'm apt to forget what it used to be like. I'll slow down a bit.'

'So your training was physical as well as spiritual?' said the Doctor.

'It's difficult to disentangle the two. In any case, I've still a long way to go. If I had the skill the tribe think I have, the skill my teacher had – I've tried to tell them – well, I wouldn't need this to find my way.'

She held up the black box.

'What is it?' asked Sarah. 'Some sort of direction finder?'

Onya nodded. 'Calibrated to the ER matrix the Entertainments Division uses for the hunt. I've programmed it for Kimonya.

'I tell you what,' she continued to Jeremy, 'why don't you stay at the front with me? Then we'll be going at your pace, not mine.' She turned, consulted the pointer on the box, and dived into the clump of greenery, followed by the sheepish Jeremy.

I wish you joy of him, thought the Brigadier as he went in behind the Doctor and Sarah.

After a few minutes of clambering up a steep incline, he could see that where the shrubs finished the terrain flattened to an open plateau which extended for fifty metres or more before the upward slope resumed.

As the two leaders emerged, the second gave a loud exclamation. 'Oof!' he said.

'Oh, Jeremy, not again!' said Sarah.

'A big lizard thingy ran right across my toes,' he said plaintively.

'Well it didn't bite them, did it?' his erstwhile guardian said. 'Now please may we –'

'Sssh!' said the Doctor. 'Listen!'

A not so distant roar – or was it a squeal? – came from the sparse woods which bounded the left of the clearing. 'That's no lizard,' the Doctor said.

Onya's eyes were darting to and fro. 'Oh my word! I told you I still had a lot to learn! I nearly led you straight into the territory of a Gargan! Quickly!' As she spoke, she shepherded them all back into the shelter of the bushes.

'He's very short-sighted and nearly deaf,' she said, hardly speaking above a whisper, in spite of her words, 'but his sense of smell... Here he comes!'

The nearest thing in size the Brigadier had ever seen was in the Natural History Museum: a dinosaur skeleton.

The Doctor said quietly, 'I haven't seen teeth as big as that since the last Tyrannosaurus I met.'

Tyrannosaurus Rex, that was the fellow, thought the Brigadier. Entirely different shape, though. This chap had short, sturdy back legs and walked on his knuckles, like a gorilla. He had a long curved neck so that he could hold his head close to the ground, like a bloodhound hot on the trail. But it was only when he stopped and raised his extended muzzle high in the air to give his squealing bellow that you could really see the crocodile rows of massive teeth.

'What a handsome animal,' breathed the Doctor.

Handsome!

His tracking brought him perilously near to their hiding place. For an interminable breath-holding age, he snuffled round the spot where Jeremy and Onya had been standing; then, with another roar, he set off again, disappearing into the woods on the right.

'He's gone after that lizard thingy,' said Jeremy in a high small voice.

'But why didn't he sniff us out?' said Sarah in a voice not much bigger. 'If he's so good at scenting things. We were only a few feet away.'

The Gargan's roar came again – from a more comfortable distance. The Brigadier found that he was still holding his breath. He let it out, as unobtrusively as he could manage.

'We're outside his territory,' said Onya in reply to Sarah. 'He builds a sort of cave, you see. Yes, look, you can just see it over there.' And she pointed to the far side of the clearing, where the slope on the left became a cliff. Against the face of the cliff, there was what seemed to be a pile of stones like an enormous cairn, several times larger than the Gargan himself.

'And he marks out his domain with a line of rocks,' Onya continued, 'and if any creature steps within its boundaries, he'll follow its scent until he finds it – and eats it. He never gives up; he'd starve first.'

The Brigadier looked across the plateau. Yes, there was a line of small rocks extending from the Gargan's lair, right round the open space. Amongst the litter of stone it wasn't immediately noticeable, unless you were looking for it. And what's more, he thought, at its nearest it's only a couple of feet away from where we stopped.

'Yes,' said Onya, following his gaze. 'If we'd put a foot over that line, we'd all be dead.'

It was always the same, Sarah said to herself as they toiled up yet another steep slope. You thought you'd got to the top and there would be another summit waiting for you, even higher, and then another – and another.

'Well, I don't mind telling you, I'm pooped,' said Jeremy.

'Oh, do stop whingeing!' said Sarah.

It was even getting the Doctor down. 'I should both save your breath, if I were you,' he said shortly.

They straggled up the last rocky incline, all tired, all irritable – except for Onya, who had bounded up the last few crags like a – like a mountain goat? Oh, shut up! said Sarah to herself. As if I could care less about clichés at a time like this!

Onya stood on the crest of the hill and waited for the others. 'There you are,' she said, with an expansive gesture. 'Kimonya, the land in the sky.'

Laid out below them like an eastern carpet woven in green and gold, the valley was shaped like a shallow bowl in the midst of the surrounding hills. A silver ribbon of water wound through the two toy villages, breaking at last into golden glints of sunlight reflected from the wavelets on a lake as blue as the arching sky.

It was the Doctor who put into words how Sarah felt – how all of them felt, maybe.

'Perhaps we've all come home,' he said.

Jeremy broke the silence. 'Hey! Look at those whopping great birds!'

The Brigadier squinted into the sun. Not birds, boy, he thought. Bats. Half a dozen or more. Giant bats.

Onya was laughing in delight. 'It's Kaido and his people, coming to meet us.'

What? He should be used to it by now, the vast range of alien races, after the catalogue of shapes and sizes he'd encountered in his time with UNIT, but still . . . 'You mean that the Kimonya tribe are bats?' he said.

'No, no, Brigadier,' said the Doctor. 'They're riding them.'

By now he could see this for himself. The creatures were not exactly the same as the bats he was used to – their faces were more like cats' – but like their Earthly counterparts they were covered with fur, albeit of a golden yellow colour, and had leathery wings spanning some twenty feet. Sitting astride each neck was a small figure dressed in a soft leather tunic, holding on to the ears, which served as a means of control, as the Brigadier could see as they all came in to land nearby.

When the leading rider jumped off, he saw that far from being a boy, as he'd assumed, he had the face of a middle-aged man – and when he spoke, he spoke in a surprisingly deep voice, a voice which had the ring of authority.

'Greetings, Mamonya,' he said, holding out both hands. 'Our Mother has returned to us.'

'Greetings, Kaido,' she replied and lightly touched his outstretched hands. 'I return with great happiness. I bring more friends to greet you.'

The Doctor stepped forward, copying Kaido's gesture. 'Greetings,' he said.

Kaido smiled and touched the Doctor's hands. 'I give a welcome to the friends of Mamonya. You have weak legs.'

Sarah stifled a giggle. Pretty strange way of greeting strangers, thought the Brigadier.

Onya laughed. 'He means that you look tired. He's offering you a lift down to the village.'

On the bats?

Sarah said, 'I'm game.'

The Doctor said, 'What are we waiting for? Thank you, Kaido.'

Bit of a dicey proposition, thought the Brigadier. Still, he'd try anything once.

'There isn't any saddle or anything,' said Jeremy.

'Hang on to the fur,' said the Brigadier.

As they climbed aboard (one per animal, sitting behind the rider), he thought of the long gone days when, as a young subaltern, he'd been stationed in Leicestershire and had ridden to hounds with some of the fashionable hunts. 'If the Quorn could see me now!' he said to himself, as they took off in a great flurry of flapping.

'Wheeee!' cried Sarah, as they swept into the sky.

I couldn't have put it better myself, thought Brigadier Lethbridge-Stewart.

Chapter Twenty-Six

Chairman Freeth had been busy. Having persuaded his father that it would be best if he let his son take the burden of hospitality from the Presidential shoulders, thus giving himself a little breathing space in which to sort out the problem of the Earth delegation, he called the Cabinet to his office and gave the Chancellor and his government their orders: he needed a strengthening of the powers to arrest on suspicion of treason; Tragan's hands were often tied by the need to provide proof.

He was in the middle of a Corporation board meeting – a full pack, bar the Vice-Chairman who had sent his apologies – when Tragan came through to announce that Rudley was about to be released into the Lackan.

'If you wish,' he said, 'we can route the transmissions of the hunt, as we record them, through to your ER receiver, on channels ninety-seven and ninety-eight.'

'No, no,' replied Freeth. 'I'll come to the control room.'

He turned back to the board. 'Very well, gentlemen. So it's understood that what I urgently need is a contingent alternative to Earth. Yes?'

A sotto-voce chorus of 'Yes'; a row of nodding heads; and the Chairman of the board rose from his appropriately oversize chair. 'Then get on with it,' he said. 'The meeting is adjourned.'

Picking up his bag of bull's-eyes, he pivoted on his heel and tripped on dainty toes from the boardroom.

It was after Darshee died that Onya Farjen had become the mother of the Kimonyans.

She had seen how it was that he was the father of the tribe. A guide, a counsellor, a sharer of grief and joy, he was also a healer. The members of the tribe treated him with cheerful familiarity, tempered with respect and love; and bit by bit, they started to behave to her in much the same way, as if she too were the bearer of wisdom.

It had turned out that the liberation which had freed her from the prison of her mind was only a beginning.

As she lived her days in the clear light which now seemed so ordinary, and yet so very far from the 'normal' way of living that she had left behind, her teacher guided her towards an understanding that saw no limits, no boundaries.

The silence of her mind was filled with the sounds, the empty space with the very presence of the multitudinous things about her, so that sometimes it almost seemed as if she were the creator of the world, and the cause of all that happened in it. And only when she was able to join Darshee in his mirth at this ludicrous misapprehension, was she able to realize the truth of it.

One morning when she went to his hut, she was surprised to find him lying on the pile of skins which made up his bed. 'It is time, my daughter,' he said. 'This old body chooses to return to the earth.'

For a moment, she could not speak. 'But what shall I do without you?' she said at last.

He smiled. 'Shall you be without me?'

She found that there were tears running down her cheeks. 'I'm not as advanced as you think I am,' she said. 'I'm not ready.'

'The time has come for me to go,' he said, 'and the time for you to grieve. When the time comes for you to be ready, you will be ready. Now, help me to sit up.'

She helped him into his usual cross-legged posture. He folded his hands. 'Never forget, Onya Farjen, that you are sky born.' He gave a little giggle. 'As we all are!' he said.

He closed his eyes and became very still.

As she wondered whether he had already died, or was

only meditating, she became aware of the sound of voices. She went outside.

Twenty or thirty Kimonyans were standing in a ragged group on the slope outside the door, swaying in time with a low, wordless chanting. At her appearance, they fell silent, looking at her. All over the village, Onya could see, the everyday business of living had come to a standstill. Men, women and children were looking up towards the hut as if interrupted by a call.

She bowed her head, having no words. A great wail rose from the group and spread throughout the village. For a few minutes it continued, filling the air with sadness, until it seemed that the whole world must be grieving; then slowly, it died; and there was silence. The group turned and walked away. The life of the village started once more. But the silence continued.

There was no sound, bar the heedless cries of small children, until late that night, when the flames of the funeral pyre of aromatic woods had consumed the body. As if someone had given a signal – perhaps Kaido had done just that, Onya thought – the crowd broke up. Everybody started chattering, laughing, running into their huts and appearing with dishes of food or jugs of sap wine, and dancing to the piping of their wooden flutes. The feast went on until dawn was breaking.

Onya had no idea for several days that she had taken Darshee's place. In an empty world, she carried on with her usual life, working in the fields, meditating as he had taught her, visiting the many friends she had made; until one afternoon as she sat outside her hut, she saw approaching a small bunch of men and women. At their head was Kaido, and in his arms he carried the small limp body of a little child.

She rose and went to meet them. As she neared the group she saw that the child was Kaido's youngest son, whose mother had died in the bearing of him.

He laid his sad burden at her feet and looked up at her expectantly. 'He is dying,' he said.

Ever afterwards, it didn't seem to Onya that it was her

doing that the boy was healed. Placing her hands on either side of the small head, as she had seen Darshee do so many times, she closed her eyes and let everything go from her mind (even the wish to help), feeling the life flowing through her, until the boy stirred under her fingers.

It was Kaido who first called her Mamonya, as he hugged his baby son to him.

No longer was Onya's world empty; she was at one with the people of Kimonya, just as before she had been at one with her master.

'Shall you be without me?'
'When the time comes ... you will be ready.'

The feast would not be taking place for several hours – it takes time to barbecue a whole deer – so the visitors were given a bite to be going on with and shown to their quarters. ('Super,' said Jeremy. 'All those little huts. Like Toytown.')

After a bit of a collapse on the pile of skins in the corner, Sarah woke herself up with an ecstatic swim in the river. The question of a bathing costume just didn't seem relevant; none of the Kimonyans who called to her to join them had bothered; and the clear cold water was so stimulating that when she put on the dress that Onya had provided for her, the touch of the soft leather on her skin made her feel 'all sliggly-hoo', as Greckle had said.

But the memory of the party brought thoughts of Waldo back with a rush. All the time she'd been swanning around as if she were on a package tour to the Costa del Chippo, Waldo was banged up on death row.

Feeling bitterly ashamed, she went in search of Onya. She found her showing the Doctor and the Brigadier round the camp, with Jeremy, fed-up, trailing along behind. She caught them up as they reached the electronics section of the main hut.

'But Mr Rance, aren't these stun-guns?' the Doctor was saying, as he surveyed the work area, now empty of technicians.

'If we're going to overturn Freeth and his gang, we've

got to have weapons,' Rance answered. 'We've a certain number of old fashioned firearms, but we've also "acquired", you might say, quite a few of the Entertainment Division's security weapons.'

'But I won't let them even consider using them,' said Onya.

Sarah hung around on the edge of the group, wondering how she could interrupt. A bit like being a child trying to get a word in with a bunch of chattering grownups, she thought.

'They sound rather effective to me,' said the Brigadier, and Sarah noticed that Haban Rance gave an approving nod.

'A barbarous weapon,' said Onya. 'Total permanent paralysis? A nasty lingering death? How can the new Parakon be based on such a thing? We'd be no better than those we fight.'

The Doctor had been examining the scattered pieces of one of the guns, which was being re-assembled. 'So you're converting them into simple old-fashioned stun-guns?'

'Which will knock out the target for only a short while. Exactly,' answered Rance. 'Though I must say, in certain circumstances I would have preferred . . .' Sarah noticed a slight narrowing of Onya's eyes. Evidently Rance noticed it too. 'All right, all right,' he went on with a grin, 'I know when I've lost an argument.'

They moved down the hut to the monitoring area. Sarah managed to get next to Onya, who seemed quite oblivious of her. She was just on the point of pulling on her sleeve out of sheer desperation, when she became aware of what Rance was saying.

'Down here, we scan the ER frequencies to try to pick up the hunts in the Lackan area. We've managed to save seven so far. How's it going, Ungar?'

'As boring as it was yesterday,' said Ungar, turning a knob in a lackadaisical manner.

'Now look here – '

But Rance stopped short, throwing a glance at the visitors.

Sarah started to speak, only to be forestalled by the Brigadier. 'Isn't that rather risky?' he said. 'Bringing them here, I mean, when their brains are transmitting everything back to Corporation HQ?'

'Not if they're deactivated, Lethbridge Stewart,' said the Doctor.

'Oh yes, of course.'

Now, thought Sarah. 'But what about –'

'All the same, we have to be careful,' Onya said. 'The rescue itself will be transmitted. We have to make it look as if they'd managed to escape without help.'

Ungar sat up, suddenly alert. 'Hang on, I thought I had something there ... Yeah, there it is again. He's on the run all right. Quite near. Just over the eastern hills. Look at the co-ordinates.' He gestured to the figures appearing at the bottom of the screen.

'Put it on the monitor matrix so that we can all experience it,' said Rance.

Ungar threw a switch and at once Sarah found herself back in the jungle she and the others had so recently left. Yet at the same time she could see and hear everything that was going on in the hut. It was like looking out of the window of a lighted house at dusk; with a change of attention, you could choose to see the garden outside or the reflection of the room behind you.

She closed her eyes and saw that she was stumbling up the same rocky slope where Jeremy had twisted his ankle; she was struggling for breath and throwing quick glances over her right shoulder. Panic was rising in her throat.

'Oh no, no!' she gasped. 'It must be Waldo!'

'Poor devil,' she heard the Brigadier say.

Concentrating on climbing the hill, as if the effort she put into it could somehow help, she was hardly aware of what was being said: 'Try scanning the other channel for the hunters.' That was Onya.

The Doctor's voice: 'Isn't that rather a tall order?'

Onya again: 'It's usually a nearby frequency. They've very little imagination, these people.'

With a jolt, the ground Sarah was walking on changed.

It wasn't so stony, and there were tussocks of grass; she was further down the hill. Although she was still climbing, she wasn't nearly so out of breath, and she was carrying a gun just like the one she carried when ... but her mind refused the dreadful image. There was a man with her, and she could hear his voice.

'Got him,' he said. 'Look, dodging behind that outcrop.'

Yes, she could see him! She opened her eyes and turned to the others, almost weeping in her frustration. 'We've got to do something!'

'Steady on, old girl,' said the Brigadier. 'We can all see him, you know.'

'There's plenty of time,' said the Doctor. 'The last thing they want is a quick death. They'll try to stretch it out as long as possible. Don't forget, they're in the entertainment business.'

'Exactly,' said Onya. 'Those two could go on chasing him for days. And we haven't a hope of going in while the sun is up. We'll have to wait for nightfall.'

The Brigadier shushed them sharply. Sarah found that a man's voice was speaking through her mouth, a deep rough voice. 'The fool's making for the Gargan territory.'

The Gargan!

'I'll have to try and stop him,' Sarah could hear herself saying. She felt herself lifting the gun, just as she had before, and carefully aiming at the distant stumbling figure.

'Do something!' she shrieked.

But just as before, her finger tightened on the trigger, the gun fired, with the same violent kick to the shoulder, and Waldo fell to the ground with a bullet in his back.

Chapter Twenty-Seven

The Chairman and the Vice-Chairman of the Parakon Corporation were, in their several ways, enjoying themselves. As they had discovered when comparing notes after sharing similar delights, their desires were, so to speak, complementary. On one point they were agreed, of course: the more helpless the victim, the greater the gratification.

Tragan, however, with his Naglon faculty of split awareness, found a plenitude of rapture in the intimate experiencing of – and simultaneous distancing from – the sufferings of the victim, whereas Freeth could only be sure of a truly memorable access of satisfaction through the exercise of absolute power, preferably lethal.

In the normal way, therefore, the latter might have been expected to revel in the bloody despatch of an unarmed fugitive. However, to have his pleasure abruptly terminated so soon was to awaken his wrath, which (as Tragan well knew) could be dangerous.

'He tried to wing him,' said the Vice-Chairman, in response to Freeth's snarl of rage. 'It's standing orders. If a quarry goes into a Gargan area, no-one can follow him. Our part of the hunt would be over. All we would have left would be the pleasure of his being eaten alive once the creature returned.'

Even as he spoke, he felt – and Freeth could see with his ER vision – the body in question stirring. He raised his head and with sobbing breath started to heave himself towards the Gargan's cave.

The hunter raised his gun – and lowered it again. Rudley had crossed the boundary of the Gargan's territory.

As if in confirmation of Tragan's words, the hunter spoke. 'That's it, then,' he said, and Freeth could feel the rumble of his voice in his chest. 'I'm not going in there after him. Come on, let's get back.'

He turned and Freeth found himself going down the hill, away from Rudley. 'Bit of luck, really,' the hunter continued. 'I promised to take the kids to the big fight tomorrow.'

Freeth switched to the other channel. By this time, Rudley had managed to make his way across the stony courtyard to reach the Gargan's lair. With a final agonizing effort, he pulled himself inside and collapsed onto the ground, amongst the scattered bones of the Gargan's prey. The transmissions ceased. He was unconscious.

Freeth gently removed his headset. He dug in his pocket for his bag of bull's-eyes. He put one in his mouth. He licked the sticky mintiness from his fingers. He spoke, very quietly. Freeth at his quietest was Freeth at his most dangerous.

'Well, congratulations, Tragan,' he said. 'Your people have proved themselves as efficient as their colleagues. They're supposed to know the terrain. Why didn't they head him off? Just idle curiosity, you understand.'

Tragan's face had by now darkened to a royal bubbling, but his voice was pale and flat. 'I suppose they made the assumption that he would know about the Gargan. After all, any regular follower of the hunts would.'

'Thank you,' said Freeth. 'You have made my point.'

He made to leave, but turned back at the door, like an actor in an ER serial. 'Have you ever heard the expression, "A fish rots from the head downwards"?' he said. 'No? Think about it in bed tonight – if you can't sleep.'

No matter what her mind tried to tell her, Sarah felt as if she were the one who had shot Waldo; but when it became apparent that he was alive, the hope that they could still save him swept away her despair. But to her amazement, nobody moved.

'Come on!' she cried. 'We've got to go and get him. Before that thing comes back.'

'We'd just be adding our own deaths to his,' said Onya.

Surely there must be some way! Sarah turned to appeal to the Brigadier, who was deep in thought.

'We could hunt the Gargan down,' he said. 'Before it gets him, I mean. Before it returns to its lair if we can. Yes, that's the ticket!'

'Impossible,' said Rance.

'Impossible for us, perhaps,' said the Doctor. 'But the Kimonyan people are hunters. Even such an enormous creature as the Gargan – '

But Onya interrupted him. 'No, no. You don't understand. All life is sacred to the Kimonyans, even the life of the beasts they eat – but the Gargan is holy. He stands for the spirit of life and death.'

'You mean they won't kill a Gargan in any circumstances?' said the Brigadier.

'Never. And if you were to do it, it would destroy everything we've built up here. It's their greatest tabu.'

Sarah was filled with the feeling of helplessness that was so familiar to her as a child. They could argue the whys and wherefores afterwards, for God's sake. It was plain that the 'grown-ups' had no intention of doing anything at all.

Lying on one of the side benches was a neat pile of direction finders like the one Onya had carried. If she were careful, she could sidle over and nick one.

'You see, when you come into this life, death is inevitable,' Onya went on to say.

'As inevitable as it is when you step into the Gargan's domain,' said the Doctor. 'Of course. The Hindus have a similar concept. The God Siva and his consort Kali ...'

But Sarah was content to lose the opportunity of improving her knowledge of the Hindu Pantheon. With a jerk of her head to Jeremy, who had been watching her wide-eyed, she walked as casually and as unobtrusively as she could the length of the hut, through the increasingly merry crowd in the club area, and out of the door.

'What was it you pinched?' said Jeremy.

She held it up to show him. 'It's just a matter of putting in the co-ordinates of the cave,' she said, doing it as she spoke. 'They were on the ER monitor screen, remember?

'There, done it,' she went on. 'Come on!'

'Stop! Wait for me!' cried Jeremy, as she took off for the eastern hills. But Sarah was as unstoppable as the Juggernaut of Bengal.

The discussion continued, with very little of consequence being said. The Brigadier suggested that Kaido and his people might know some way to entice the Gargan from his den. Ungar had reported that Waldo had stirred briefly before lapsing into unconsciousness again. If the creature could be kept from him, they might be able to call to him to come out, to escape the immediate peril at least.

But then what? As Onya pointed out yet again, the Gargan's hunt for its prey was inexorable. Once it had found Rudley's scent it wouldn't rest until it had made a meal of him.

Reluctantly, and with great sadness, Onya and Haban Rance came to the conclusion that this was one rescue attempt which had failed even before it was set in motion.

'But what other option is there?' said the Brigadier when he was alone with the Doctor. 'We can't just leave him there waiting to be killed.'

But the Doctor wasn't any more sanguine about Rudley's chances than the other two.

'Our hands are tied, Lethbridge-Stewart. Even if we did manage to lure the beast away, the poor boy would still be doomed.'

The Brigadier had never known him to take so negative an attitude at a time of crisis.

On the other hand, he thought, the Doctor was usually right in his assessment of a situation. It did look as if Captain Rudley was a goner. Unless... Of course. Of course!

'Unless we took him right away from here,' he said. 'We've got the flycar, after all. What's to stop us all getting away? This can't be the only place on the planet where we can hide from Tragan and Co.'

But it seemed that the Doctor was determined to be pessimistic. 'It had crossed my mind. The snag about that is . . .'

He stopped and looked around. 'Where's Sarah?' he said sharply. 'And Jeremy?'

The Brigadier shrugged. He hadn't seen them for some time.

'The little fools!' said the Doctor. 'They've gone to try a great romantic rescue!'

He set off down the hut. 'Let's just pray we're in time to stop them.'

The Brigadier started after him but immediately turned back. He picked up one of small stun-guns and slipped it into his pocket. No way was he going up there unarmed.

The camp was backed by a thick wood. Even after she got through that, Sarah found that the grassy slope leading up into the hills was dotted with clumps of trees, varying from small thickets to quite extensive spinneys. Some of them were quite thick; it was quite a fight to get through them; but she reckoned it was safer to stay as close to the line the direction finder indicated as possible.

She had got through the last of them and was more than halfway up the rocky slope to the thinly forested area which topped the eastern hills before she realized that Jeremy wasn't actually with her. Indeed, when she looked round, she saw him coming out of a small copse nearly a hundred yards behind.

What did he think he was doing? Didn't he realize that the longer they took, the more likely it was that the Gargan would get there first? 'Come *on*,' she shouted. 'Can't you go any faster, for Pete's sake?'

His shout back was interrupted as he tried to get his breath. 'You go on . . . ahead. I'll . . . catch you up.'

'No, you'll only lose your way.'

202

He stopped. 'I'm sorry, I've got to have a bit of a rest. I'm... puffed out!'

'Oh Jeremy!'

She would not cry. *She would not cry!* She sat down on a handy tussock by a tumbling mountain stream to wait for him. Perhaps it was just as well; she was pretty fagged-out herself.

The Brigadier wasn't much better off. 'Are you sure this is the way?' he said, using the query as an excuse to stop for a breather.

'Of course I am. We flew over the whole area, didn't we?'

The Brigadier smiled privately at the irritation in his voice. He was rather pleased to see that the Doctor was also making rather heavy weather of the climb.

As they emerged from yet another difficult wood, he stopped again and peered upwards. 'No sign of them,' he said.

'Well, they're younger than we are,' said the Doctor, also stopping, 'by several hundred years.'

'Speak for yourself,' said the Brigadier, and set off again with all the vigour of a man past his first youth and determined not to show it.

When Sarah reached the top, she was almost certain that they had arrived at the very place where Kaido had met them with the bats. It certainly looked the same. Logical really, she thought, as she caught her breath. They'd been walking along the – what was it? She searched amongst her (almost buried) package of girl-guide memories; yes, that was it – the direction finder had pointed along the 'reciprocal bearing' of the one Onya had followed. That was great. She knew the way from here.

Hardly waiting for the puffing Jeremy, she started a desperate scramble down the steep rocks. If only the Gargan hadn't returned!

When at last she reached the bottom – for her guess had proved right – she stopped at the edge of the stony clearing and looked, and listened. The enormous Gargan construction was off to the right. From this angle the arch of its entrance could clearly be seen. There was no sound coming from it or, for that matter (apart from the usual racket), from the surrounding forest. There was certainly no hint of the squealing roar of the Gargan after its prey.

She held up a shushing finger to Jeremy as he slid down the last few feet with a clatter of falling rock. With a jerk of her head for him to follow, she made for the pile of stones.

'Wait a mo'!' cried Jeremy in an alarmed squeak. 'Onya said that if we crossed the line of rocks, the thingy would eat us up!'

'We can't worry about that now,' she hissed. 'Now, come *on*!'

Treading with exaggerated care, she led the way to the cave. Pausing at the entrance, she kept herself pressed against the cliff wall and peeped inside. At first, it was difficult to see anything at all. The sun had gone and dusk was near, so the inside of the lair was almost black.

Gradually her eyes became accustomed to the lack of light. Thank God, the Gargan wasn't there! But where was Waldo?

More confidently she moved into the darkness; and then she saw him, lying on a pile of white bones and strangely shaped skulls. Even in this light, she could see that those under him were stained a dark red.

She ran forward and knelt down by him. She called his name. He didn't move.

'I say,' said Jeremy, 'he hasn't half been bleeding.'

'Waldo!' said Sarah again. 'It's Sarah! Wake up! Please!'

But her only answer was the heavy, stertorous breathing of the desperately wounded.

If anything, the Brigadier found it more difficult to hurry downhill than he had coming up. It was lucky that, thanks to Haban Rance, he was at least more or less dressed for mountain climbing, instead of still being in the uniform he had thought appropriate to his visit to Space World –

only yesterday, was it? Ridiculous. Talk about the relativity of time.

The Doctor seemed to have got a second wind of some kind. All very well for some. The man had two hearts, hadn't he?

His internal grumbling was cut short as the two of them arrived at the base of the steep slope.

'There's the creature's cave,' said the Doctor, indicating it with a nod. 'But there's no sign of Sarah and Jeremy... No! There they are!'

But even as the Brigadier looked over and saw the two youngsters, each with one of the wounded man's arms around their shoulders, supporting him, dragging him, he heard what he had been dreading to hear: the bellow of the Gargan as it crashed through the trees towards its lair.

Chapter Twenty-Eight

Sarah wasn't immediately aware of the imminent arrival of the Gargan. The dead weight of Waldo – for he was still utterly unconscious – made it impossible that they would be able to drag him very far. But as she looked up at the Doctor's shout and saw him and the Brigadier, heedless of crossing the boundary of the Gargan's domain, running towards her, she also saw, a way behind them, the fearsome figure of the creature itself, whipping its great snout high in the air to utter a bellow of triumph as it sighted its prey.

'I can't hold him any longer!' she gasped as the Doctor arrived.

'We'll take him,' said the Doctor. But as he seized Waldo's arm, the Gargan came forward at a run, its long neck outstretched, its great mouth agape.

'Hold on,' cried the Brigadier, pulling out the gun.

As the animal came nearer, it slowed down and stopped, its neck rearing up in the air and swaying like a snake-charmer's cobra as if it were puzzled by the embarrassment of riches laid out before it.

There was nowhere to run to; behind them was the cliff wall and the mouth of the cave. The Brigadier was aiming two-handed at the creature's head, his arms swaying as he tried to get it in the sights.

'Wait!' said the Doctor, 'I've got a better idea.'

To Sarah's astonishment, he started to sing:

> 'Klokleda partha mennin klatch,
> Aroon, araan, aroon.

Klokleeda mertha teera natch,
Aroon, araan...'

For a moment, it seemed as if it were going to work. The Gargan stopped swinging its head and looked straight at the Doctor. But then, with a roar louder and more menacing than any they had yet heard, it drew its head back with the evident intention of attack.

The Brigadier pulled the trigger.

Oh, what a fall was there! If the Brigadier hadn't skipped out of the way like a ten-year-old, he would inevitably have been crushed. The great head slammed down with a thud which shook the ground; the body, larger than two elephants, quivered momentarily, then sank down as the forelegs collapsed, rolled massively on to its side and came to a shuddering halt.

The forest, which had fallen silent at the last great bellow, came back to chattering squawking life.

'Now you've done it,' said the Doctor.

Sarah sat down on a rock, her legs giving way under her. 'Is it dead?' she said faintly.

The Brigadier cautiously approached the huge body. 'It doesn't seem to be,' he said. 'Not yet, at any rate.'

With Jeremy's help, the Doctor laid Waldo onto the ground. 'Captain Rudley! Can you hear me? Captain Rudley?'

There was no reaction.

He made a quick examination of the wound. 'His scapula must be shattered,' he murmured to himself, 'but at least there's no bullet in there. With an exit wound like that...' He looked up and spoke aloud. 'He's lost a great deal of blood,' he said.

Jeremy was fidgeting backwards and forwards as if he were about to take off into the trees. 'I say,' he said, 'don't you think we ought to get out of here? That thing might wake up – and suppose he's got a wife or something?'

'A good point,' said the Doctor. 'We'd better make a stretcher.'

The Brigadier produced a knife, remarkably large and

sharp for one carried in a trouser pocket, and he and the Doctor quickly constructed a stretcher from a couple of saplings and the whippy branches of young trees, bound together with creeper.

As Sarah brought back a bundle of leafy twigs, she caught the end of a slightly acrimonious exchange.

'You were singing an old Venusian lullaby? Really, Doctor!'

A lullaby! Yes, that's just what it sounded like, she thought.

'It's been remarkably efficacious in the past,' said the Doctor huffily. 'Unfortunately, the Gargan didn't seem to have the same ear for music as my old friend Aggedor.'

'That gun thingy was certainly efficacious,' said Jeremy, warily eyeing the recumbent monster. 'I mean to say! Wallop!'

'Yes. Handy little weapon,' said the Brigadier, taking the twigs from Sarah and weaving them into the stretcher.

'That's all very well,' said the Doctor, sitting back on his heels and letting the Brigadier get on with it. 'If he's dead, Lethbridge-Stewart, Kaido's people will probably throw Onya and the rest of them out of Kimonya. If he's not, he'll track us down and have us for dinner.'

'Yes, well,' said the Brigadier, as he tucked in the last twigs, 'if we'd stayed with Rockabye Baby, he'd be onto the port and walnuts by now.'

It was the Brigadier, too, who had the Bright Idea.

Having managed, with a great deal of difficulty, to get Waldo up the slope to the top – they'd had to tie him onto the stretcher at the steepest bit – they were on their way down the rather more gentle incline on the far side. Sarah and Jeremy were carrying the front end of the stretcher, with the Doctor at the back. The Brigadier was leading the way, following the line of the stream, when he suddenly stopped. Sarah nearly cannoned into him.

'Eureka!' he said.

'That's usually my line,' said the Doctor. 'What have you found?'

'I was only thinking earlier today,' he answered, with a half-grin on his face, 'about my fox-hunting days as a young man. Do you know, there was one run where hounds lost the scent time and time again. And do you know why?'

'Yes, I do! Indeed I do!' said the Doctor in high glee. 'Well done, Lethbridge-Stewart.'

What were they on about? thought Sarah. Why did they have to speak in riddles?

'Why then?' said the Brigadier.

'Because the fox took to the water. Am I right?'

'Quite right,' said the Brigadier, shortly. He seemed to be quite miffed at having his moment of triumph pinched from under his nose.

Thus it was that the next hundred yards or so were uncomfortably spent wading down, clambering down or falling down (in Jeremy's case) the cascading waters of the little tributary. It was quite dark by now, and becoming really cold. Sarah found it very nearly impossible at times, even though the Doctor and the Brigadier had taken over the carrying of the stretcher, but the thought that the Gargan might be fooled by this stratagem, and Waldo's life saved, gave her a glow inside which made up for everything.

Even though the welcome with which Onya received them seemed somewhat reserved, her first concern was for Waldo – but whether he would survive was another matter. To Sarah's horror, Onya and the Doctor agreed that there was nothing they could do, apart from cleaning him up and bandaging the wound.

'They shot him with a simple old-fashioned firearm, you see. They always use them in the hunts – the audience prefers it. We can't replace the blood he's lost.'

Sarah wanted to stay and help, but she was shivering so much that Onya insisted that like the others she should go to her hut and dry off.

This wasn't ordinary shivering, she thought to herself, as she desperately rubbed herself with the Kimonyan equivalent of a towel. What was the matter with her? Yes, of course she was wet and cold, but this terrible shaking had come on when everybody seemed to be insisting that Waldo was going to die.

She had never felt anything remotely like it before. She'd had her quota of tears, of course, but this? It was as if – as if she were weeping inside; grieving for the loss of something which had never been hers, and now never could be. And yet – Oh, Waldo! she said in her mind. If only it was me instead!

Having wrapped herself in the soft knitted robe she found waiting on her bed, and tied the scarf around her neck, she hurried back. As she ran through the neat streets of the camp, she could hear the joyful chatter of the Kimonyans preparing for the feast, and just across the bridge, she could see them starting to gather by the warm glow of the fires.

As she neared the hut, she heard the voices of Onya and the Doctor. Onya was clearly displeased. Sarah stopped. She didn't want to walk into the middle of a row.

'What else could we have done?' the Doctor was saying. Onya didn't answer. Then he said, 'In any case, I think the point may be an academic one.'

Onya said, 'I'm afraid you're right,' and fell silent again. Sarah went in.

Waldo was lying on the bed with a neat bandage on his upper chest. The Doctor was covering the blanket which lay over him with a skin of close grained fur which looked like sable, whilst Onya folded his bloodstained clothes. Apart from his almost imperceptible breathing, he lay quite still. His skin, waxen in the light of the flickering oil lamp, was drawn tight to the bones of his face.

There hadn't been much point in her haste. 'Is he . . . is he going to be all right?' she said. What a stupid question. You only had to look at him.

There was an appreciable pause before the Doctor spoke. 'We've made him as comfortable as we can,' he said. 'We just have to hope for the best.'

She sat down by the bed. She wanted to take his hand, but it was hidden under the blanket.

The door opened. It was Kaido. He was wearing a full-length multi-coloured robe and his face was ceremoniously painted in a whirling pattern. Behind him, Sarah could see Jeremy lurking – and the Brigadier too.

'The meat is roasted, Mamonya,' said Kaido. 'The feast awaits our guests.'

Jeremy poked his head in the door. 'Smells like Sunday dinner at school,' he said. 'Wouldn't surprise me if they'd got Yorkshire pud and all.'

Oh Jeremy!

Kaido politely stood to one side. For a moment nobody moved. Sarah became aware that everybody was looking at her.

'Oh. Oh, Doctor, I couldn't eat a thing. I'd rather stay here with Waldo.'

'I think you should come, Sarah. It's important that we should all be there. The feast is being held in our honour, you see.'

When she didn't move, he came over to her. 'We shan't be far away,' he said gently.

They were all waiting for her. Reluctantly, she rose and went out. She stood by Jeremy and waited for the others. The Brigadier put a hand on her arm. 'Stiff upper lip, old girl,' he said.

Except in so far as Kaido was their leader (and he seemed to be treated more like a big brother), there appeared to be very little awareness of class in the Kimonyan society. There was no question of the best venison being reserved for the chief and his guests. People sat where they liked, and wandered round the circle of fires, chatting to their friends and claiming a favourite tit-bit of meat from whichever spit was the nearest.

The whole village was there, all dressed in their most colourful robes. Even the little children running from group to group as though the whole village belonged to the same family had their faces painted in intricate patterns. The sap-wine was as freely available as the succulent meat (though nobody seemed to drink it immoderately) and before long the general tone of merriment and celebration had risen to a height which even drowned out the rival party going on in the camp club, which sounded to be a far less decorous affair.

'Your food warms the belly as your welcome warms the heart, Kaido,' said the Doctor. 'We thank you.'

'I hear your words as the words of a brother,' replied Kaido. 'Fill your hearts with our love and your bellies with our meat.'

Sarah looked at the wooden platter piled with choice pieces. What was the use of even trying? The first (and only) bit she'd put in her mouth had been chewed a thousand times and still wouldn't go down. She'd had to surreptitiously remove it and hide it in a clump of grass.

'My belly's almost full already. It's super. Sort of melts as you chew it,' said Jeremy. He leant over and spoke quietly. 'Do try a bit, Sarah. You must eat, you know.'

She gave him as much of a smile as she could manage. Poor old Jeremy. Everybody was always getting at him, but he wasn't so bad really.

Suddenly she became aware of a distant noise which cut through the sounds of jollity – even through the piping of the wooden flutes and the rhythmic chants. A cold whiteness flooded her; her skin tightened. It couldn't be, could it? 'Listen!' she said sharply.

The Doctor heard her and spoke quietly to Kaido, who stood up and held both hands in the air, calling for silence. The chattering and laughter on the fringes went on, but enough villagers obeyed to make it possible to be certain, even though the squealing roar was still a way off.

'The Gargan, by jiminy!' said the Brigadier.

'Even angrier – and hungrier,' said the Doctor.

'He's after Waldo Rudley,' said Onya with a glance at the Doctor.

'He's after us all,' the Doctor said.

Chapter Twenty-Nine

'You all went into his territory?' Sarah heard again the anger – or was it concern? – in Onya's voice.

'We had no choice,' replied the Doctor. He got up and walked away from the group; he was staring at the hill, so brightly lit by the twin Parakonian moons, down which the Gargan must come, as if he were trying to work out what it was going to do when it arrived.

Jeremy was also starting to move away, for quite another reason. 'Well, come on,' he said in a high-pitched voice, 'what are we waiting for?'

This time Sarah, even as frightened as she was, did recognize the note in Onya's voice. It *was* anger – but it was the anger of a mother with a toddler who had run into the traffic. It was no good running away, she reiterated, the Gargan would just follow their scent, just as it had done to find them now. Even when the Brigadier told her of his Big Idea, she dismissed it as useless. The creature was far too intelligent to be fooled by such an elementary trick.

'We'll just have to finish him off then,' said the Brigadier.

'No!' said Kaido in a powerful voice.

'If you want to save your lives, that's the last thing to do,' said Onya, grimly.

'But we can't just hang around waiting to be eaten,' wailed Jeremy.

'Got it!' said the Doctor, turning back; and he demanded from each of them a piece of their clothing: a

sock, a piece torn off a shirt, the scarf Sarah was wearing
– anything at all.

'Of course!' said Onya. 'Well done, Doctor.'

'Would you be so good as to get me a piece of Captain
Rudley's clothing, Onya?' said the Doctor briskly, as he
started wrapping a sizable lump of meat in the large
handkerchief he'd taken from his pocket.

'I'll go,' said Sarah, but Onya was already running
towards the bridge. Nevertheless, she took off after her.
As she ran over the water, she could hear the squeal of
the Gargan, much, much closer. Suppose the Doctor's
idea didn't work? How could she leave Waldo all by
himself, unconscious and utterly defenceless?

As she reached the row of huts, Onya came out at a
rush, clutching Waldo's bloodstained shirt, and ran back
across the bridge.

When Sarah got inside it was to see that though Waldo
had moved – he was no longer lying so straight and his
arms were outside the disarranged covers – his eyes were
closed.

She sat down beside him and took his hand. 'Waldo!'
she said. 'Can you hear me?'

The Brigadier watched the Gargan coming down the hill,
its nose to the ground (reminding him irresistibly of
Mickey Mouse's dog, Pluto), stopping every so often to
thrust its snout into the air, opening its gargantuan mouth
and once more threatening the world. Behind him he
could hear the Kimonyans, crowded round their leader,
joining in an incomprehensible chant of fear and praise.

In front of him was the little pile of parcels of meat,
now topped with Rudley's shirt. 'How good are you at
lobbing grenades?' the Doctor had asked. Good thinking.
But the essence of an attack with grenades was to put
them in precisely the right place at precisely the right
time. He had to catch the creature's attention, and that
meant waiting until it was near enough for him to place
the bundles of meat right under its nose.

'Go on!' cried Jeremy. 'What are you waiting for?'

'Quiet, boy!' said the Doctor.

'I'm sorry,' he said, 'but unless something happens soon, I don't think I shall be able to stop myself running away.'

The Gargan came nearer. The Brigadier judged the distance. Not yet – not yet.

Now! With the easy overarm action learnt at Sandhurst all those years ago, he lobbed the haunch of venison wrapped up in Waldo Rudley's shirt high into the night sky, to land less than a yard from the creature's nose.

'Hole in one,' said the Doctor.

The Gargan lifted its head to the full extent of its serpentine neck and glared suspiciously around. It uttered a tentative squeal. Hearing no response, it lowered its head and sniffed the bundle. Then, picking it up in its front teeth it tossed it into the air, caught it and, with a couple of quick chews, swallowed it down.

'One might almost say, "Howzat?" ' said the Doctor.

The Brigadier was waiting with the meat wrapped in the tail of his own shirt in his hand. Like being watched by the Sergeant-Instructor, he thought, as he sent it on its way.

'He likes the taste of you,' said the Doctor as the animal chewed the new morsel.

Sarah's scarf ... the Doctor's handkerchief ... Jeremy's sock ...

'Did, you *have* to leave me to last?' said Jeremy, the quaver still in his voice, as the Gargan mouthed the latest offering.

The chanting had stopped, as the villagers watched their sacred beast devouring its dinner. Its occasional roar had turned into a continuous purring growl of satisfaction. It gulped Jeremy down, sniffed the ground as if to make sure that there was nothing left, turned and ambled away up the hill the way it had come. It was evidently satisfied that it had devoured its prey.

'You make gifts to the Gargan,' said Kaido to the Doctor. 'You are indeed my brother.'

'Waldo!' said Sarah, 'Can you hear me?'

His hand remained still in hers. His eyes were shut, and his breath was slight.

Sarah gripped his hand fiercely, as if to force some of her own vitality into the lifeless body.

'Please wake up,' she said. 'It's Sarah.'

She was aware that there were tears running down her face, but she didn't wipe them away. They were an irrelevance, a small hiatus in the intensity with which she was willing Waldo to live.

Whether she sat like this for minutes or for hours she was never to know. There was nothing to indicate the passing of time and nothing in the world to be aware of, bar that too still face.

Was that a movement?

But no; it was nothing but the flickering of the light as a rogue draught caught the wick of the lamp.

But that – yes, it was a tiny movement in the hand she held so closely.

'Waldo!'

A flicker of his eyelids and then he was looking at her, straight into her eyes.

'Oh, Waldo,' she said, taking his hand in both of her own.

'Sarah,' he said, his eyes looking deep into hers. He took a shallow, rasping breath. 'I'm sorry that we . . .' His voice trailed away as he struggled to take another breath.

'Don't try to talk,' Sarah said in anguish.

But he persevered, and in a surprisingly strong voice, he spoke again. 'I wish we . . .' His voice stopped. A look of surprise came over his face and he gave a rattling sigh which seemed to go on for an impossibly long time. His eyes unfocused and his fingers went limp in her hand. His mouth dropped open.

'Waldo,' she said yet again. But even as she said the word, she knew there was nobody there to hear it.

Suddenly the Doctor was there, with his fingers on the pulse point in Waldo's neck. After a long moment, he closed Waldo's eyes. 'I'm sorry,' he said.

She looked up at him.

'If I hadn't come back, he would have died alone. I wanted to stay with him, but you wouldn't let me. We just went away and left him. Nobody should die alone.'

The Doctor looked at her as if he understood everything she was feeling. 'You were right; and I was wrong,' he said.

She got up wearily and went out of the hut, past Onya and the Brigadier, past Jeremy; out into the moonlight.

On the bridge, with the sound of rushing water filling her ears, she stopped and looked up into the sky with its unfamiliar constellations of stars. Where was he now?

There was a numbness within her that seemed even more unbearable than pain. It was as if Waldo's death had left a black hole in her heart: all the things of the world that had given her delight were crushed into a heaviness, contracted to a nothingness, from which no light could emerge.

What difference did it make where he was?

'Be brief, Tragan,' said Chairman Freeth. 'I have an eager young soufflé lying in front of me, trembling in anticipation of ravishment by my fork.' His voice was thick with desire.

Tragan's expressionless voice, amplified and distorted, bounced off the polished surface of the panels of Blagranian fernwood. 'It's Rudley,' he said. 'We picked up a contact.'

'Is that all?' A large forkful slurped into the capacious mouth.

'It was very short. But before he lost consciousness again, he spoke to the Earth girl, Sarah Jane Smith. And wherever the girl was, the Doctor and the others must have been nearby.'

Freeth put down his fork. 'Ah. Now that is of considerably more interest. What did you use to destroy them? A missile, presumably.'

There was a pause before Tragan answered, his voice flatter than ever. 'The contact was too short to establish the co-ordinates, I'm sorry to say.'

'Then send a gunship on a search and destroy mission! Do I always have to do your thinking for you?'

'If we alert them too soon, they'll just go to ground. The Lackan is a large area.'

Freeth's soufflé was already losing its virgin nubility, sagging into a despairing middle age before his very eyes.

'Running true to form, are we, Tragan? You ruin my dinner just to tell me that nothing can be done?'

The Vice-Chairman's protest at this was ignored; Freeth went straight on: 'These people must be eliminated! Get on with it!'

He picked up his fork, sighed, put it down again and waved petulantly for the soufflé to be removed.

If it had not been for the dream, Onya Farjen would have been content to live out her life as the mother of the Kimonyan tribe.

It had seemed quite natural that a forest beast should speak, and while speaking should metamorphose into a canjee, the small furry piglet which the Kimonyans kept as pets, and then into a sailbird, soaring with its companions high above the island which was the Lackan. Although she could not remember the words, the message was clear: personal liberation was not enough.

Appalled as she was at the enormity of the task – that she, Katyan Glessey as was, should seek to turn the world upside down, to open the gates for all in Parakon, even for those who had no idea that they were in prison – she nevertheless found herself exulting in the thought of it, dangerous though it was.

To seek out those who felt as she did, without exposing herself to Security; to help those who could bear no more to escape as she had done; to build a fellowship with the ones who dared to stay and work unseen (as she did herself as servant to the President); and ultimately to plan with the trusted few the steps which must be taken to destroy the evil that held Parakon in its grip; all this had been the manifestation in the world of her own freedom – a small return for the love that had set her free.

Was it all to be lost now, to be thrown away because of a stupid mistake on her part?

'It's my fault, Rance. Because the boy was unconscious, I quite forgot that the transmission needles should be deactivated.'

It was not until the next morning, going to Sarah in the hope of offering comfort, that she had learnt that Waldo had come back to consciousness, albeit for a very short time. She knew the malignity of Tragan's organization too well to hope that it would have gone unnoticed.

She had at once sought out Rance, as leader of the newcomers, and found him with the Doctor and Brigadier, dissecting the latest Security weapon they had 'acquired', a maser-powered gun which would ground a flycar as swiftly as a stun-gun would paralyse its occupant.

'So we can expect an attack at any time?' said Rance bitterly. 'All our plans go for nothing? We just give up?'

'How advanced are your plans for the coup?' said the Doctor.

'Just about complete.'

'Then why wait?' said the Brigadier. 'Attack is the best form of defence and all that; why not go ahead at once?'

If only we could, thought Onya.

'It's not so easy,' she said. 'Yes, we have completed our plans for the takeover at the Palace and the Corporation – all the strategic points in fact. But the difficulty is that –'

'We're here and they are there,' interrupted Rance, with even more bitterness in his voice. 'We have to make a preliminary foray to capture enough transport. Or are you suggesting that we should ferry three hundred and seventy-two people in Onya's flycar?'

'See what you mean,' said the Brigadier.

'Yes. A seemingly insuperable problem,' said the Doctor, slowly. 'There might be an answer though. If our new friend Kaido can be persuaded to play ball. Do you agree, Brigadier?'

What was he talking about? thought Onya. The Brigadier also seemed to be nonplussed, but only for a moment.

His face brightened. 'I'm with you,' he said. 'Airborne troops. Splendid notion.'

Rance was looking suspiciously from one to the other. Onya said, 'Would you care to share it with us, Doctor?'

'How many passengers could one of the Kimonyan bats be persuaded to carry?'

Of course!

'And what's their maximum range?' added the Brigadier. 'Given auxiliary fuel, of course. Nose bags or whatever.'

Now why didn't they think of that?

Chapter Thirty

The next morning, Kaido, more out of love for Onya and respect for the Doctor than a true apprehension of the situation, agreed to the use of the bats as troop carriers. Unfortunately, since they had only sixty-eight fully-grown animals and since the maximum practical load would be four apiece (the Kimonyan rider plus three), the attack force would have to be scaled down to some two hundred troops.

Luckily, Haban Rance was an example of that rarity among leaders, one willing to relinquish his position to a better qualified candidate. In the discussions that followed, it soon became apparent that the Brigadier's professional expertise far outweighed the amateur tactics of an electronics engineer.

Jeremy had been detailed off to run the Brigadier's messages, much to his disgust. ('Poor old Jeremy,' he'd overheard Sarah saying, 'one of life's dogsbodies.') He came back from the bat stables, with their rows of hanging giants, after a futile attempt to 'liaise with the bat handlers' to find the Brigadier with Haban Rance, poring over a map of Parakon City, putting the final touches to the revised plan.

'... and by the time I and Mr Ungar have secured our position at the Security HQ,' he was saying, 'your squadron should have effective control of the ER transmission station. Who will you have as your two I/C?'

His what? thought Jeremy, as bemused as always; he was fed up with not knowing what people were talking about. But satisfactorily, Rance was just as foxed.

'Your second in command. I beg your pardon, Mr Rance.'

'I'll take Medan. He's a good man in a fight.'

'Well, the important thing to get across to him is that when you join me for the final takeover at the stadium, he must keep the transmissions of the Games going.'

Eh? What did the silly old Games matter?

'Why?' said Jeremy.

'The whole essence of the strategy,' the Brigadier said emphatically, 'is to effect a swift transfer of power while everybody is distracted by the finals of the Games.' He became aware that he was talking to Jeremy. 'What are you doing here? You're supposed to be liaising with – '

'They won't take any notice of me.'

'The job of a staff officer's aide is to take the weight of detail off his principal's shoulders.'

Jeremy was righteously indignant. 'But I'm not a staff officer's whatnot. And I'm not a dogsbody either! I'm an investigative journalist – like Sarah.'

That was telling him!

'Ah yes, of course,' said the Brigadier. 'Well, go and investigate the – the kitchens, there's a good fellow. See if you can rustle up a cup of that disgusting coffee stuff that tastes like roasted turnips.' He turned back to Rance.

Jeremy sloped off. Sarah was right, he thought. Everybody's dogsbody was what he was.

It could hardly be said that Sarah was feeling better. The dead feeling persisted as the ground of her being; but the necessity for concentration on the plans for the coup – and the thought that she was doing what Waldo would have wanted – kept her on course.

She was flying back to Parakon with Onya and the Doctor. Onya had two purposes: firstly to alert the crypto-dissidents in the city of the approaching coup-d'état; and secondly to see the President. The hope that a coup would succeed was based on the premise that the Parakonians were so conditioned to obedience that they would obey anybody who was clearly in charge, especially if they had the backing of the President.

'But surely he won't join a plot against his own son,' Sarah had said when she was first told of the plan.

'He's a good man,' the Doctor had said, 'and an idealist. He really thinks that he's set up the best of all possible worlds for his people, and the people of the other planets in the Federation. If he can be made to see what's really going on...'

'That's why we're going in ahead,' said Onya, 'to show him proof of the evils that are being committed in his name.'

It was when she heard of the Doctor's own intention that Sarah had said that she would come too. As acknowledged leader and de facto tyrant, Freeth – and his creature, Tragan – would always be in the best position to foil the attempted rising. The Doctor meant to find them, in order to provide a distraction while the takeover was in progress.

At first he would not hear of Sarah's proposal. 'There's no point in our both putting our heads into the noose.'

Cliché! she thought, despite herself. So she answered with another one. 'Two heads are better than one,' she said. 'You must admit I've been a help to you in the past.'

In the end, at her insistence, he acquiesced. 'I shall be glad of your company,' he said courteously, when she had rebutted every objection he could think up.

As they approached the tall buildings on the outskirts of the city, the Doctor said to Onya, 'Before we part company, is it possible you could get us into one of the Parakon Corporation buildings?'

'Which one?' said Onya. 'Apart from Parakon House, they have buildings all over the city.'

'I want to find out about the rapine set-up on other planets,' replied the Doctor.

'You need the Corporation Data Store,' she said. 'I held onto my Katyan Glessey pass, so we shouldn't have any trouble getting in. But what are you trying to find out?'

The Doctor's face was grave. 'There's something missing

in the rapine story. It's been nagging me from the start. And if what I suspect is true, then I'm quite sure you'll have no trouble at all in getting the President on our side.'

'Why?' said Sarah. 'What do you suspect?'

'Something more horrible than anything we've found out so far,' he said.

In spite of the fact that the ER recordings which the Doctor had come to consult were contained on small discs the size of a saucer, the Data Store was, as Sarah exclaimed, 'the size of St Pancras Station.'

The hall was divided into different levels and galleries, and in the innumerable cubicles sat a scattered bunch of researchers lost in their own ER worlds.

They had had no trouble getting in, apart from the moment Sarah's heart gave a jolt when the little old man at reception punched up the name Katyan Glessey on his screen. It transpired, however, that he was merely looking for a reservation, a booking of the facilities needed. But even though he couldn't find one, he still let them in.

The Doctor was soon immersed in his research.

'I must say,' he said, 'these ER reports are remarkable. I'm there, really there. Or rather, that's how it seems.'

For a moment, Sarah's last experience of ER was as immediately present to her as it had been when she held Waldo's back in the sights of her gun. She shuddered and pushed the image away.

'Are they any help, though?' said Onya.

'Yes, they are. Undoubtedly.' The Doctor went on to explain that the Federation planets – the colonies, or whatever one wanted to call them – formed a chain, a string of worlds exporting rapine and importing goods, flourishing just as Freeth had promised; everybody prosperous, everybody happy, at least on the surface.

So what was worrying him? Sarah wanted to know.

The planets where the supply of rapine was dwindling, he said. The economies were starting to break down; poverty growing; and discontent. The fertility of their soil had been all but eaten up and had to be replaced by massive doses of fertilizer.

Onya said, 'I could have told you all that.'

The Doctor said, 'Of course. It's what I expected. But what is the end term of the progression? And where does the fertilizer come from? Let's find out.' He selected a disc from the rack in front of him and asked Onya to patch three ER channels together.

'Right,' he said, when they were all wearing the headsets, 'let's go to Blestinu, where the TARDIS first landed. This is the latest recording.' Sarah took a deep breath. What horrors was she in for this time?

At once she was in the middle of a nightmare landscape of mud. A few stumps of shattered trees showed that this had once been a normal piece of countryside, but now the terrain was as covered with craters as the surface of the moon. To the sound of shooting and distant explosions was added the whistling shriek of a shell which heralded an explosion nearby which created a hole the size of half a tennis lawn. Sarah felt herself being covered with flying mud and debris. She uttered an exclamation of dismay.

'Yes,' she heard the Doctor's faint voice, 'we're in the middle of a war; a conventional shooting war.'

She pulled off her helmet. Back in the Data Store, she saw Onya lean forward and adjust one of the controls.

'I suspect this is only the tip of the iceberg,' the Doctor was saying. 'A body that's been blown to bits isn't much use to anybody.'

'What do you mean?' said Onya.

'Let's have a look round,' said the Doctor in reply. Sarah replaced her headset. The Doctor's voice came through much more strongly now that Onya had altered the volume and the sounds of war were gratefully distant.

For Sarah found herself present at a series of the most horrendous scenes of death and devastation she had ever seen. Dead bodies were everywhere, lying where they had fallen or stacked in neat piles. The smell of decaying flesh pervaded the air. A few survivors wandered aimlessly through the ruins of their world; elsewhere ragged soldiers ran for cover and let off sporadic bursts of automatic fire at their unseen brothers.

But none of this was what the Doctor was looking for.

'Ah. Now this is what I was afraid of,' she heard him say at last. She was wearing what could only be a gas-mask. Through the eyepieces she could see that they had arrived at a country road thick with the fallen, mostly women and children, still clutching pathetic bundles of belongings, or lying beside handcarts overloaded with inappropriate household goods.

'Refugees,' said Onya.

'Look over there to the left,' said the Doctor. 'A mechanical lifter, loading them into a truck. Can you see the driver? He's wearing a gas-mask, too.'

'And the truck has the badge of the Parakon Corporation,' said Onya. 'I'm beginning to understand.'

Sarah was still in the dark. 'What are you getting at, Doctor?' she said.

'Can you take any more?'

'I must.'

Once more she was thrown into a bewildering, dizzying series of quick snatches of a planet at war with itself, stopping inside a cavernous building, some sort of factory, with the din of machinery fighting the roar of a queue of Parakon trucks.

'Oh, my God,' said Sarah. 'They're tipping the bodies into that machine!'

'A processing plant,' said the Doctor. 'And look, coming out the other end, all neatly bagged and labelled ... Well, what do you think it is?'

'I don't think I want to know,' said Sarah.

'Fertilizer,' said the Doctor.

The Doctor told them what he thought had happened. The President must have handed over to his son about the time that it was becoming apparent that the normal sources of nitrogenous plant food was becoming too depleted throughout the Federation for the operation to continue. Freeth, probably by the chance discovery of a warring planet, hit on this macabre solution to the problem. The protein of animal flesh was an ideal source of nitrogen.

The trouble was that there could never be enough for a self-sustaining operation. Every world growing rapine would inevitably be reduced to desert in the end. Hence the constant search for new worlds to supply the greed of Parakon.

'You were right, Doctor,' said Onya. 'When the President finds out that this, this nightmare is how his dream has ended . . . Give me that disc. I must go to him at once.'

She hurried away, as the Doctor tidily replaced all the other discs which he had been using earlier.

'But why do they keep a record of it all?' said Sarah. 'It's evidence against them.'

'Why did President Nixon keep the Watergate tapes? Why did the Nazis keep neat registers of the horrors that they perpetrated? They think they're all-powerful – invulnerable.'

As he spoke, a distorted and muffled voice sounded from somewhere below the Doctor's waist: 'Trap One, Trap One, this is Greyhound. Do you read me? Over.'

'Oh, for Pete's sake,' said the Doctor, his hand diving into his pocket and producing what appeared to be a small button with a hole in the middle. Glancing round at the oblivious researchers sitting nearby, he spoke softly into it.

'Hello, Brigadier. Yes, I can hear you. Over.'

'Trap One, Greyhound. All in order? Over.' The Brigadier's voice sounded tiny and thin, like one of Mickey Mouse's chipmunk friends.

'As far as we can tell, yes, everything is in order and quite probably tickety-boo. Over.'

'Trap One, Greyhound. Approaching perimeter. Dashed windy up here. Maintaining radio silence. Out.'

The Doctor put the receiver back in his pocket. 'He does so love playing soldiers,' he said.

That's not fair, thought Sarah. 'He's not exactly playing at the moment, is he?' she said.

The Doctor gave her a startled look. 'True, true. Sorry. Sorry, Lethbridge-Stewart. Right then, we'd better join in.

227

Action stations, Sarah Jane Smith. Now, the object of the exercise is to find out where friend Freeth is lurking – '

But he was saved the trouble of searching for, as he spoke, a voice like the voice of God boomed through the hall.

'Stay where you are! Put your hands in the air! You are surrounded!'

Sarah's hands shot up. All over the Data Store, figures rose to their feet, hands in the air. The only exception was the Doctor who turned casually towards the main door, where a figure stood flanked by two Security men.

'Good afternoon, Mr Tragan,' he called out. 'The very man! I wonder if you could help us? We're looking for Chairman Freeth. Have you any idea where he might be?'

Chapter Thirty-One

Freeth was at this moment playing the dutiful son.

Even if Onya had carried out her original plan and flown straight to the palace, she would probably have missed the President, for this was the day on which he fulfilled one of his few remaining public functions, bestowing his official presence on the final evening of the Games. Freeth always joined him, as a discreet reminder to the watching multitude of where the real power lay; though he always made sure that there was a conspicuously armed guard nearby, as a deterrent in case the reminder was too provocative.

As always, the President greeted him with joy. In his turn, he affected the half-mocking tone which stood for affection in his dealings with his parent.

'My, my!' he said. 'Aren't we the beau of the ball? The people will think that their President has discovered the secret of eternal youth. Thank you, Yallet.' He nodded a dismissal to the smooth-haired youth who had been titivating the sparse, tired hair into an elaborate coif. As he left the small retiring room behind the Presidential box, the sound of the crowd in the stadium swept through the open door like a massive wave breaking on a rocky coast.

'You're a dear boy, Balog,' said the President, peering with rheumy eyes at the rouged old countenance in his mirror. A look of discontent passed over his face as he caught sight of the result of Yallet's efforts. 'I wish, though, that my Onya hadn't left me. She really understood how to do my hair for these public occasions.'

Freeth's thick lips pouted in disapproval. 'A bondservant,' he said. 'A middle-lower, or at the most a lower-middle.' He spat the words out as though they tasted rancid. 'You can't trust these people, Father. They have no sense of integrity – of loyalty.'

The President sighed. 'But Onya of all people!' He swung his wheelchair away from the looking-glass and gazed admiringly at the grotesque caricature of an overweight toddler standing before him, as if it were the apotheosis of manly beauty.

'I just give thanks that I have you,' he said. 'It's a great comfort to an old man to know that our heritage is in safe hands.'

Freeth smiled puckishly. 'Our heritage if not our hair, eh, Father?'

The President started to laugh, but the wheezy sound turned into an asthmatic gasp. Freeth pressed the requisite button on the arm of the chair and watched, still smiling, as a precisely appropriate dose of medication saved his father's life yet again.

The blare of music which had been melding with the distant roar came to a discordant end.

'Ready, Father?'

The old man shook his head. 'I'm beginning to dread these public occasions, Balog,' he said.

'You don't have to stay after the opening march of the combatants,' answered Freeth. 'You can come back and loll in here until the award ceremony.'

His father nodded unhappily.

The double doors slid open, with a surge of sound like the blast of heat from a furnace. A fanfare struggled to be heard.

'Your cue, I believe,' said Freeth. 'Now, don't go over the top. Three pirouettes and a double somersault will be quite enough.'

As the wheelchair carried him through the doors to the rapturous greeting of nearly five hundred thousand of his loving people, the President was still laughing his creaky laugh.

* * *

The action of a flying bat the size of those from Kimonya, with the beats of the immense wings being echoed in the up-and-down motion of the body, felt remarkably like that of a small boat in a choppy sea. It reminded the Brigadier of a wildly improbable cutting-out expedition (landing from canoes behind the enemy lines) that he had led when he was seconded to the SAS as a captain. He felt again the rush of adrenalin and the fierce eagerness for action which had possessed him then, carrying him through the hail of fire which greeted them – they had been betrayed – ultimately to carry the day.

His sentiments were not shared by Jeremy. 'I think I'm going to be sick,' said the small voice behind his left shoulder.

'Nonsense,' he called back. 'Just a few pre-battle butterflies, that's all. Soon be in the thick of it. Concentrate on that.'

'That's what's making me feel sick,' replied Jeremy.

The Brigadier was relying on two factors to allow his bat-battalion to get through to land its troops at the relevant targets for the coup.

Firstly, although Rance had warned him of the echo-location scanners – a form of radar, thought the Brigadier – he had also pointed out that they were not geared to the expectation of attack. Their function was to police the occasional flycar demonstration by the braver dissidents, allowing the air patrol wing to destroy them.

So if the bats came into the city at a relatively low altitude, they would not only be shielded by the towering factories at the perimeter, but stood a good chance of being beneath the level of the echo-location pulses.

Secondly, it appeared that wild bats, who did not have the advantage of warm stables in the winter, were given to seasonal migration. Although it was still rather early in the year, Kaido (on whose bat the Brigadier was riding) was confident that, for a while at any rate, the flock would be mistaken for their itinerant cousins.

'I do believe we've got away with it,' the Brigadier said

to himself as they approached the centre of the city, where all their early targets were grouped.

As if to punish his over-confidence, from all directions, vectoring in at top speed, came the purple-liveried flycars of the Security Force.

The Brigadier glanced round at his amateur army, hanging on grimly to the fur of their flying steeds, clutching their stun-guns and projectors. He hoped to God they'd remember their orders. If they tried to turn this into a shooting match, they'd have lost before they began. It was a coup, not a war.

'By jove, they're fast,' cried the Brigadier as the cars swooped towards them.

'Too fast,' said Kaido.

'What do you mean?'

'You'll see. Hold on tight.'

Just as it seemed that the approaching patrols must inevitably blast them all out of the sky, Kaido's bat, in common with all the others, pulled in its wings and dropped like a shot pheasant.

'Good grief!' exclaimed the Brigadier over the despairing wail of his alleged aide-de-camp which came from behind him.

The flycars, taken by surprise, swung through the emptiness where the flock had been and sped away into the distance, curving round in circles half the city wide before they were able to return to the attack.

The bat had unfurled its wings and, as suddenly as before, with a couple of quick flaps, it turned and shot off to the left, then swooped up into the air once more. All around, its companions were employing similar tactics, jinking and dodging and fluttering like autumn leaves in a playful breeze.

Kaido was laughing with glee. 'This is our game – and the game of our animals. They enjoy it as much as we do. Kimonyan children chase each other on baby bats.'

As best he could, the Brigadier, ignoring the squeaks from immediately behind him – and indeed the oaths proceeding from an unhappy Ungar behind Jeremy – gave the pre-arranged signal for all groups to disperse to their several destinations.

He saw Haban Rance giving him a cheery wave as his bat zig-zagged away towards the ER station. Good, he thought as he pointed Kaido in the direction of the Security HQ, morale was still high. Everything was going well.

It's doubtful if Sarah would have agreed with him. She and the Doctor had been hustled into a Security flycar and whipped across the city to an area different from anything she had seen so far. Even though it was starting to get dark, she could still make out that the buildings, of a style which reminded her of the pavilions of Space World, were not residential; nor were they industrial.

Dominating them was a colossal construction which, as they flew over it, could be seen to be a mighty floodlit stadium full of people. Sarah had often seen shots on TV, during the Olympic games for example, which looked similar, but this was on a scale breathtakingly larger.

'The Games, I presume,' said the Doctor, as they started to descend. Tragan didn't bother to reply.

'I've never seen the point of these places,' said Sarah, determined to behave as if nothing was wrong. Desperately trying to hide the tremor in her voice, she added, 'You're so far away you can't see anything.'

Tragan turned round and eyed her. His face was still, bar one large dripping pustule which was pulsating like a glabrous sea anemone. 'You are forgetting ER, Miss Smith,' he said. 'Every position is equipped with a multichannel, multi-viewpoint receiver. Even if you're in the farthest seat, you can have a ring-side view.'

'Then why bother to come at all?'

'Real blood. Real death. So much more fun to know that you're actually taking part. We could fill the stadium five times over.'

A dribble of pus trickled onto his purple lips. He put out his tongue and licked it off.

Freeth arrived shortly after they reached the area, deep

under the centre of the stadium, which Sarah could see had been designed as a place to bring troublemakers. There was a row of lockups in the corridor; the circular main room had doors all round, obviously leading to different sectors of the stadium. There were manacles fastened to the wall, and trestles and frames the purpose of which she felt no impulse to ask, especially in view of the rack containing different types of whip and scourge next to them. And why should there be a drain in the corner?

Freeth's peevishness at being summoned from the Games vanished in a moment when he saw the reason for it.

'Two sitting ducks, Chairman,' said Tragan.

'Congratulations,' he said, wonderingly. 'I must admit you have surprised me.'

'I'm afraid that the others are still missing,' said Tragan, 'including the woman who pretended to be the dead Katyan Glessey.'

The computer check at the Data Store!

'No matter,' said Freeth. 'This is the one I want. Well, Doctor, what am I going to do with you?'

'If you're wise, you'll listen to what I have to say to you.'

'Oh, but I'm not. Wise? The very idea! Cunning and devious will do me.' His playful tone faded. 'What is more to the point is that I am powerful – and vindictive. I have been made to look a fool.'

'Appearances are not always deceptive,' said the Doctor.

Freeth's thick lips drew back over his little teeth in a cross between a sneer and a smirk. 'A cheap gibe, Doctor,' his face lit up, 'and one that is going to kill you. You have given me a simply top-hole idea!'

'I can't wait,' said the Doctor.

So the Chairman explained. 'You see,' he said, 'it has been an immemorial custom, for at least five years, that before the championship final, the audience is given an hors d'œuvre, an antipasto, a little snackette, so to speak. Two fierce gentlemen come on dressed as clowns and perform a send-up – is that right, Miss Smith?' He twinkled briefly in Sarah's direction. 'Yes, a *send-up* of the final combat.'

He turned back to the Doctor. 'And since you're in the market for making people look like fools, it struck me that it would be a splendid wheeze if you were to be the understudy, so to speak. Dressed as a clown.

'Oh, not to *pretend* to fight another clown, of course, but a real fight to the – if you'll forgive the expression – death.'

His face was illuminated by another bright idea. 'And to make sure that you lose, we'll put you up against Mr Jenhegger. You know – the favourite to win the championship? Now, isn't that the most spiffing notion?'

'And if I refuse?' said the Doctor coldly.

'Ah, but you won't! You see, we shall take you to the changing rooms, and Miss Smith will stay here with her dear old friend, Mr Tragan.'

In spite of herself, Sarah shrank back – and saw that the Doctor had noticed.

'Every time you jib,' Freeth went on, obviously enjoying himself, 'we shall bring you a piece of your lady friend. Only teensy-weensy pieces, of course – we're not barbarians – and *you* can decide how much of her you want. There! What could be fairer than that? You can even choose which bits, if you like.'

'You'll leave Sarah alone!' said the Doctor.

Freeth smiled charmingly. 'Entirely up to you, dear boy.'

Tragan had been listening apparently impassively, but his face was boiling like a thick purple soup. 'You haven't said anything about the Toad,' he said in an empty voice.

'Nor I have!' said Freeth in delight. 'The cherry on the icing, the Toad is. You see, the fighting circle is in the middle of a – well, I suppose you would call it a catwalk – over a pit. And in the pit – and this is where the fun comes in – in the pit is the Toad. The Great Butcher Toad, they call him, though he's not so big as all that; about the size of a bull, I suppose. Yes, a small bull. And you see, he simply adores tearing people into bite-

235

sized munchies, and eating them. Especially when he hasn't had his usual, ah, meat and two veg? Is that the right colloquialism? Please do correct me if I get these things wrong.'

Freeth produced his handkerchief; he wiped away the drool of saliva at the corner of his mouth.

'The Games will be over if you don't get a move on,' said Tragan.

'As practical as ever,' said Freeth. 'Ready, Doctor?'

The Doctor moved over to Sarah and put his hand on her shoulder. He looked deep into her eyes. She was shaking with anger and with fear, but whether it was fear for herself or fear for the Doctor she couldn't tell.

'Please don't go,' she said, hating the part of her that hoped that he would.

Freeth was watching them with a kindly smile. 'I don't want to rush you,' he said. 'It's an important decision, I can see that. Do please take two or three seconds to make up your mind.'

The Doctor turned back to him.

'What are we waiting for?' he said.

Chapter Thirty-Two

Servants are as invisible as postmen. Who would suspect a chambermaid with an armful of sheets of ulterior intentions, or for that matter a uniformed bondservant carrying a tray of cool drinks and tempting snacks?

'I didn't order refreshments,' said Yallet, at the private door to the retiring room. 'Well, never mind. Thank you.'

Avoiding his attempt to take the tray, Onya made to bring it through the door. Yallet frowned and stood in her path.

'I wish to see the President,' she said.

'The President is resting. Now please go away.' He took the tray from her.

A thin, tired voice came from inside. 'Who's that? Did I hear... Is that really you, Onya?'

'Yes, President.'

'My Onya. Come in, come in!'

Yallet tightened his meagre lips and stood to one side. When the President saw her, he smiled with the unaffected joy of a child greeting a long-lost parent.

'You've come back to me,' he said.

On the roof of the Corporation Security HQ, the Brigadier spoke in a low voice to his second-in-command, Ungar. Jeremy, who was standing behind him, was wondering to himself whether he dared to suggest that he should remain on the roof as a kind of lookout or something, while the others went off to do the actual fighting. He had a mental picture of twenty or thirty of the sort of thugs who'd guarded them when they first got caught near the

TARDIS all firing guns at him, and him sort of going pop as they all hit him at once.

The Brigadier interrupted himself. 'Sssh! What's that noise?'

Jeremy became aware that they were all looking at him.

'Only my teeth chattering,' he said meekly.

'Try to keep them under control, there's a good chap,' said the Brigadier.

'Now listen everybody,' he went on, 'there's a slight change of plan. It seems that Tragan's people have concentrated themselves in the communications area, which is here.' He pointed to the map in his hand. 'Now, Ungar's recce suggests that if we approach from here ... we can take cover here ... and here ... and with any luck give them the surprise of their lives.'

Jeremy was concentrating on his teeth. No matter how hard he clamped them together, as soon as he stopped trying, they were off again.

'Are you listening, Jeremy?'

'What? Yes. Yes. Jolly good idea.'

'Wait for my signal. Don't go rushing out getting yourself killed.'

'Who, me?' said Jeremy.

'Anybody. We don't want any dead heroes. Right? Off we go, then.'

Jeremy opened his mouth; and closed it again. It was too late now to talk about lookouts and stuff. In any case, he didn't want to be left all by himself. He took a deep breath and scuttled after them.

As Ungar had found, there was a strange dearth of personnel, even for the late shift. One unfortunate they encountered was silenced with a blast from the Brigadier's stun-gun and propped in a corner, staring at nothing, to recover his strength in a few hours. Apart from him, nobody.

Nevertheless, Jeremy was glad that the plan entailed their taking cover. As they crept through the darkness of the open-plan communications floor towards the lighted area in the corner, he kept close behind the Brigadier, on the principle that generals and people like that didn't usually get killed. You only had to look at Napoleon and Wellington and that chappie with the funny voice and a beret in the desert with all those guns going off (he'd seen it on the telly) – Montmorency or something.

They'd arrived behind a bank of control desks which were not in use at present, and were peeping over the top. It was clear why the rest of the building was so deserted. A whole bunch of Security officers – getting on for fifty, Jeremy reckoned – were scattered round the duty area, nearly all wearing ER headsets.

'The Games,' the Brigadier breathed in Jeremy's ear. He looked at his watch, seemed to do a countdown under his breath, and stood up. 'Freeze!' he shouted. 'Hands above your heads!' At his shout, the encircling assault troops stood up, stun-guns at the ready, and Jeremy crouched down, as small as he could manage, and put his hands over his ears.

The noise was considerable. Most of the enemy chose to disregard the Brigadier's instruction, and went for their guns. The raucous whine of the stun-guns on both sides of the conflict was mingled with the swish and bang of the portable missile launchers carried by the more senior of the Security forces.

With such utter surprise, and with the enemy being blinded at first by their ER helmets – and, for that matter, by their absorption in the Games – there was no possibility of a real defence. In a matter of minutes, the Brigadier was calling for a cease-fire. The noise ceased.

In the incredible hush that followed, Jeremy peered over the desk again. A large number of the Security men were lying paralysed (but conscious) by the stun-guns; the rest had their hands in the air. Nobody in the attacking force seemed to have been hit outright. Two had an arm dangling uselessly from a near miss, and Ungar was staring in surprise at his left hand, which had a finger missing.

'Well done everybody,' said the Brigadier. He looked down at Jeremy. 'You can come out now,' he added.

Jeremy rose slowly to his feet. 'As it's all over,' he said tentatively, 'does it matter if I let my teeth chatter a bit?'

What were they all laughing at? he thought bitterly. All very well for them, they were used to all this stun-gunnery stuff. He was only a journalist, wasn't he? He thrust down rising memories of war correspondents on the telly, flak jackets and all.

'Quiet!' called the Brigadier, and the relieved hubbub died away. Jeremy saw him pull out of his pocket one of the little mini-intercom thingies they'd all got (except him, of course!); it was quacking away like billyo.

Hang on a moment, he thought, that sounds like Sarah.

It was too; a mini-Sarah in a great old state. 'Brigadier!' she was saying. 'Can you hear me? Over!'

'Yes, Sarah, I can hear you. What is it? Over.'

'Listen, I haven't got much time. They've got us – Tragan's got us in the stadium – the Games place – in the security bit and they're going to – '

Her voice abruptly ceased. The Brigadier lifted the thing to his mouth, but stopped himself from speaking. He switched it off.

'Ask her!' said Jeremy urgently. 'Find out what's happened!'

'That could place her in the gravest danger,' snapped the Brigadier. 'Ungar! Take us to the flycar area. At the double!'

As the door opened, she managed to slip the little button back into her pocket, just in time. Tragan, returning with a portable ER headset, looked at her suspiciously as if he might have heard her voice. He was evidently satisfied, however. He just told her to sit down.

It was only after the Doctor had left that she had realized that when he put his hand on her shoulder, he had slipped something into her side pocket with the other hand, the one hidden from Tragan and Freeth; and only when Tragan, after a look round the sparsely furnished room, followed Freeth and the Doctor out, had she been able to find out what it was.

The sound of his feet outside the door had warned her that he was coming back. Whether the Brigadier had understood her hurried message, she had no idea.

'Can't I at least go somewhere to watch the fight?'

'And escape? And spoil all the Chairman's plans? No, no, my dear. You must stay here in case we need you – or part of you, at least.'

'What about ER? Can't I watch it on ER?'

'Unfortunately, there is just the one set,' he said, holding it up, 'and I need it myself. However, if you sit down like a good girl, I'll tell you what's going on.'

Reluctantly she sat down and watched him while he donned the headpiece and adjusted the controls.

'Nothing happening at the moment,' he said. 'It would be the interval before the announcement of the big fight, and of course the new attraction.' The lower part of his face, below the helmet, was rippling gently; it was so pale that it was almost white, with just a tint of lilac – like a naff new paint for the ceiling, Sarah said to herself.

Silence; and in the silence came the pain of thought. Could she have stopped the Doctor going? Was it her fault that he was going to be killed? But if he had refused, what would have happened to her, to both of them? The thoughts went round and round in an endless loop – like a Moebius strip, the Doctor would have said – and that thought caused a pang which started them all over again.

'Ah!' said Tragan at last. 'Something's happening. Yes, here comes Jenhegger into the Presidential box.'

'The President's box?'

'Yes, of course,' he said, as if it were self-evident. 'They always introduce the finalists from the President's box, and they can walk straight onto the catwalk from there. Jenhegger looks like an angry ape. I expect he's annoyed at being made to fight a clown. So much the better. Ah! Here comes the Chairman – and the Doctor.'

'Does he, does he look all right?' No answer, bar a faint smacking of the lips. 'Please! Please tell me!'

So Tragan told her exactly how he looked, and while

she listened, Sarah was praying, praying, praying; praying that the Brigadier would get there in time.

Freeth had gone to a great deal of trouble deciding what the Doctor should wear. 'I sometimes think I missed my vocation,' he said. 'I should have been very happy in show business. You can just imagine me dancing through the fairyland of theatre, now can't you? Or perhaps I should say prancing! To be at one with the aristocrats of the stage, the very princes of dramatic art, and put on pantomime, for example – the acme of histrionic achievement! Let's face it, Earth has a great deal to offer to dull old Parakon.'

While he rattled on, he was selecting the Doctor's fighting gear: item, one long striped frock suitable for a comic bondservant in an old-fashioned farce; item, a pair of skinny boots, twice the length of the Doctor's own feet; item, one frizzy ginger wig.

The Doctor silently dressed himself.

'And of course, we mustn't forget your weapon!' He produced a traditional cook's rolling pin, with which the Doctor was to oppose Jenhegger's hefty broadsword.

'Now, I know what you're going to say, Doctor. "That's not fair," that's what you're going to say; and I shall come back with the lightning riposte, "No it isn't, is it?"'

The crowd were certainly taken with the Doctor's get-up. He was greeted with hoots of glee, which were doubled and redoubled after Freeth's introduction to the fight.

'My friends,' his rich voice boomed through the amplifier, 'what can I say? We all know that Jenhegger didn't have a Dad...'

The mountainous Jenhegger glowered as the audience roared their appreciation.

'...but even he must have had a Mum. And here she is, to give us all a glimpse of the happy home life of the Jenheggers!'

Uproar.

The gate swung open and the gargantuan fighter led

the Doctor along the perilously narrow catwalk to the fighting circle.

As wide as the square of a boxing ring, the circle had no ropes or safety rails. If a combatant were to be thrown out of the fighting area, it would not be to land in the comfortable lap of a correspondent from the sports pages of a friendly tabloid, but to be greeted with open arms – and mouth – by the Toad (which was 'Great' indeed), who could now be seen below leaping up with the eagerness of a dog being offered a marrow-bone fresh from the butchers.

Jenhegger turned and struck an arrogant pose, moving with the lightness and grace of a star dancer. Dressed only in a breech clout, his tanned seven-foot frame was solidly clad in iron-hard muscle. He lifted his stubby sword, six inches wide at the hilt, as heavy as a bludgeon but as sharp as a new carving knife, and pointed it at the Doctor.

'Clown,' he rumbled, 'you are dead!'

Raising the sword ready for the first slashing blow, he advanced across the ring.

The Doctor held up his hand. 'Wait!' he said.

'Why do you stop me?'

'Do we have to fight?'

'Yes.'

'Why?'

Jenhegger looked puzzled, as if this was a question he had never considered before. 'If I do not,' he said slowly, 'they will kill me.' He frowned. 'And you make a clown of my mother,' he added.

'Not I, my friend,' said the Doctor. 'Very well, so be it. You will not attack me before I am ready?'

Jenhegger grunted. 'We kill each other, but we do not cheat.'

'Thank you,' said the Doctor, and pulled off the ginger wig, which he dropped with the rolling pin into the pit of the Toad. The dame frock followed, to be torn to pieces by the infuriated amphibian below.

Jenhegger watched in puzzlement as the Doctor dragged off the elastic-sided boots. 'What are you doing?'

'I have no wish to mock your mother. If I am to face death, it will be as myself. Besides, this ridiculous footwear would trip me up.'

The actions of the Doctor, who was by now clad only in his underpants, were highly unpopular with the spectators. One in particular, the Chairman of the Parakon Corporation, was shouting at the top of his voice, over the crescendo of catcalls and jeering, for the Doctor to stop what he was doing and fight.

'Your boot has hit the Toad in the eye,' said Jenhegger, apparently still bewildered by the uncommon turn of events. 'You're making it very angry.'

'I think I'm making Chairman Freeth even angrier,' said the Doctor. And indeed, he could be seen jumping up and down, insofar as his bulk would allow, and screaming with rage: 'What are you waiting for, Jenhegger? Kill him!'

The perplexed face cleared. The sword was lifted once more. 'Are you ready now?'

The pale wiry body of the Doctor straightened. He raised his hands and settled into a fighting position.

'Ready,' he said.

Chapter Thirty-Three

'What's happening? Please tell me! Please!'

Tragan gave an irritated shake of his head – and then relented. 'Nothing very much,' he said. 'They're slowly circling each other. I can't think why Jenhegger doesn't attack. One stroke would do it.'

Sarah's anguish was such that she could hardly bear to listen. She wanted to know but dreaded to hear. Where was the Brigadier? Had he heard her plea for help? And even if he came to the rescue, how could he be in time to save the Doctor?

'They're speaking to each other again. I can't hear what they're saying. I'll switch to the Jenhegger channel. It's a pity the Chairman didn't see fit to implant transmission needles in your friend; I should have enjoyed experiencing his death. Ah, that's better!' And to Sarah's chagrin, he lapsed into his former absorbed silence.

'Come and fight, coward! Come and taste Jenhegger's sword. Or are you too terrified?'

Jenhegger had never encountered an opponent like this. Why did he not seem frightened? His air of confidence, the aura of skill which surrounded him, quite confounded the gladiator.

'It may be your custom to taunt one another before engaging,' replied the Doctor, 'but I can see very little advantage to you on this occasion.'

Why was he not afraid?

'Why should I be afraid?' the Doctor said, as if he had read the other's mind. 'When I stepped out here, my life ended. If I return alive, I shall be returning from the dead.'

He was just trying to confuse him by talking nonsense!

'Enough! You talk too much!'

'So I have been told.'

'Die then!'

At last Jenhegger attacked. Charging towards the Doctor with an inarticulate battle-cry of frustration and rage, he swung his sword to the side in anticipation of his famed decapitation blow.

But when he delivered it, somehow the Doctor was no longer there to be decapitated. He had stepped to one side the better to help Jenhegger on his way, and with the cry of 'Hai!' and a twist of his hand he achieved his aim. Jenhegger flew through the air and landed with a heavy thump on the edge of the platform.

He scrambled to his feet and turned quickly, bracing himself to take the certain attempt to topple him over into the pit – and saw the Doctor quietly watching him, his hands by his side, for all the world like a casual bystander, rather than a participant in a fight to the death.

His vision blurred momentarily as the fury rose thickly in his throat.

'For that alone I kill you!' he snarled, and once again he charged – and once again found that he was charging the empty air.

'Stand still and fight like a man!' he roared. Changing his tactics, he advanced on the Doctor with his sword arm windmilling round, up, down, across, in the attack which had been known to dismember an opponent so fast that he fell instantly, sliced into several discrete pieces.

'Thank you... for your... kind invitation,' said the Doctor, bending and swaying and jumping as the heavy blade whistled past. 'Please forgive me... if I don't... Oh, well done! That was a beauty!' he added, as an overhead cut missed him by a hair and thudded deep into the wooden floor.

He couldn't last much longer, surely; and there was no

sign of the Brigadier! It must be that he hadn't got her message!

Sarah, wound up to a pitch of irrational desperation that would have taken her over the top at the Somme screaming defiance, found her mind working at lightning speed. There was only one thing to do: get up there while the Doctor was still holding out and somehow create a diversion. But that meant escaping now, right now. Of course! She'd seen the blow on the back of the neck which Onya had used to lay out the guard – and Tragan was in the ideal position, leaning forward slightly in the intensity of his concentration. She looked round for something to use as a weapon.

Nothing.

Onya had just used her hand.

She stood up, but in spite of being blinded by the headset, somehow he sensed her movement.

'Sit down, Miss Smith.'

'What's going on?' – still moving forward – 'Let me see! Oh, please let me see!'

He grunted. His face was no longer off-white, and as she got nearer she could see the little pimples which peppered the larger blisters. 'Ah!' he suddenly said. 'He nearly lost a foot! Good, good. If he hadn't . . .'

Now!

With all the strength of her insane courage, she brought down her clasped fists on the exact spot at the base of Tragan's skull. But instead of obediently collapsing on the floor, he leapt to his feet, tore off the headset, and seized her by the arms.

'You little vixen,' he hissed, his swollen face inches from hers. Dragging her across to the wall, he snapped the manacles hanging there onto her wrists.

'No more "fun," ' he snarled, pulling a multi-tailed whip from the rack. 'It's time you were taught a lesson!'

He drew back his arm – and dropped it again as a confused shouting and the squawk of stun-guns came from outside.

The whip fell to the floor and Tragan went for the

missile projector in the holster at his side, even as the door flew open and the Brigadier appeared, stun-gun raised – and was stopped in his tracks by the sight in front of him.

For Tragan had his gun pointing not at the Brigadier but straight at Sarah's head.

The clatter of boots behind the Brigadier died away as his backup arrived, and took in the situation.

For a moment there was silence. Then the Brigadier spoke quietly.

'Don't be a fool, Tragan,' he said. 'You haven't a hope. Give up and I'll make sure that you get a fair trial.'

'You don't understand, Brigadier,' he replied, 'I am a Naglon. Imprisonment means death for a Naglon. You may kill me if you wish, but first, I shall have the satisfaction of blowing Miss Sarah Jane Smith's head off.' His face, a deep muddy purple, was swelling alarmingly into ballooning hemispheres.

He raised the gun – and the two doors behind him burst open. He spun round, to receive the full blast of Rance's and Ungar's stun-guns.

The missile launcher clattered to the floor; Tragan's knees gave way and he sagged to the floor. Sarah could see his eyes, wide open, staring at her without expression, but clearly still seeing. As she watched his face, which by now was almost black in the intensity of its colour, the swellings were becoming so large they were merging one into another, and yet still they grew, until his eyes were hidden from sight.

Surely his face must burst!

And so it did; not with a bang; not with an explosion which splattered the walls; but with a juicy burp, a whoopee-cushion raspberry, a despairing fart, which slopped his purple lifeblood on to the bare stone floor, still stained with the blood of so many of his victims.

Jeremy, peering over the heads of the group behind the Brigadier, reckoned it was probably okay to go in now. As he sidled through the door, he saw Rance signalling to his men to remove the body. The Brigadier had turned to Sarah. 'Are you all right?'

'Yes, yes, but – '

'We'll soon have you out of those things.'

'Never mind about me! Jeremy! See what's happening to the Doctor!'

'What?'

'The ER set. There on the floor.'

He picked it up and shoved it on, and immediately found himself in the middle of a hand to hand fight with – of all people – the Doctor!

'Well? What's going on?'

He tried to tell them as well as concentrate on the fight. It was funny but, though he didn't want to hurt the Doctor, he couldn't not do his best to spifflicate him.

'Jeremy!'

'He's twisting my wrist... and I've dropped my sword... and I've thrown him off and... Oh no!'

The Doctor has fallen off the edge; he was hanging on by his finger tips. Jeremy walked slowly over, listening to the astonishing roar of the audience, which was so loud it had stopped being a sound; it was just an intense sensation in the ears like a pain that didn't hurt.

'For God's sake, Jeremy!'

'Sorry, I... there's an enormous frog thingy jumping up and trying to grab his legs and...'

He lifted his foot to push the Doctor's fingers off the edge, but the Doctor heaved himself up with one hand and grabbed his ankle with the other!

Over the crowd, he could hear a voice he seemed to recognize, shouting, 'Finish him off, Jenhegger!'

The Doctor was climbing up his leg! And he – the fighter chappie, rather – was trying to shake him off and...

'Switch channels!'

'What?'

'Give it to me!'

The helmet was snatched from his head and with a sort of a bump he was back in the cell place.

'The Doctor's rolling away from him and going for the sword,' Sarah said, urgently. 'He's got it! And the gladiator is right on the edge and about to go over... and the Doctor is rushing across and he's grabbed his hand and... he's pulled him back! The Doctor's saved his life!'

Even over the thunder of the crowd, Freeth's scream of rage could be heard. He turned to the guard standing next to him. 'Shoot him!' he cried. 'Shoot them both!'

But even as the man raised his gun, a voice boomed through the stadium, quietening the clamour and halting the guard.

'No! The killing will stop! I, your President, order it!'

Unnoticed, the double doors had opened behind Freeth and the President's wheelchair had appeared, pushed by Onya Farjen.

The President spoke again into the microphone in his hand. 'Doctor. Jenhegger. Your fight is at an end.'

By the grumbling groundswell it was clear the audience was not pleased. But it was their beloved President who had spoken. There would be no trouble.

By now, the two combatants were walking back along the catwalk. As Jenhegger opened the gate into the Presidential box, he turned back to the Doctor. 'You could have killed me,' he said, trying to understand. 'Why didn't you kill me?'

The Doctor smiled. 'My dear fellow,' he replied, 'what possible reason could I have for doing such a thing?'

They were greeted by Onya. 'Are you all right, Doctor?' she said.

'A little puffed, I must admit,' he answered.

The President wheeled himself forward. 'I am a blind and foolish old man, Doctor. Can you ever forgive me?'

The Doctor nodded. 'The past is dead, President – and I am still alive.'

'But not for long, Doctor!'

The rolling tones of Chairman Freeth had completely lost their teasing, bantering note. His voice was sharp, decisive, vicious.

'No, Balog,' said the President, quavering with the effort of resumed authority. 'As long as I am President of the world, and of the Corporation, there will be no more – '

But his son rode over the old man with all the callousness and cruelty he had for so long contrived to conceal. 'Hold your tongue,' he said. 'You *are* a foolish, blind old man. It's time you opened your eyes. You are not in charge any more; I am. Stand out of the way, everybody!' And he snatched the gun from the guard and aimed it at the Doctor.

'Goodbye,' he said.

But before he had time to pull the trigger, the weapon was dashed from his hands. 'No!' cried Jenhegger. 'You shall not! He is a good man!' Picking up the great body as if it were stuffed with feathers, he lifted it high above his head.

Freeth was screaming in a paroxysm of terror, and squirming in the big man's grip like a prime codfish about to be gutted. With one stride, Jenhegger carried him to the rail of the President's box, and pitched him over the edge into the depths of the pit.

'President! Don't look!' cried Onya, over the gleeful croaking roars and hog-killing squeals coming from below.

'I have turned away my face too many times,' answered the President. 'If I had not, I might still have a son.'

The squealing stopped. The Great Butcher Toad was not to be cheated of his dinner after all.

Sarah sat in the high-backed tapestry chair which the others had insisted she should take (rather than the rickety old deck chairs also on offer) and tried not to listen to the Brigadier and Jeremy behind her, swopping arcane male anecdotes about life at Holborough, and wondered briefly what it must be like at public school. A cross between a high-security jail and a kindergarten, judging by the sound of it.

The Doctor's head was hidden underneath the TARDIS console. Occasional grunts and imprecations were the only indications of the progress of his repairs. It was when it became clear that they were going to be stuck in the Time Vortex for some while that he had rather grumpily found something for them to sit on.

Ought she to be afraid that they would never get back to Earth? Maybe. Yet it felt so safe to be in the TARDIS with the Doctor, especially after all the really scary things she'd encountered during the last few days.

Only a few days? Ridiculous. It seemed that she was leaving a large part of her life behind on Parakon. 'I left my heart in San Francisco . . .' The song lilted through her mind. God help us, she thought, I even feel in clichés.

It was no good. She couldn't keep Waldo out of her mind forever, and though the pain of her grief wasn't extinguished, it was cushioned by the clear knowledge that the world could still be joyful. The memory of how the weight of fear fell away when the Doctor was saved and all was well, all was very well, rang through her like a peal of triumphant bells.

And what had Jeremy said, that other time? 'Life must go on – that's what he would have wanted.'

She got out of her regal chair and went over to address the feet sticking out from under the console.

'Doctor,' she said, 'where do you keep your teapot? I could murder a cup of tea.'

Already published:

TIMEWYRM: GENESYS
John Peel

The Doctor and Ace are drawn to Ancient Mesopotamia in search of an evil sentience that has tumbled from the stars – the dreaded Timewyrm of ancient Gallifreyan legend.

ISBN 0 426 20355 0

TIMEWYRM: EXODUS
Terrance Dicks

Pursuit of the Timewyrm brings the Doctor and Ace to the Festival of Britain. But the London they find is strangely subdued, and patrolling the streets are the uniformed thugs of the Britischer Freikorps.

ISBN 0 426 20357 7

TIMEWYRM: APOCALYPSE
Nigel Robinson

Kirith seems an ideal planet – a world of peace and plenty, ruled by the kindly hand of the Great Matriarch. But it's here that the end of the universe – of everything – will be precipitated. Only the Doctor can stop the tragedy.

ISBN 0 426 20359 3

TIMEWYRM: REVELATION
Paul Cornell

Ace has died of oxygen starvation on the moon, having thought the place to be Norfolk. 'I do believe that's unique,' says the afterlife's receptionist.

ISBN 0 426 20360 7

CAT'S CRADLE: TIME'S CRUCIBLE
Marc Platt

The TARDIS is invaded by an alien presence and is then destroyed. The Doctor disappears. Ace, lost and alone, finds herself in a bizarre city where nothing is to be trusted – even time itself.

ISBN 0 426 20365 8

CAT'S CRADLE: WARHEAD
Andrew Cartmel

The place is Earth. The time is the near future – all too near. As environmental destruction reaches the point of no return, multinational corporations scheme to buy immortality in a poisoned world. If Earth is to survive, somebody has to stop them.

ISBN 0 426 20367 4

CAT'S CRADLE: WITCH MARK
Andrew Hunt

A small village in Wales is visited by creatures of myth. Nearby, a coach crashes on the M40, killing all its passengers. Police can find no record of their existence. The Doctor and Ace arrive, searching for a cure for the TARDIS, and uncover a gateway to another world.

ISBN 0 426 20368 2

NIGHTSHADE
Mark Gatiss

When the Doctor brings Ace to the village of Crook Marsham in 1968, he seems unwilling to recognize that something sinister is going on. But the villagers are being killed, one by one, and everyone's past is coming back to haunt them – including the Doctor's.

ISBN 0 426 20376 3

LOVE AND WAR
Paul Cornell

Heaven: a planet rich in history where the Doctor comes to meet a new friend, and betray an old one; a place where people come to die, but where the dead don't always rest in peace. On Heaven, the Doctor finally loses Ace, but finds archaeologist Bernice Summerfield, a new companion whose destiny is inextricably linked with his.

ISBN 0 426 20385 2

TRANSIT
Ben Aaronovitch

It's the ultimate mass transit system, binding the planets of the solar system together. But something is living in the network, chewing its way to the very heart of the system and leaving a trail of death and mutation behind. Once again, the Doctor is all that stands between humanity and its own mistakes.

ISBN 0 426 20384 4

THE HIGHEST SCIENCE
Gareth Roberts

The Highest Science – a technology so dangerous it destroyed its creators. Many people have searched for it, but now Sheldukher, the most wanted criminal in the galaxy, believes he has found it. The Doctor and Bernice must battle to stop him on a planet where chance and coincidence have become far too powerful.

ISBN 0 426 20377 1

THE PIT
Neil Penswick

One of the Seven Planets is a nameless giant, quarantined against all intruders. But when the TARDIS materializes, it becomes clear that the planet is far from empty – and the Doctor begins to realize that the planet hides a terrible secret from the Time Lords' past.

ISBN 0 426 20378 X

DECEIT
Peter Darvill-Evans

Ace – three years older, wiser and tougher – is back. She is part of a group of Irregular Auxiliaries on an expedition to the planet Arcadia. They think they are hunting Daleks, but the Doctor knows better. He knows that the paradise planet hides a being far more powerful than the Daleks – and much more dangerous.

ISBN 0 426 20362 3

LUCIFER RISING
Jim Mortimore & Andy Lane

Reunited, the Doctor, Ace and Bernice travel to Lucifer, the site of a scientific expedition that they know will shortly cease to exist. Discovering why involves them in sabotage, murder and the resurrection of eons-old alien powers. Are there Angels on Lucifer? And what does it all have to do with Ace?

ISBN 0 426 20338 7

WHITE DARKNESS
David McIntee

The TARDIS crew, hoping for a rest, come to Haiti in 1915. But they find that the island is far from peaceful: revolution is brewing in the city; the dead are walking from the cemeteries; and, far underground, the ancient rulers of the galaxy are stirring in their sleep.

ISBN 0 426 20395 X

SHADOWMIND
Christopher Bulis

On the colony world of Arden, something dangerous is growing stronger. Something that steals minds and memories. Something that can reach out to another planet, Tairgire, where the newest exhibit in the sculpture park is a blue box surmounted by a flashing light.

ISBN 0 426 20394 1

BIRTHRIGHT
Nigel Robinson

Stranded in Edwardian London with a dying TARDIS, Bernice investigates a series of grisly murders. In the far future, Ace leads a group of guerrillas against their insect-like, alien oppressors. Why has the Doctor left them, just when they need him most?

ISBN 0 426 20393 3

ICEBERG
David Banks

In 2006, an ecological disaster threatens the Earth; only the FLIPback team, working in an Antarctic base, can avert the catastrophe. But hidden beneath the ice, sinister forces have gathered to sabotage humanity's last hope. The Cybermen have returned and the Doctor must face them alone.

ISBN 0 426 20392 5

BLOOD HEAT
Jim Mortimore

The TARDIS is attacked by an alien force; Bernice is flung into the Vortex; and the Doctor and Ace crash-land on Earth. There they find dinosaurs roaming the derelict London streets, and Brigadier Lethbridge-Stewart leading the remnants of UNIT in a desperate fight against the Silurians who have taken over and changed his world.

ISBN 0 426 20399 2

THE DIMENSION RIDERS
Daniel Blythe

A holiday in Oxford is cut short when the Doctor is summoned to Space Station Q4, where ghostly soldiers from the future watch from the shadows among the dead. Soon, the Doctor is trapped in the past, Ace is accused of treason and Bernice is uncovering deceit among the college cloisters.

ISBN 0 426 20397 6

THE LEFT-HANDED HUMMINGBIRD
Kate Orman

Someone has been playing with time. The Doctor Ace and Bernice must travel to the Aztec Empire in 1487, to London in the Swinging Sixties and to the sinking of the *Titanic* as they attempt to rectify the temporal faults – and survive the attacks of the living god Huitzilin.

ISBN 0 426 20404 2

CONUNDRUM
Steve Lyons

A killer is stalking the streets of the village of Arandale. The victims are found each day, drained of blood. Someone has interfered with the Doctor's past again, and he's landed in a place he knows he once destroyed, from which it seems there can be no escape.

ISBN 0 426 20408 5

NO FUTURE
Paul Cornell

At last the Doctor comes face-to-face with the enemy who has been threatening him, leading him on a chase that has brought the TARDIS to London in 1976. There he finds that reality has been subtly changed and the country he once knew is rapidly descending into anarchy as an alien invasion force prepares to land . . .

ISBN 0 426 20409 3

TRAGEDY DAY
Gareth Roberts

When the TARDIS crew arrive on Olleril, they soon realise that all is not well. Assassins arrive to carry out a killing that may endanger the entire universe. A being known as the Supreme One tests horrific weapons. And a secret order of monks observes the growing chaos.

ISBN 0 426 20410 7

WHO ARE YOU?
*Help us to find out what you want.
No stamp needed – free postage!*

Name _____

Address _____

Town/County _____

Postcode _____

Home Tel No. _____

About Doctor Who Books

How did you acquire this book?
Buy ☐   Borrow ☐
Swap ☐

How often do you buy Doctor Who books?
1 or more every month ☐   3 months ☐
6 months ☐   12 months ☐

Roughly how many Doctor Who books have you read in total? _____

Would you like to receive a list of all past and forthcoming Doctor Who titles?
Yes ☐   No ☐

Would you like to be able to order the Doctor Who books you want by post?
Yes ☐   No ☐

Doctor Who Exclusives

We are intending to publish exclusive Doctor Who editions which may not be available from booksellers and available only by post.

Would you like to be mailed information about exclusive books?
Yes ☐   No ☐

About You

What other books do you read?

Other character-led books (which characters?) _____

| Science Fiction | ☐ | Thriller/Adventure | ☐ |
| Horror | ☐ | | |

Non-fiction subject areas (please specify) _____

| Male | ☐ | Female | ☐ |

Age:
| Under 18 | ☐ | 18–24 | ☐ |
| 25–34 | ☐ | 35+ | ☐ |

| Married | ☐ | Single | ☐ |
| Divorced/Separated | ☐ | | |

Occupation _____

Household income:
| Under £12,000 | ☐ | £13,000–£20,000 | ☐ |
| £20,000+ | ☐ | | |

Credit Cards held:
| Yes | ☐ | No | ☐ |

Bank Cheque guarantee card:
| Yes | ☐ | No | ☐ |

Is your home:
| Owned | ☐ | Rented | ☐ |

What are your leisure interests? _____

Thank you for completing this questionnaire. Please tear it out carefully and return to: **Doctor Who Books, FREEPOST, London, W10 5BR** (no stamp required)